Book One of the Modern Prophet Series

Two Doors

Karl J. Morgan

Book One of the Modern Prophet Series:

Two Doors

Two Doors may be purchased or ordered through book-sellers or at www.karljmorgan.com, or www.sacredlife.com.

ISBN: 978-0-9860270-7-9
ISBN: 0986027073
Library of Congress Control Number: 2014945338

Cover Design By: Miko Radcliffe, drawingacrow.net
Text Design By: Sabrina Lueck, SLdesigns54@gmail.com

Sacred Life Publishers™
www.sacredlife.com
Printed in United States of America

**Dedicated With Love To
Sadie Audrey**

This book is dedicated to Sadie Audrey, the newest member of our family and the infant child of my beautiful daughter Annette and her husband Tim. I try to write stories that are life-affirming, with the good guys ending up on top, and a sincere belief that God is watching over us and helping us to attain our dreams. Little Sadie is a constant reminder and even embodiment of those things. Every person was once like her, looking at the world with wonder and joyous for the opportunity to play for a time in this incredible reality we have been given. I would like to think that my heroes, Dave Brewster, Bill Marshall, and now Peter Smith, feel the same way, humbled by their special talents and inspired to go forward and make the most out of life.

Thank you Sadie for reminding me of the incredible gifts we have been given: this world, the human race, and the infinite possibilities awaiting us all. As I like to say in each book, the universe is a much more magical and mysterious place than any of us can imagine. I look forward to growing with you and discovering the magic that lies ahead.

Contents

Dedication iii

Chapter 1 1

Chapter 2 7

Chapter 3 13

Chapter 4 19

Chapter 5 27

Chapter 6 33

Chapter 7 43

Chapter 8 53

Chapter 9 65

Chapter 10 73

Chapter 11 85

Chapter 12 97

Chapter 13 107

Chapter 14 117

Chapter 15 125

Chapter 16 137

Chapter 17 153

Chapter 18..169

Chapter 19..179

Chapter 20..189

Chapter 21..201

Chapter 22..213

Chapter 23..225

Chapter 24..237

Chapter 25..249

Chapter 26..259

Chapter 27..267

About the Author 281

Other Books by Karl J. Morgan 283

Chapter 1

Peter Smith hated the subway. He never had to deal with crowds back home in Iowa. Now he was here in the Big Apple. His dad told him the big money was here, but so far it was a big headache. He was staying with his cousin in Westchester County. Alice and her husband were nice enough, but the small room they gave him was almost as claustrophobic as this packed subway car. Pete was looking for a room to rent in Manhattan, near the office where he was to start as an accountant in one week. He knew taking the train both ways would wear him out, and he was hoping against hope to find something he could afford. His cousin's house was only a short-term solution anyway, since Alice was already six months pregnant.

Today was even worse than the previous days when he made this journey into the city. Even though the city tried to keep the cars as clean as possible, there was no way to control the people riding in them. Today someone close by was ripe. He tried to ignore the smell by turning his head away, but the bodies were so tight he couldn't move. He looked to his right and saw another man grimacing at the smell, which made Pete smile. The man smiled back and waved his hand in front of his face and rolled his eyes. He felt something sharp and looked down to see the blade of a knife poking into his shirt. He looked at the man in front of him who was grinning menacingly at him, motioning Pete to give him his cash. This was the stinky man, he was certain, and now he was being robbed in a car full of disengaged witnesses. He stared at the man's dark-brown teeth and felt his horrible breath on his face. He slowly reached into his pocket and withdrew a small wad of cash to hand over. When he looked at the man again, he could see he was staring over Pete's right shoulder with a look of abject terror on his face. The knife dropped out of his hand and the robber clutched at his chest with both hands and fell to the floor. Several women nearby screamed. Another man in a dark suit pushed through the crowd and kneeled near the robber saying, "Back up! I'm a doctor."

Pete felt a hand on his right shoulder pulling him back. He turned to see the same man smiling at him. "Come on, buddy, give the doctor some room," he said. The subway car entered the station and slowed to a stop. When the doors opened, one of the riders shouted for the police. The stranger led Pete out of the car onto the platform, away from the action. "That was really something. What happened there?"

"I don't know. I was just standing there smelling that guy when he put a knife to my ribs," Pete replied. Several more police officers arrived and removed the robber from the car. The doctor began to give CPR to the crook while the officers pushed back the crowd. "Then he got a strange look on his face and collapsed to the ground. Maybe I should tell the cops about the knife."

"Did he cut you?" the man asked, looking down at Pete's body.

"No, I don't think so," he replied.

"Well, it's up to you, but I think that guy has enough problems already," the man said, pointing at the group of officers. One of the police had removed his jacket and placed it over the dead man's face. "I'm getting out of here. Was this your stop?"

"I think so," Pete replied, removing a piece of paper from his pocket and showing it to the other. "I'm looking for this address. I'm trying to rent a room there."

"That's funny, pal," he replied. "That's my address. You must be Peter Smith." He offered his hand to Pete, who shook it weakly. "I'm Gabe Prospect. Come with me, and I'll make us some coffee. You look like you're going into shock or something." The men left the subway station and walked along the busy sidewalk for two blocks before Gabe approached a glass-encased high-rise and signaled Pete to follow.

The doorman smiled and opened the door, saying, "Good morning, Mr. Prospect. How are you today, sir?"

"I'm good, Sam. How are Shirley and the kids?" Gabe asked.

"Just fine, sir, and thank you for asking," the doorman replied and quickly closed the door behind them.

"Hey, Bob!" Gabe shouted to another man behind a large marble desk.

"Gabe, it's good to see you sir," Bob replied. "What's happening with your cousin, Mike? We haven't seen him in a while."

"Oh you know, family business stuff," Gabe answered. "Have a good one." Gabe pushed a button and the elevator doors opened. When they were inside, he typed a code into a keypad and pushed the button for the penthouse level."

"I really appreciate the offer of coffee, Gabe, but I can already see this place is out of my range," Pete said. "Maybe I'll just go to the next place on my list."

"Nonsense, Pete," he replied. "I'm not looking to make a lot of money here." He leaned in and said, "My family owns this whole building and lots more. If you can afford to refill my liquor cabinet, I'm a happy guy. Anyway, after what we've been through with the smelly guy dying right in front of us, at least you can have a cup of coffee with me."

When the doors opened, the skyline of Manhattan stretched out in front of them. The main room was massive, with glass all around. Several sitting areas were spread around the room. There were two fireplaces in the room and one giant flat-screen TV. Gabe led Pete through the room and into the large kitchen. He pointed to a table for Pete to sit and then walked out of the room. Pete had never seen such a place. It was right out of the movies about the rich and their extravagant life styles. The poor bastard in the subway would have had a better payday if he had picked on Gabe. All the appliances were top of the line and copper pans were hung from a large rack on the ceiling. There was even a small fireplace in this room, to offer warmth during a quick kitchen breakfast. Pete was not in Iowa anymore.

Gabe returned with a middle-aged woman who came over and introduced herself as Maria, the housekeeper. She went to make coffee while Gabe sat across from Pete at the small table. "Maria's the best!" Gabe began. "Are you hungry, Pete? She makes the most amazing *chilaquiles*. I haven't eaten yet, how about you?"

"I guess I could eat something, but I don't want to be any trouble," he replied.

"Great! I don't like eating alone. Maria, *dos chilaquiles verdes, por favor*." She smiled and nodded. "While we're waiting, let's get down to it. How does five hundred dollars a month sound?"

Pete was stunned. "Gabe, you could get five times that amount easily. I mean, look at this place: it's amazing!"

"Yeah, I know, but you seem to be a down-to-earth kind of guy to me," Gabe replied. "I already told you I don't need the money anyway. After the incident on the subway, I can see you're having some issues and where you live shouldn't be one of them."

"I still feel like there has to be a catch in here somewhere," Pete said. "If you don't need the money, then why get a roommate anyway? You could probably have parties here all the time."

"Unfortunately, it's the family that has the money, Pete," Gabe noted. "I can live here free, with food and Maria to help out. But, then there's my cousin."

"Ah, the catch."

"No, not at all. Mike is a great guy and I love him like a brother, but he is a bit of a stick in the mud. Anytime I get out of line or have too much fun, he's on the phone to his dad or my granddad about it," he answered. "His side of the family is a bit prudish, if you know what I mean."

"But what has that got to do with me?" Pete replied.

"First of all, Mike doesn't live here all the time," Gabe said. "He stays here when he is in town or when Granddad thinks I'm getting out of line. If I have a normal roommate like you, maybe he'll stay away more. If the family thinks I've matured, then they might stop grilling me on everything."

"What about your father?" Pete asked. "Is he still living?"

"Dad? Of course, but my whole side of the family is the black sheep. Everyone looks down on us because we aren't the saintly bunch of do-gooders they are. You have no idea how hard it is for a whole family to work together. Everyone is constantly in everyone else's business, poking around," Gabe replied.

"What kind of business is your family in?" Pete asked.

"That's a bit complicated, too," Gabe replied. "Let's just call it a conglomerate. Each part of the family is involved in different parts of the business, with Granddad sitting at the top. He is really the only one who can see it as one whole."

Maria set cups of coffee on the table along with cream and sugar. Then she returned with two plates brimming with food. The *chilaquiles* were covered with cheese, eggs, and sauce. She patted Gabe on the cheek and left the room with her own plate of food. Gabe immediately began to shovel the food into his face. "Man, that's good! This is my favorite breakfast. Go on, jump in there, roommate."

Pete tasted the fried tortilla strips and rich sauce with cheese and sour cream. "Wow! This is fantastic. I've never had this before. But I don't think I've decided yet about this place."

Gabe laughed. "Okay, man. Look around! If I turn out to be some kind of freak, you can leave any time you want. But remember Maria is part of the package. She'll keep doing the cooking and cleaning. Try it for a month. If you don't like it, I'm sure you can find some dark, stinky hole nearby for twice the price."

"You've got a point," Pete replied. "But I should tell you about my one problem."

Gabe dropped his fork and looked at the other man. "You're the freak, right?"

Pete laughed. "No, I'm no freak. In fact, I'm probably more like your cousin in that regard. I just have a bit of a sleeping disorder."

"You're not going to walk off the balcony and splatter onto the sidewalk, are you?" Gabe asked.

"No, nothing like that." He looked both ways to make sure they were alone. "It's just that I tend to have lots of bad dreams. My parents tell me that I talk in my sleep and often wake up screaming. To make things worse, I usually remember each dream for hours afterward."

Gabe smiled and said, "No worries. Our sound proofing is excellent here and the rooms are quite separate, so I don't think it's a problem. I guess we'll both try it for a month and see if we can still stand one another after that, okay?"

Pete extended his arm to shake the other's hand. "That's a deal, roomy."

"Great! Welcome to my humble abode," Gabe replied. "I guess you'll have to go get your stuff. After we eat, I'll go down to the lobby with you and get you set up with Bob. He can get you a key and pass-code for the elevator. You can't get to this level without one. Do you have a lot of stuff?"

"No, not really. I've been living with my cousin and her family. Back in Iowa, I was still at my folks' house. I just have a bunch of clothes, some books, and my laptop. It might take a couple trips, but it's no problem," Pete replied.

"Well, you might consider a cab for the return trip. Sam and Bob can help with your stuff. That way you can get it done in one trip if you like."

"Thanks. That's a great idea. When do I get to see the room?" Pete asked.

"Just eat your breakfast, Pete. We'll check that out before we head downstairs," Gabe answered.

Chapter 2

Gabe Prospect sat hunched over his laptop. He was reviewing the latest quarterly results from the family business. Every few minutes he took a sip of soda and stretched to relieve the tension in his shoulders. Pete had been impressed by the room, which was quite large and included its own bathroom and view of the city. He had left two hours ago to collect his personal effects, and so Gabe was doing his bit to earn the allowance the family provided. He was a magician at seeing patterns in the numbers so the family could discover trends in time to adjust their strategies. His phone rang and he picked up the receiver, saying, "It's Gabe."

"Hello, Gabriel, it's your father," said the voice on the phone.

"Hey Dad, what's up?" he replied.

"Your grandfather has been giving me crap all day about the subway incident. What did you do?" his father asked.

"I swear I didn't do anything, Dad. The scumbag just had a heart attack. I can't be held responsible for that. People die all the time!" Gabe replied.

His father sighed. "Yes, I know you're right. But as you know, your granddad is always suspicious when one of us is around when it happens. It did seem oddly coincidental though. That piece of shit jeopardized our plans. If it had been me, I might have encouraged him to have an arrest."

"I already said I didn't do anything like that," Gabe protested. "I'm not you, remember?"

"I keep telling your grandfather that, but you know how he is, son. Don't worry about it, Gabriel. I believe you. Unfortunately, it probably means Michael will come by for a while to keep an eye on you," he said.

"Great, just what I need," Gabe sighed. "That's okay. Now that we have a new roommate, it's probably best that Mike gets to know him too. This whole situation is very strange. If Mike can help me figure it out, that's a good thing. Hey, I've got an idea that will shake everyone up. After this call, I'm going to call Mike and ask him to come here for a while. What do you think about that?"

His father laughed. "That's my boy, throwing a curve they'd never expect. I've got your granddad on the other line, so I'll have to let you go. I love you, son."

"I love you too, Dad," Gabe said as the line was cut off. He dialed another number and said, "Mike, what's happening?"

"Gabriel, this is a surprise," his cousin said.

"I got that new roommate today and was wondering if you'd like to stay here a few days and help me with him," he replied.

"Wow! I'm surprised. You're asking me for help? This is a first of some kind, isn't it?" his cousin laughed.

"Maybe," Gabe laughed. "But seriously, I could use your help on this."

"Say no more, cousin," Mike replied. "I'll be there later this evening. I've got a ton of stuff to do with the uncles, as you can imagine. When I'm finished, I'll head over there."

"Perfect!" Gabe replied. "I look forward to seeing you tonight."

"I'll see you then. And Gabriel, thanks for the invitation," Mike said and then hung up the phone.

Gabe laughed and said, "Well, I guess my stock just went up in this family!" He turned back to his computer. There was a new trend in the Middle East data that no one else had seen yet.

§

Pete was able to squeeze all of his belongings into the taxi cab. He hugged Alice and promised to call her soon. She had been surprised by the address of the new room in Manhattan. Somehow, it seemed too good to be true. She had written down the phone number and promised herself to check out this Gabriel Prospect on the internet as soon as her cousin left. Pete kissed her on the cheek and climbed into the front seat of the cab, as the trunk and rear seat were chocked full of his stuff. The car pulled away and headed for the nearest expressway into the city.

After the car turned the first corner, Alice turned and walked back into her small home and went to her computer. First she searched for Gabriel Prospect and found almost nothing. There was an article mentioning a Gabe Prospect as a member of the family running The Prospect Enterprise, a massive, but shadowy business that seemed to reach into many different industries and global markets. As a private company, there were no financial statements, but she did find a listing of properties owned by the company, which included the address her cousin had given her. It also mentioned another member of the family named Michael. He was all over the net. She found images of him at dozens of charitable events, where his family was a major contributor. At least the family did not seem to be a criminal enterprise from the first look.

Pete sat quietly in the cab, hoping to unpack his things as soon as he arrived at his new home. The driver seemed content not to talk, and that was better for Pete. He was never good with strangers. On the downside, the driver did not smell very good. Pete wondered if this was his fate in New York to be constantly surrounded by stinky people. At least this man was a licensed and bonded taxi driver, the opposite of the man on the subway. He closed his eyes to relax and put the man's odor out of his mind. Within seconds, he had fallen asleep.

Pete opened his eyes to see the cab exiting the expressway in the Bronx, far from his destination. He turned to the cabbie and said, "What the hell is this?"

The driver held a pistol in his right hand and pressed it against Pete's temple. "You just shut up and sit tight, or I'll blow your brains out right here and now!"

Pete was frozen in fear. Now he would be robbed and probably killed for the clothes and stuff in the back of the cab. Maybe he should jump out and hope not to be killed by the car behind them. The cabbie pressed the gun into Pete's ribs and smiled at him.

"Don't worry, Pete. This won't hurt for very long." The cab turned off the road into a small garage where five other men stood with rifles aimed at him. Two of the men began to pull his stuff from the back seat. The cabbie was laughing. "You stupid bastard. I don't know what you did to Lenny in the subway, but I'm going to kill you and sell your shit online." He hit Pete over the head with the gun again and again. The last things he remembered before passing out were the cabbie's laugh and body odor.

"Here we are, sir," the cabbie said. Pete woke up suddenly, still sitting in the taxi. All of his belongings were still packed into the back seat. It had all been a dream. He fumbled for his cash to pay the fare and gave the man a twenty-dollar tip to compensate for the dream when he was attacked and murdered. He climbed out of the cab as Sam was finishing unloading the vehicle. When the car was empty, Sam pounded on the trunk and the vehicle pulled away into traffic.

"Don't worry, Mr. Smith," Sam began. "Bob and I will make sure everything gets to your room." He looked closely at Pete and said, "Are you okay, sir? You look a little confused."

"No, I'm okay, Sam," Pete said. "I just fell asleep in the cab and had a bad dream. I guess I was startled when we arrived here." He held out another twenty to tip him.

"No tips needed, sir. It's all included in the rent, but thanks for the offer," Sam said.

"Okay. And you and Bob should just call me Pete. I'm not a sir to anyone," Pete replied.

"Okay, Pete, and welcome home," Sam said. Pete walked into the building where Bob was waiting for him with a key-card.

"Welcome home, sir," Bob said. "Here is your new key-card. I'll go up with you now and show you how the elevator works. Sam will keep an eye on your stuff."

"Thanks, Bob. You should call me Pete. I'm not really comfortable with sir," Pete replied as he followed Bob into the elevator car.

"Sure, Pete, as you wish," Bob said. When the doors had closed, he began, "Rule Number 1: Try to have an elevator car to yourself. If you can't, you can press the penthouse button and slide your key-card, but don't enter the pass-code. When everyone else leaves, the car will go up to your floor, but the door won't open until you enter the code."

"Okay," Pete said.

"It's important since the elevator opens directly in the foyer. We don't want others running around in the apartment, do we?"

"No we don't. Okay, I got it," Pete replied.

"You're not a superstitious person, are you?" Bob asked.

"No."

"Good, because the code is six, six, six, asterisk, six, six, six," Bob said.

"That's an interesting choice," Pete laughed.

"Gabe wanted something easy to remember," Bob said. "Don't worry. If you forget, just contact me or Gabe. Please don't write it down though. If anyone else finds out, just let me know and I'll change it immediately."

"Okay, I got it," Pete replied. "What's Rule Number 2?"

"If anyone comes to visit you, either you or Maria will have to come to the lobby to escort them," he answered. "The only way to the penthouse is with a key-card and the pass-code. So only someone with both can get there. That's it!" Bob said. He pushed the open-door button and walked out. "That's all my rules, Pete. Sam and I will bring up your stuff. Just relax and enjoy your new home." As the doors started to close, Bob inserted his hand to re-open them. "I forgot. If the elevator stops before the penthouse to let someone else go up, the system will disable the pass-code. You'll have to wait for them to leave and then re-enter it, unless it's a guest you've invited, of course. Have a good day, Pete."

When the elevator opened again, Pete was standing in the foyer of the penthouse. Since he had time to wait for his belongings, he sat in one of the groupings of furniture and turned on the television. A breaking news alert flashed on the screen. "This is a breaking news bulletin. Police have confirmed the identity of the man who died of a heart attack in the subway this morning. His name was Leonard Manson of the Bronx. He was an indigent who had been living on the streets for a number of years. He had a long history of run-ins with authorities. His body was found with a knife which had his fingerprints on it. Anyone with information regarding Mr. Manson or the events of this morning should contact the NYPD."

"That is too weird!" he gasped.

"What's weird, Pete?" Gabe said.

Pete turned to see the other five feet behind him, holding a glass of soda in his hand. "I'm sure it's nothing, Gabe. I fell asleep in the cab and had a stupid dream."

Gabe walked over, sat on an adjacent couch and set his glass on the coffee table. "Tell me about it."

"It seems silly, really," Pete protested.

"Come on, man. You already told me you have freaky dreams. Tell me already," Gabe demanded.

"It's just that in the dream, the taxi took me to the Bronx and the cabbie threatened to kill me. He said something about revenge for Lenny," Pete said.

Gabe was laughing. "You're nuts. There was probably a story on the radio about the incident, and your subconscious mind pulled those things into the dream. Don't sweat it." He got up and went to the kitchen for more soda.

Pete chuckled but was not convinced. The cabbie never turned on his radio. It was off when he fell asleep and still off when he awoke. He promised to forget it and continued watching television.

Chapter 3

Pete was happily putting away his belongings. The room was much larger than he could have hoped for at this price. It was not surprising, given the size or location of the building, however. He also still had most of the week to learn the neighborhood before his job began. There had to be local stores and eateries just waiting to be discovered. The incident on the subway and his dream in the taxi were fading away quickly. He was thrilled to have cable and internet connections for his small television and computer. He felt he could live happily in this room alone if Gabe and his family demanded it. Perhaps this change of locale was just what he needed to get beyond the nightmares of his youth. He looked forward to a long night's sleep for the first time in ages.

Gabe was preoccupied with his thoughts. He paced the floor wondering what was going to happen next. The phone rang and he grabbed the receiver. "Hello?"

"Gabe, it's Bob," the front desk man said. "You should check out Channel 27. There's an interesting story you need to see. I'll hold while you watch."

Gabe turned on the set and changed to the appropriate channel. Trent Michaels, the new field reporter was talking to a man in the street. "We're live on the street in the Bronx this evening with Vincent Manson, whose brother died in a subway this morning. How is your family, Mr. Manson?"

"How do you think we're doing?" he replied. "It's a mess right now. Lenny was a good man. He didn't have a heart attack. Somebody killed him."

"Mr. Manson, the police say there was no evidence of any assault on your brother. Why do you say he was murdered?" the reporter asked.

"I know my brother was no saint, but he didn't have any heart problems. He was as healthy as an ox. I'm hoping someone out there can help me find my brother's assassin. We're poor people, but we didn't deserve this!" the man finished.

Gabe switched off the television and returned to the call. "Okay, what's the big deal? The guy is grieving for his brother."

"Gabe, Sam is confident the cabbie who brought Mr. Smith is that same Vincent Manson."

"Shit! Is he sure?" Gabe asked.

"One hundred percent certain, Gabe," Bob replied. "And one more thing: your cousin Michael just got out of a cab in front."

"Perfect timing, just like always!" Gabe laughed. "Please tell him everything. Bye." He hung up the phone and sat on the couch. They were in for it now!

Within a minute, the elevator doors opened and Mike walked out and found his cousin sitting on the couch with his head in his hands. Mike was taller than Gabe, at around 6 feet 2 inches. He was very fair with blonde hair and icy blue eyes, while his 5-feet-10-inch cousin had black hair and dark brown eyes. Mike's family was one of their grandfather's favorites, probably only surpassed by his Uncle Michael's, for whom Mike was named. It was ironic that Gabe was named after Mike's father. Mike strode into the room and left his two suitcases for Maria to put away. He walked over to the liquor cabinet and poured himself a double whisky over the rocks. Then he sat on the couch next to his cousin. "Well, this is another great mess your family has gotten us into!" he laughed.

"I didn't do anything!" Gabe argued. "I swear I was just riding in the subway when that man had an attack. This is totally unfair, especially to blame my whole side of the family for a random occurrence."

"Okay, okay, I apologize," Mike said, offering his glass to his cousin. "You probably need this more than me." He walked back to the cabinet and prepared a second drink, then rejoined the other. "Here's to Granddad!" he said as the two touched glasses and sipped the drink. "Where's our new friend? You didn't let him go wandering about, did you?"

"No, he's just setting up the stuff in his room," Gabe replied. "He could come out at any time, so keep it down."

"Okay," Mike whispered. "What do you think is happening with him?"

"It's very strange so far. The incident with the cabbie is too coincidental. We have to keep an eye on him. This could devolve into something very sinister if we're not careful," Gabe replied in hushed tones.

"You know this hasn't happened in a very long time," Mike said. "Everyone has bad dreams, but when they start to be based on unknown realities, it gets our attention."

"I know. That's why we brought him here. Perhaps it's nothing. If his dreams occur here, maybe we'll be able to react if they presage something," Gabe replied. "We don't want to get ahead of ourselves though. I have to believe this was a one-time deal. A few more dreams that don't match up and we can forget all about it."

"And you can send him packing," Mike said.

"Maybe, maybe not," Gabe answered. "I really like the guy. Maybe I'll let him stay until he has enough dough to get a decent place."

"Just keep our secrets!" Mike urged. "We don't want him to know too much."

They heard a door open and turned to see Pete walking towards them. He was looking at Mike and offered his hand. "You must be Gabe's cousin Mike. I'm Pete Smith."

Mike shook his hand firmly and replied, "Nice to meet you Pete, but I prefer Michael, if that's okay."

"Of course, sorry if I offended you, Michael," Pete answered.

"No worries, Pete. Come sit down and join us," Mike said. "Let me get you a drink too." Mike poured two fingers of whisky over ice and handed the glass to Pete. Then he sat next to his cousin. "So, Pete, tell me about yourself."

"Not much to tell, actually," Pete replied. "I grew up in Iowa, just got my degree from the University of Iowa and came to the big city to make my fortune."

"Gabe tells me you have a job nearby starting next week. That's great in this economy," Mike said. "If it doesn't work out, let me know. We're always looking for good people in our family's business."

"Cool. I was talking to my cousin Alice a little while ago and she mentioned the Prospect Enterprise. Is that your family's company?" Pete asked.

"That's us. What kind of work do you do?"

"Well, my degree is in finance, but this will be my first job since getting it," Pete answered. "I guess I'll see where life takes me. I love finance but, really, I just want to fit in and move up as best I can."

"That's what it's all about, right?" Gabe interjected. "Is your new company big?"

"I googled them and they have annual revenue around five billion. So, pretty big, I guess," he replied. "How does that compare to your company?"

"Well, since we're private, I can't really say, but we're definitely bigger than that," Mike said. "To find that out, you'll have to marry one of my sisters or another female cousin, right Gabe?"

"That's right," his cousin agreed. "Granddad has a tight circle he trusts. Everyone else only knows what they need to. I hate to change the subject so much, but I thought I'd make sure you understand our house rules, Pete."

"Okay, just tell me what to do," he replied.

"First, we should discuss privacy," Gabe began. "We'll both stay out of your room and you will stay out of ours. Of course, none of us have anything to hide, but I'm sure you wouldn't want one of us rummaging around in your stuff." He took a sip of whisky and smiled at Pete. "Second is the house phone. Please don't use or answer any of them. They are part of the business and we use them for business use only. You can use your cell phone wherever you like. Is that a problem?"

"Of course not," Pete said. "I use my cell for everything anyway. What else?"

"No parties without our approval," Mike said. "If we have any gatherings, you are welcome to join in, unless Granddad comes. He's kind of special and doesn't generally like to meet our friends. If he comes over, you'll have to stay in your room. We'll have Maria bring you dinner."

"Don't make such a big deal, Mike," Gabe laughed. "Pete, honestly, my grandfather has never been here. I told you before we were the black sheep of the family. I'll probably have to stay in my room too if he shows up."

"But you understand my point, right, Gabe?" Mike asked.

"Yes, you are right, Mike," Gabe replied. "No one meets Granddad." He winked at Pete.

"Seems kind of strange, but if that's the rule, I'm okay with it," Pete replied. "Anything else? DNA samples? Microchip implanted in my head?"

The two cousins laughed. "What a comedian!" Gabe smiled. "Nothing like that, although I feel like there's a chip in my head most days. But besides the monthly rent, it would be cool if you could give Maria fifty bucks a week for food and odds and ends. She cooks all the meals and will do laundry if you like. How does that sound?"

"That's very fair, especially if the rest of her food is like the breakfast," Pete agreed.

"She didn't make *chilaquiles* for him, did she?" Mike asked. "It's too bad I missed it."

"Well, that's what you get for being a workaholic, cousin," Gabe replied.

"If that's all, I'm pretty bushed," Pete began. "It's been a long day for me. I think I'll go to bed." He stood up.

"Have a good night, Pete," Mike replied. "By the way, what's your plan for tomorrow?"

"I thought I'd wander around the neighborhood and see what's happening," Pete replied.

"If it's okay with you, I'd like to hang out with you tomorrow. I don't come here very often, and I'd like to take a look around too. I can help you navigate," Mike asked.

"That would be great. I'll talk to you both tomorrow." Pete stood, walked to his room, and closed the door behind him.

"What the heck was that about?" Gabe whispered.

"I'm not taking any chances on this one, Gabe," he answered. "If there is anything to that man, I want to find out before something bad can happen to him."

"I think it might be provocative for you two to be seen together," Gabe replied. "I should be the one to hang out with him. No one knows who I am. You're in the press all the time."

"I hadn't thought about that," Mike sighed. "The last thing Pete needs now is publicity. But I'm not sure about you either after the subway incident, cousin."

"We're not going to talk about that again, are we?" Gabe moaned. "I didn't do anything."

"We should sleep on it, Gabe. Tomorrow, I'm sure the right solution will emerge," Mike replied.

Chapter 4

Pete was having one of his favorite dreams. The first cup of coffee was the best part of the morning to him, and he was sitting in a small coffee shop savoring every drop. He sat at the front window, watching the traffic and pedestrians walk by. It was a busy day in the city, and the sidewalks were packed with people heading to work. It was cool and a gentle rain poured over the field of black umbrellas. He took a bite of his scone and looked to his left. A stunning blonde with blue eyes sat on the stool next to him. She smiled when he looked at her. Her perfume smelled like strawberries. He tried to say something to her when an odd smell hit his senses, but it was not like the body odor of the cabbie. It was more sinister, like sulfur or chlorine. A young man walked into the coffee shop to grab some coffee before heading to classes. His backpack was brimming with books. He saw Pete looking his way and smiled before heading over to the counter to place his order.

Pete noticed the beautiful woman had picked up her bag and walked out the door. That would be him soon, with places to go and things to do. Today, he was just happy to explore this new neighborhood. Another smell caught his attention. He turned to his right and saw the cabbie sitting on the other stool. He turned back quickly to avoid being recognized, and began to climb off the stool. As he turned back to grab his cup of coffee, he noticed the young man walking out of the store, but he had somehow forgotten his backpack. He smiled at Pete again as he began to type numbers into his cell phone. Pete tried to get his attention when the store exploded.

Pete, the other patrons, furniture, and broken glass flew out onto the sidewalk and the street. The mass of people on the sidewalks began to scream and run away from the scene. Pete was on the bottom of a pile of people and debris. He could hear others shouting for help. He was able to see the cabbie's lifeless body a few inches away. Blood poured from a large chunk of plate glass that was embedded in the cabbie's chest.

Pete sat up straight in bed with the sounds of sirens and screams for help still ringing in his ears. He was drenched in sweat and trembling. He slowly rose to his feet and walked into the small bathroom. He washed his face and sat on the toilet, allowing the images from his dream to fade. Looking at his watch by the sink, he noticed it was three-thirty in the morning. After five minutes he felt calmer and returned to bed, although he doubted he would sleep again. Under the covers, the images of the dream filled his head still. He pushed the thoughts out of his mind, and after fifteen minutes fell asleep again.

He awoke again and looked at the alarm clock, which read four-thirty. That would be it, he thought. He sat up and turned on the light on the bedside table. He was startled to see Gabe in his room, sitting on the easy chair beyond the end of the bed. "What the hell are you doing in here?" he demanded. "What about the privacy rule?"

Gabe stood up and walked to the end of the bed. He was smiling but said nothing. Pete stood up and walked over to the other and thumped him on the chest with his index finger. "Hey, I'm talking to you, Gabe! What the devil are you doing in here?"

Gabe only smiled and stood his ground. Pete smelled that same sulfurous odor he had in the coffee shop dream, but now it was overpowering. He covered his nose with his hand. Suddenly, the walls of the room were ablaze. The curtains were consumed instantly and the fire spread to the ceiling, where waves of flame raced toward the center of the room. The temperature was soaring and noxious black smoke covered the ceiling and was moving toward them. Pete could feel his pajamas catching on fire and tried desperately to put out the flames. Gabe was laughing now and pushed Pete back down onto the burning bed. Pete screamed in pain as the fire covered his body.

Pete awoke to a knock on the door. He was still shaking from the last dream and weakly said, "Yeah?"

Maria opened the door and said, "Mr. Pete, breakfast will be ready in fifteen minutes." She smiled at him and closed the door. He was panting for breath and his skin felt like it was still on fire. He rushed to the bathroom and turned on the shower. He pulled off his pajamas and stood under the cold water. As the water warmed, the dream began to fade into another miserable memory. Clearly, one day in this new place had done nothing for his sleep.

Twenty minutes later, he left his room and walked into the kitchen to find Michael and Gabe sitting and eating. They motioned him to sit between them and Maria brought a plate of food and a cup of coffee for him. "How are you today, Pete?" Mike asked.

"Not too good, I'm afraid," he replied. "More bad dreams. I'll be okay, just let me get something into my stomach." The two cousins had been watching a morning news talk show. Pete began to watch as well. It was the typical format with small snippets of news between various local interest stories and celebrity interviews. It was the kind of television Pete hated, but he was the guest here. He preferred scientific or historical programs where he could feed his mind.

The host on the show said, "This just in. There has been an explosion at a coffee shop in Manhattan this morning, approximately thirty minutes ago. That is all we know now, but the area is now cordoned off by police. We will keep you advised as more information becomes available." Pete's fork dropped to his plate and he sat slack-jawed, staring at the screen.

"Are you okay, Pete?" Gabe asked.

"No, I'm not," he replied. "This can't be happening."

"It's probably just a gas line explosion," Mike said. "What a terrible tragedy. I'm sure the police will get to the bottom of it."

"You don't understand," Pete argued. "I had a dream about that last night." The two cousins exchanged worried glances. "It's probably a coincidence, but I saw a young guy come into the shop with a backpack. I thought he was a college student or something. Then I saw him leave without the backpack. The bastard smiled at me and dialed a number on his cell phone. That's when the bomb exploded."

"It must be a coincidence," Gabe insisted. "The odds of a terrorist attack are very small. What else do you remember?"

"There was a beautiful blonde sitting next to me. She left just before the blast. Sitting on my other side was the cabbie who brought me here. He died in the blast," Pete recounted, panting for air.

"You have to know your mind put him there, Pete," Gabe said. "You saw him yesterday and your mind plugged him into the other dream. I'm sure he's fine."

"I know you're both right," Pete sighed. "The coincidence caught me off guard. I'll be okay."

"Anything else?" Mike asked.

"Not in that dream, but I did have another one," Pete admitted. "It was very strange. I woke in my bed and Gabe was in my room." He turned to Gabe and continued, "I asked you why and you just smiled at me. Then the whole room caught on fire and you pushed me down on the burning bed."

"Well, that part is definitely a dream!" Gabe said. "Pete, excuse Mike and me. We have a conference call in a few minutes. It shouldn't take too long and then we'll both go out with you to look around, okay?"

"Sure, that would be great," Pete replied as the other two hurried out of the room. He turned to Maria who looked horrified by his revelations. "The pancakes are awesome, Maria. Thanks. And don't worry about my dreams. I get them all the time." She smiled and returned to cleaning the dishes.

Michael and Gabe rushed into Gabe's room and closed and locked the door behind them. "It's got to be a coincidence," Gabe began. Mike raised his hand to silence the other and dialed a number on his phone.

"It's Michael . . . what can you confirm about the explosion today . . . okay, I understand . . . what about a Vincent Manson . . . really . . . okay, tell Granddad we have a situation. Bye." Mike collapsed onto one of the large chairs in the room, held his head in his hands and sighed. "It's all confirmed. Every last word."

"We have to keep this from Pete. If he knew, who knows what he would do? He might start thinking he is causing all of this," Gabe said.

Mike laughed weakly. "You have to know that is a possibility, cousin."

Gabe laughed and said, "You know better than that! He's just a guy, not some evil demon or terrorist. And what about the room on fire? You know I would never do that!"

Mike stood and walked over to the window and looked down on the city. "Yeah, you're right. But something is going on here. We have to keep our eyes on Pete, and we absolutely can't let him take that other job. That would provide too many hours a day when we cannot watch out for him."

"I'm sure your dad or mine can find a job for him," Gabe replied. "Or there is another possibility. We could tell him everything."

Mike laughed out loud. "You must be nuts, Gabriel. It may come to that eventually, but it's way too early. This could be a once in a lifetime premonition. As you said, the burning room was just a dream. Even his dream when he thought Vincent Manson would rob and kill him was just a dream. That poor bastard is dead now. He won't be hurting anyone anymore."

"What about the bomber?" Gabe asked. "Pete saw his face. I'm sure the police would love that information."

"There were lots of witnesses who saw the student with the backpack, so the police don't need Pete. Besides, are they going to believe a man's dream?" Mike laughed.

"We sure do," Gabe remarked. "You even told Granddad we have a situation. That's not something he'll be happy to hear."

"It had to be done," Mike sighed. His phone buzzed and he looked at the caller ID. "And speaking of the old man, here he is." He pressed the connect button. "Hi, Granddad, how are you . . . yes, Gabriel is here with me . . . yes, I said a situation . . . okay, let me put you on speaker."

§

While he was waiting for his roommates to wander the sites, Pete was typing into his journal. Years ago, he had decided to keep track of his nightmares. He hoped to find a trend in the data, or closure, but so far nothing. He thought it might make a good book someday, so he kept at it. As he was finished with the dream about the room burning, his cell phone rang and he looked at it. It was his cousin calling. "Hi Alice, how are you?"

"I'm so glad to hear your voice," she sighed. "You heard about the bombing today, didn't you?"

"I heard about an explosion, but didn't know it was a bombing yet," he replied.

"Get off your computer and check out the news!" she said. "It was definitely a bombing, although no one has claimed responsibility yet. At least ten people were killed and dozens injured. Many of the injured are reporting a young man with a backpack left it behind just before the blast. That's not far from you, is it?"

"They said backpack?" he groaned. "It's just like my dream."

"What are you talking about?" she asked. "I want you to move back here. Don't worry about the job. I want you to be safe."

"Relax, Alice, I'm fine," he replied. "I'm living in one of the most secure buildings in the city. My new job is only a few blocks away. I'm not going to hide from some maniac with a bomb, and the cops will probably nab him today anyway."

"I'm afraid, Pete," she said. "Your folks asked me to keep an eye on you. I don't think the city is safe anymore."

There was a knock at his door. "Alice, my roommates are taking me out on the town. I'll call you later. Bye." He walked over and then opened the door to find Gabe standing there. "Are we ready to go?"

"There's a bit of a change in plans, Pete," Gabe said. "Can I come in? I promise not to set your room on fire."

Pete laughed. "Sure, sorry about that stupid dream, come on in." When the two had sat down, Pete said, "If you guys can't go, that's okay. I just want to look around."

"Bob and Sam tell me the streets are a real mess right now," Gabe began. "Cops and the FBI are everywhere. Bob has brought in another ten security guards until things cool down. "It's probably better we stay here today. Hopefully things will be back to normal tomorrow."

"No problem," Pete replied. "I don't want to get caught in a mob. That would just fuel more bad dreams."

"There is one other thing," Gabe said. "My dad, Mike's dad, and Granddad are coming for dinner at six."

"I know the rules," Pete said. "I'll stay here. I've still got lots of stuff to put away."

"Well, that's the thing. They all want to meet you," Gabe said.

"Me? Okay, that's fine too," Pete said. "Any special things I need to know about them? I don't want to mess up."

"My dad's cool. Mike's is a lot like him; another stick in the mud. Granddad is the greatest, but to some folks, he can seem a little overwhelming," Gabe answered.

"So, he's like a superhero? He sounds great!" Pete replied.

"Something like that, Pete. Just let him do the talking. If he wants small talk, he'll lead the way. And sometimes he says some stuff you'll find hard to believe. Don't worry about that. He's fine, but a little eccentric," Gabe stated. "And wear something nice. No suit and tie, but no jeans either, okay?"

Chapter 5

The bomber hurried down the empty sidewalk. He was out of breath from running to evade the police. He leaned against a brick wall to catch his breath, looking about to make sure he wasn't followed. The sun was setting now, and it was time for Joe Martin to collect his reward. This job had been the most distasteful of his criminal career. With no education and no prospects, he did what he could to eat. When Sheila came to him with the chance to make a quick twenty thousand, he could not pass it by, no matter what the crime. He knew he would be hunted, but the chance to get out of the city and make a new life in another country was enough to risk capture. It was early that morning when he met with her to take the bomb. She said it was designed to be identical to a terrorist weapon so they would not be suspects. All he had to do was leave it behind.

As he had walked into the coffee shop, he saw her again, sitting on a stool in the window, with another man next to her. She had winked at him, which he thought was unnecessarily familiar. He ordered his coffee, and when it arrived he slipped off the backpack near the cream and sugar counter and walked out. He saw her again, twenty feet down the sidewalk with a small device in her hand. Was it a cell phone? He did not know or care. He turned the other way and took his own phone to check on his flight reservations. The blast knocked him off his feet. Hundreds of people were shouting and blood was everywhere. He climbed back to his feet and ran away with the rest of the crowd. He found dark hiding places to disappear into throughout the day, but whenever he heard another siren, he fled on his circuitous route to this building. He looked at his phone. It was 5:45 p.m., the exact time she requested. Joe went down the alley and found the door which she said would be open. He pulled the handle and walked inside.

"Sheila, are you here?" he shouted.

"Keep it down, Joe," she replied from across the room. Then he saw her. She was sitting on a lone chair with her legs crossed. She was a real beauty and knew how to show off her long legs. As he crossed the room, she unfolded her legs and stood up. She picked up her briefcase and set it on the chair. "You did a great job, Joe. Worth every penny."

"I hope so," he replied. "Half the NYPD is out for my blood right now. Just give me the cash and let me get out of here."

"Of course," she smiled. "It's right here in this case."

"Open it," he demanded. He had stopped five feet away.

"Okay, but give me a second to unlock it," she said as she turned to open the case.

"This job is a real lifesaver," Joe said. "You can't imagine how this is going to help me out."

Sheila opened the case, removed a revolver, turned and shot Joe in the chest. He fell back to the ground, groaning in agony. "You're such a dumb ass, Joe." She shot him in the head twice. Then she wiped down the gun and put it in his hand. "Oh, I forgot the money," she laughed. She picked up the brief case and poured the cash out around him. "Don't spend it all in one place, Joe." Sheila tucked the briefcase under her arm and rushed out into the alley, where a limousine was waiting. She climbed into the back seat and it raced away.

She poured some whisky into a glass and swallowed it. Then she pressed a button to raise the screen between the seats and took her cell phone, dialing a number quickly. After a moment, she said, "Master, the job is done . . . of course, the courier is dead . . . my flight leaves in an hour . . . I'll see you tomorrow morning . . . Good night, Master." She clicked off her phone and refilled her glass.

§

Gabe's cell phone was ringing. He pressed the contact and said, "Yes, Bob."

"Your grandfather's helicopter has just landed on the roof. They'll be there any time now," the deskman said.

"Thanks for the warning," Gabe said as he closed the connection. He walked out of his room and noticed Mike and Pete watching television. "Show's on, everyone." Mike switched off the set and pulled Pete to his feet.

"Just stay calm and try to have fun," Mike said.

"Sure. I'm actually looking forward to this," Pete replied just as the elevator arrived in their foyer.

The resemblance between the grandfather and one of the men was startling. The grandfather looked like an older clone of the other. Both looked very much like Michael, so Pete assumed the man was his father. The other was several inches shorter and had darker skin and black eyes. The grandfather's hair was pure white and he sported a neatly trimmed mustache and beard. The other men's hair was sprinkled with gray, but they still seemed quite young to be the fathers of his roommates.

As the men crossed over to the younger ones, it was clear the grandfather ran the roost. The other men stayed a few feet behind him. The grandfather hugged both of his grandchildren and then came over to Pete. "You must be Peter," the man said. "Please call me Granddad, everyone else does."

Pete shook the man's hand. "It's a pleasure to meet you, sir. But it's just Pete, if that's okay." The other men looked horrified by his comment.

"Pete, sure, that's fine," the grandfather said. "We have a very close friend named Peter, so that's why I said that."

"Don't even think about it, sir," Pete laughed. "You can use either name."

"Thank you, Peter," the man replied. "Let me introduce you to two of my sons. This is Gabriel, whom my grandson is named after. Some folks tell me we look very much alike."

Pete shook the other man's hand. "The resemblance is amazing, sir. Nice to meet you."

"It's nice to meet you as well, young man. You can call me Gabriel. Since my nephew prefers Gabe, that will keep us from getting confused. And this is my brother, Luce."

"It's nice to meet you too, sir. Luce is an interesting name," Pete said.

"One of a kind, I assure you," the man replied. "Let me get us all some drinks. I know I could certainly use one."

After drinks and small talk, the group sat down for dinner. Maria had outdone herself yet again. Cooking for Granddad was a serious affair. No one wanted to be on his bad side. The three older men sat on the opposite side of the table from the younger ones. Pete was given the seat of honor, facing the old man. Pete was trying his best to avoid the man's eyes, but each time he looked in his direction, Granddad was watching him. Both Gabe and Mike were fidgeting like mad, deathly afraid one of them would slip up.

"So, Peter, I'm told you are an accountant," the old man said.

"Yes, Granddad. But I haven't really started working yet. My job starts next week and I'm looking forward to it," Pete replied.

"You seem like a nice boy. How would you like to work for me instead?" he asked. The other four men sat in stunned silence.

"That's very generous of you, Granddad," Pete replied. "But I already committed to the other company."

The old man was laughing. "I'm not used to being turned down, Peter. But I appreciate your honesty. May I ask the name of your new company?"

"Bertrand Industries," Pete replied. "They are just a few blocks from here."

"I know them well," the elder Gabriel said. "Real estate and property management, I believe. Oscar Bertrand is a good man."

"Well, if you change your mind, just let one of my grandchildren know," the old man replied. "I wish you all the best."

Gabe's mind was reeling. No one ever turned down his grandfather. He could not believe the old man was taking this in stride. Something else had to be going on here. He promised to discuss it with his father later.

"Thank you, Granddad," Peter replied.

"You know, son, a job is like walking through a door," Granddad began. "Unlike in most of life, there are many doors to choose. You can select one, and if it is not to your tastes, you pick another."

"Granddad, I'm not sure what you meant by 'unlike in most of life,'" Pete noted. The other men held their heads in their hands and groaned softly.

"Don't listen to their bellyaching, Peter," the old man complained. "This is one of my favorite stories and they have heard it a million times. May I continue?"

"I've never heard it. Please do," Pete said.

"Almost every choice you make in life is like choosing between two doors," he began. "One door leads to good while the other leads to evil. Take, for example, the young man who left the bomb in the coffee shop this morning. By doing such a heinous act, he chose the wrong door. Even if it was his first such choice, he can never go back. If his first choice was to cheat on a test in school or steal a candy bar, perhaps he could learn to choose better. Once he made the choice he did, though, he was lost forever. He chose to be an evil person. Life may yet smile on him and give him a good life, but the odds are highly stacked against him."

"But what about his childhood and the environment he was raised in," Pete argued. "Maybe he didn't have a choice. Maybe he was forced into a life of crime." The two older men got up and walked away from the table. Mike was mortified, while Gabe sat smiling. Finally, he thought, someone was standing up to the old man.

"Come back here you cowards!" the old man commanded his sons. "Peter is just stating a hypothesis and is entitled to his opinion, whether I agree with it or not." He turned back to the young man and said, "Peter, you have to come to work for me. I'll triple any offer you have. You can work directly for me. Please think about it."

"I'm flattered and will seriously consider it, Granddad," he smiled.

"Good. But back to what you were saying. Do you believe in free will?" the old man asked.

"Of course, I do. But I think some people are put in terrible conditions that push them in the wrong direction. That's not an excuse for their actions, but it has to have an impact," Pete said.

"You are absolutely correct!" Granddad laughed. "All of our lives are different. Some are born rich and become paupers or criminals. Others are born destitute and become magnates of industry or religious leaders. While I would agree we have some predispositions in one direction or another, we still choose. That man with the bomb today did not use it to rob a bank to feed his family. He put a bomb in a crowded restaurant, took his coffee, and walked away. He had no concern for the lives of those poor people. He could have chosen to rob a store or panhandle for change or even steal a woman's handbag. I could understand that. We all need to eat. But his act was brazen and cowardly. His only goal was to make people suffer or die. He made that choice when he left the backpack behind. There was no gun to his head."

"I can't argue with your logic, Granddad," Pete admitted. "Maybe his life was terrible and he felt pushed in the wrong way, but no one forced him to do it. He made his choice."

"Marvelous!" Granddad laughed. "Now you understand the two doors. I think we have time for one more drink before we have to leave."

Chapter 6

Sheila Farness woke early as usual. Jetlag was not a problem, as she was accustomed to traveling around the globe to help her master with critical jobs. She traveled well and was paid exceptionally well. The Satori Industries GV landed in San Francisco at 11:00 p.m., and a company limousine had Sheila back in her townhouse before midnight. The sun was up and the air was cool and foggy. After her shower, she sat in her breakfast nook sipping a cup of fresh coffee. It was going to be a busy day, which was also normal. She was thumbing through her agenda on her smart phone, trying to prioritize the meetings for the day, when the front doorbell rang. Her nerves were instantly on edge. No one ever came to her house without an invitation. Something had to be wrong. She walked to the bedroom and removed her handgun from the drawer of the nightstand and slipped it under her belt in the back.

She moved down the stairs very deliberately, trying to guess who would be coming here. Were there any witnesses to the slaughter of the courier? Certainly not. Her planning had been too good for that to happen. She held her breath as she strained to look out the peephole. She sighed deeply with relief and opened the door. "Master, what an honor and privilege to welcome you to my home," she fawned. "Please come in."

Bill Satori was a short and stocky man with a dark, ruddy complexion and dark brown eyes deeply sunk in his face. He smiled briefly and walked past her and up the stairs. "Nice pistol, Sheila," he noted without looking back. She hurried to follow him upstairs. When she arrived in the kitchen, he was sitting at the small table opposite her coffee. "I'll have some coffee too, if I may, Sheila?"

"Of course, Master, it will only take a moment," she replied. She took a K-cup from the cupboard and slid it into her coffee maker and pressed the brew button. Almost instantly, the fragrance

33

of coffee filled the room. She looked at him and asked, "Cream and sugar, like usual, Master?" He nodded and turned to look out on the city. After she had prepared his coffee, she put some cookies on a small plate and brought everything to the table and sat down. "Master, is anything wrong?"

He laughed and smiled at her. "No, Sheila, everything is fine. The episode yesterday was perfect, and I'm very proud of you. But I wanted to find out how you are feeling about all of this. Many people died senselessly yesterday in our little attack. We both know that Manson was the only real target. The rest were, shall we say, collateral damage to hide our true intent. If someone discovered we were behind this, they might think us extreme. I can imagine that is difficult for a young, beautiful woman to cope with."

"Master, I never question your decisions," she replied. "Besides, people die every day. None of them would have lived forever."

Bill chuckled, "My, you are a cold-blooded one, aren't you Sheila?"

"Just trying to do my job, Master," she said. "Am I not meeting your expectations?"

"Quite the contrary, my dear. You are one of my most trusted advisors and friends. I do have to admit I was surprised that you left the cash though. You could have kept it, you know."

"Never, Master," she demanded. "You told me to leave it, as we had an arrangement with Mr. Martin."

"But he won't be spending it now."

"A deal is a deal, Master."

Bill laughed again. "You're quite the woman, Sheila, and I'm proud to have you on my team. I've deposited one hundred thousand dollars in your account today as a small bonus for the New York job."

"You are too generous, Master. Thank you very much."

"There is much yet to do, Sheila. I have several such missions for you in Western Europe over the next weeks," Bill began. "We need to get as many countries fearful of terrorist attacks as we can.

That will drive billions of new business to our company. Already today we have been contacted by the City of New York for a video surveillance system worth a few hundred million."

"These are very exciting times for Satori Industries, Master," she smiled. "I'm happy to do my part."

"Please take a few days off. You can fly to Madeira tomorrow if you like, and stay at my residence there for three or four days. Then I will contact you with the next steps. You'll be much closer to the Continent from there."

"Again, Master, you are very generous," she said.

He leaned across the table and whispered, "There is a brewing problem though. The Prospect Enterprise is becoming more interested in our activities, although I'm not certain how they can trace anything to us."

"What would you like me to do?"

"Nothing yet, Sheila. You handle things in Europe. I have a few friends inside the Prospect organization, and I'll use them to learn more. If your unique talents are required, I'll contact you right away," he replied.

§

The intercom button on Emmanuel Prospect's desk phone chirped. He pressed the button and said, "What is it, Liz?"

"Sorry to bother you, Granddad, but your son Josh is here with two women and would like to meet with you briefly," his assistant for too-many-years-to-recall said in her velvety Southern drawl.

"Is there time in my schedule for this? This is very unusual."

"Your schedule is open for one-half hour before the Mayor is due to arrive, Granddad."

"Okay, send them in," he said, closing the connection. Joshua was Granddad's youngest son, and his siblings thought the favorite as well. But Joshua chose to stay outside the family business, preferring to live a simple life in a small apartment in a poor Bronx neighborhood. Joshua always said they should stay close to the poorest people to remain humble and best able to accomplish that which was truly important.

As they stepped into the old man's office, Joshua looked the same: tall, lean, and with his long hair tied into a tight ponytail running down most of his back. Like his father and brother, he wore a neatly trimmed mustache and beard. He rushed forward to hug his father tightly. "Dad, it's been a while," he whispered. "I'm sorry for that."

"We should chat later, son," he replied. "Please introduce me to your friends, and by the way, I only have a half hour before the Mayor arrives."

"I'll keep it brief, Dad," Josh said as he walked back to the two women. "This is Rachel Manson and her daughter Shirley. They live in a small house just down the street from my place. Rachel's husband, Vincent, was killed yesterday in the bomb attack downtown."

Emmanuel walked over to the women and shook the older woman's hand. "I'm so sorry for your loss, Mrs. Manson." He touched the younger woman on the shoulder and said, "Poor child, please accept my condolences." He motioned toward two couches, and the women sat on one and the two men on the opposite. He put his hand on his son's knee and asked, "What can we do for these poor people, Joshua?"

"Actually, Mrs. Manson wanted to talk to you. I just facilitated this. Please go ahead, Rachel, we're listening."

Rachel cleared her throat and blushed. "This is very difficult for me, Mr. Prospect."

"Would you prefer to come back in a few days when you're feeling more secure?" the old man asked. "I cannot imagine what you're going through right now."

"No. I think it's best to clear the air as soon as possible," Rachel said. "The deaths of my husband and his brother were not random.

They were murdered deliberately, and I think I know who was behind it."

"His brother?" the old man asked.

"He was the man who suffered a heart attack in the subway two days ago," Joshua reminded him.

"Ah, yes, I remember that now. But how was a heart attack a murder, Mrs. Manson?" Emmanuel asked.

"Please let me be frank, Mr. Prospect. My brother-in-law Lenny was not a good man," she replied. "He's been on the wrong side of the law his entire life. Vince tried to sever all connections with him years ago, but whenever Lenny was down and out, he would show up at our door, begging for a place to stay and some money. Vince could never turn him down. They were brothers, after all."

"Your husband was a good brother, Mrs. Manson," Granddad said.

"Thank you, sir. But the night before Lenny died, he stayed at our house. Shirley had gone to bed and Vince and I were sitting in the kitchen with him. He told us a beautiful woman came looking for him that day and offered him twenty thousand dollars to plant a bomb in a coffee shop. She said her boss wanted to shake up the Mayor's office in order to secure a new contract for surveillance equipment. Lenny was horrified. He said he turned the woman down flat and threatened to tell the police," she said.

"Did he call the police?"

"No. Lenny would never do that. He's been in too much trouble with them and the cops would never believe a man like him. But when he told us, my husband blew his stack. He screamed at Lenny about how much danger he was in. He told him he should have made an excuse or something. Vince was so mad that he physically grabbed his brother by the scruff of the neck and threw him outside. I couldn't believe my eyes," Rachel said. "The two of them argued through the door for a few minutes. Then Lenny just left, and that was the last time we saw him alive."

"And that was it?" Emmanuel asked.

"Not quite," the younger woman added. "I heard the commotion downstairs. When things got quiet, I couldn't sleep, so I went over to the window to say goodbye to my uncle. When he walked around the side of the house, I called to him. Uncle Lenny turned to look at me and made a sheepish smile. Then he just turned and walked away. That's when I noticed the white limousine parked across the street from our house. I thought that was really weird. No one in our neighborhood has the money to rent a limo. As Lenny walked down the street, the limo drove away. While I can't be sure, I thought there was a blonde-haired woman sitting in the back."

"Wow!" Emmanuel exclaimed. "That's a frightening story. But what can I do?"

"Dad, there is another detail that Shirley does remember," Joshua noted.

"Yeah. The license plate on the limo was unusual. It read SATORI9," she said.

"Joshua, are you suggesting that Satori Industries is involved in this?" Emmanuel asked.

"You already know the answer to that question, Dad. Video surveillance equipment is one of their specialties. And you know Bill Satori will do anything to grow his business. I bet you even know who the blonde is, don't you?" Joshua asked.

Emmanuel sighed, nodded and held his head in his hands, lost in thought. After a moment, he looked up at his son and said, "These women are in extreme danger. Can we put them in a safe house?"

"I'm not leaving my home, Josh," Rachel argued. "I've already lost my husband and I'm not about to lose all my friends and possessions."

"Rachel, I'll take care of everything. You can stay in your house for now," Joshua noted. "But I want you to tell my dad about the conversation you had with Vince before he went to work two days ago."

Rachel sighed and looked downward. Her eyes were welling with tears. "Vince was working the afternoon shift in his cab that day. He got a call from the police around noon telling us that Lenny was dead. He and I cried together for a long time. He called his dispatcher and asked for the day off, but was told there was one long-distance fare from Westchester County he'd have to take. So, we had a cup of tea together to calm his nerves. Then he told me how he knew Lenny was murdered. He wanted revenge. He told me if God would put that killer in his cab he would bring him here and kill him in the garage. He said his friends would help out and dispose of the body and any personal effects. He prayed that would happen so his brother would not have died for nothing. When he left for work, he took his pistol with him, confident that God would help him out, but nothing happened. He brought that one fare into the city and then clocked out and came home."

"Joshua, please do whatever you can for these ladies. Make sure they are safe and provided for," Emmanuel said.

"I've already made the arrangements, Dad. I'll stay with them until the team is in place. Then I'd like to go meet Gabe's new roommate. After what you've just heard, I hope you agree with me."

"Yes, that seems like a prudent plan," Emmanuel said. "This story gets more complicated by the hour. And try to find out what the burning room means too. That seems to be the only loose thread left."

§

The early morning clouds had disappeared and it was becoming a warm sunny day in the city. Pete Smith slipped out of the Prospect residence at noon to take a look around the neighborhood. He would be starting his new job in a few days and wanted to scope out any eateries or coffee shops on the four-block stroll to Bertrand Industries. He had skipped breakfast today since he did not want Mike and Gabe following him around. It seemed odd that those two seemed to have nothing better to do than tag along with him. Perhaps they knew the best places around, but Pete was just not in the mood for company. He came to the city to build a new life and career, far from the cornfields of Iowa. Two doors ahead on the left was a delicatessen, so he decided to stop for a bite to eat. Opening the door, he ran into the end of a line of people waiting for tables, so he took his place with them. A line was a very good sign. It not only meant that the food was good, but also the service had to be quick to get this many folks through lunch in one hour. As he waited, a waitress came up and asked, "Table or counter?"

"The counter's fine with me," he replied. She pointed to an empty chair at the counter and moved along to the next person in line. Pete sat and looked at the menu. There were no Jewish delis in his hometown and he had no idea what to order.

"What'll it be, sonny?" an older waitress behind the counter asked.

"What's good?"

"If you'd order already, that would be good," the waitress replied.

"Excuse me," said the woman sitting next to him at the counter. "I'd recommend the pastrami on rye. It's incredible. But you should get a half sandwich. The full one is huge!"

"Thank you," Pete smiled at her, and turned to the brusque waitress. "I'll have what she said and an iced tea."

"Suit yourself," the woman said and walked away.

"Don't worry about her," the young woman said. "You'll get used to that kind of attitude around here."

"I hope not," Pete laughed.

"You know, you look awfully familiar to me," she replied. "Aren't you Peter Smith?"

He was stunned. He had been in the city for two days, almost always in the Prospect cousin's apartment, and now a young woman recognized him in a tiny deli. "I'm sorry, but I guess you have the best of me."

"I guess you don't remember me, but I was only one of the four people on the call." She stuck out her hand and he shook it warmly. "I'm Isabel Garcia, and I'm the HR Director at Bertrand Industries. Remember that Skype call we had?"

The waitress returned and slammed a plate and glass in front of him. Without saying a word, she turned and walked away again. "I do remember the call, Ms. Garcia. I was actually headed over to your office after lunch. I wanted to check out the area between my apartment and the office. It's good to see you again."

"Pete, please just call me Isabel," she smiled. "I'll walk back with you after we eat. There are some problems we need to discuss."

"Problems? Do I still have the job?"

"Yes, of course, but we don't know for how long," she replied. "Just this morning, the Prospect Enterprise made a tender offer to acquire our company."

"You're kidding me!" Pete gasped. "I can't believe they did that."

"That's an interesting reaction! Whatever do you mean?"

"Well, I had dinner with Mr. Prospect, two of his sons, and two grandsons last night. He asked me to go to work for him instead of Mr. Bertrand, but I told him I had to stand by my commitment to Bertrand Industries," he recalled.

"I'm sure they are unrelated, Pete. Pardon me for saying this, but you're just a recent college graduate with no experience. I hardly see how the Prospect Enterprise would buy our company just to get you," she laughed. "But I am totally impressed that you know the Prospect family. You'll have to tell me all about them later."

"Are you two dating or eating lunch," the old waitress said as she interrupted their conversation. "We need the seats, so eat and go." Before they could react, she walked into the kitchen.

Chapter 7

Gabe was sitting in front of his three computer screens, trying to figure out what was going on in the Middle East region. The revenue projections were dropping by the day. The regional VP, another of his uncles, could not figure it out either; and, as usual, Gabe was called upon to work his magic on the numbers. There had to be some clue buried in the columns and rows of figures, but after two hours of looking, nothing had caught his eye. He sighed and sipped his now-cold coffee and sat back, just as his phone chimed in his pocket. He extracted the device and looked at the screen, then pressed the connect button. "Uncle Josh, this is a pleasant surprise. How are you?"

"I'm fine, Gabe. How are you?"

"I'm just going a little crazy looking at the Middle Eastern projections. Something's wrong over there and I can't see it in the numbers," Gabe confided.

"Well, I'm sure you'll figure it out. You do have that unique talent. But you know what I would do, don't you?"

"You'd fly over there and talk to the people," Gabe replied. "In fact, that's a great idea! Why don't you do that? I'm kind of busy myself."

"Gabe, you know how I feel about the family business," Josh replied. "But I'm actually calling about your new roommate. Dad and I met with two very interesting ladies this morning, and we both think it's important I meet him."

"Sure, you know you are welcome anytime, Uncle Josh," Gabe said. "Hang on a second and let me ask Pete about his schedule…"

"No problem, I'll hold . . ."

Two long minutes later, Gabe grabbed the phone and replied, "He's not here."

"I thought you and Michael were keeping an eye on him?"

"We were! Mike left town again and I told Pete I'd walk around with him later. Maria said he just left about an hour ago," Gabe said. "What do we do now?"

"Do you have any idea where he might have gone?"

"Since he arrived, he's been talking about checking out the local eateries and the route to his new job at Bertrand Industries. Do you think he's there?"

"I'm leaving Dad's office now and heading to Bertrand's location. You take the most direct route and we'll meet there. If you see Pete, grab him, and let me know where you two are," Joshua explained.

"Let's just calm down a minute, Uncle Josh," Gabe said. "Don't you think we might be a bit overzealous on this?"

"Gabriel, Bill Satori is involved now."

"Whoa! I haven't heard that name in a long time," Gabe gasped. "Okay, I got it. I'll be out on the street in two minutes. Goodbye, Uncle Josh." He closed the connection and headed for the elevator. As he reached the elevator and pressed the call button, he turned and shouted, "Maria, call me if Pete comes back, okay?"

"Si, Senor," she replied as the elevator doors closed behind him.

§

The sidewalks were packed with people as Pete and Isabel walked out of the delicatessen. "Pete, I'm going to hold onto your arm so we don't get separated in this mob," she said as passersby pushed them back and forth. This was yet another unique experience for the man from the small town in Iowa. There appeared to be more people on this one block than in his entire town. Most of the people were wearing business attire, as Pete knew he would be soon. Suits and ties were not his favorite attire, but in Manhattan, it was the norm and would take some getting used to. The crowd was not the real problem though. Everyone seemed to be lost in their own worlds and not averse to bumping into him as they passed. He thought about what his mother told him about pickpockets in big cities and casually moved his wallet from his rear to front pocket. They stopped at an intersection to wait for the walk signal. It had been an incredible coincidence to run into Isabel in the deli, he thought. In a city as packed with as many folks as Manhattan, the odds must have been astronomical, yet here she was, casually holding onto his right arm. He had certainly never dreamed about anything like this!

As he stood waiting for the light, a thought arose in the back of his mind and quickly pushed its way to his prefrontal lobe. In his mind, he could see a car racing toward them. He could see the people scrambling to get out of the way, but many acted too late. He saw a pregnant woman hit by the car and flying through the air. Blood was everywhere and people were screaming in pain. He was frozen and couldn't seem to move as the car continued toward them. "Pete, the light changed, let's go," urged Isabel while pulling on his arm. Instantly, he snapped out of his dream and began to walk forward, along with the throng of people who had been waiting for the light to change. He quickly realized it was just another dream and prayed that it would never happen here or anywhere else. Let this vision be just a dream, he thought. They walked another block in the teaming crowd, which seemed to be thinning quickly as people stepped into buildings to return to work, or arrived wherever they were headed.

They arrived at the next intersection and stopped to wait for the signal again. That was when he thought he heard someone shouting his name. He turned around but was completely surrounded by the others waiting for the light. It sounded like Gabe's voice, he thought. But why would Gabe be here? He realized that there must be thousands of men named Peter in New York City. He smiled to himself at his presumption that the shout was aimed at him; but did notice that the voice was coming closer, which made him pause for a second. Again, Isabel was pulling on his arm. "Where's your mind at, Pete?" she asked. "We're almost there." They joined the crowd as they began to move across the intersection.

"I'm sorry, Isabel. I guess I was just distracted by the number of people here. I'm not used to this where I come from," he replied, as they continued to cross in front of a line of yellow taxis waiting their turn to enter the intersection and deliver their fares.

Then he heard someone shout "Pete!" again. He turned his head back to the sidewalk and saw Gabe standing there. The air filled with the sounds of taxi horns honking. The crowd around them began to scatter in different directions. Isabel said something about running, but her voice was drowned out by the horns. Still looking back at Gabe, he could see his lips move as if to say "Look out!" but couldn't hear him over the din. His head snapped around to see a black sedan racing toward them. Isabel was pulling him away, but his feet felt like lead, or perhaps it was just the sensation of slowing time that made it seem so hard to move. Then the car slammed into the crowd. Pete saw the pregnant woman hit by the car and flying through the air. Now it became really strange. As her body came down, somehow Gabe was there to catch her, but that could not be true since Gabe was behind him only a second ago. More people were struck or managed to jump out of the way of the careening vehicle. After what was probably a tiny fraction of a second, only Isabel and Pete stood in front of the onrushing car. Nothing could save them now. Then Pete felt a hand in his back shoving him and Isabel out of the way. He turned to see a man with a beard and long ponytail being struck by the car and pinned between it and a taxi which it slammed into, coming to a stop at last.

After being shoved away, Pete and Isabel tumbled onto the hard pavement. Pete felt his face being scraped by the concrete and then come to rest. When he sat up, he could see Isabel holding her badly scraped knee, where blood was oozing out and down her shin. It had to be a dream, he thought. Soon he would wake up, preferably in his old bedroom back in Iowa, and give up on his search for fame and fortune in the big city. "Pete, are you okay?" said a voice nearby.

He turned his head to blearily see Gabe kneeling next to him. "I think so," he replied. "My brain's a bit confused by all of this right now. Is Isabel all right?"

Gabe moved over to the woman and touched her knee. He turned back to Pete and said, "Yeah, she'll be fine. Look, the wound has already stopped bleeding."

"Oh my God, Gabe, what about the man who pushed us out of the way? I saw his body getting crushed between the car and a taxi," Pete asked.

"I think you mean me," said another voice above him.

Pete looked up, and there was the man with the beard and ponytail, standing and smiling at him. "I'm pretty agile, Peter. As you can see, I'm okay."

"But how?"

"All that matters now is that no one was killed in this crazy mess," the man said. "By the way, my name is Joshua Prospect, and I'm one of Gabe's uncles." He extended his hand. When Pete shook it, the other pulled him up to his feet. Pete hugged Joshua and thanked him again for the miraculous rescue. "Pete, as you can see, ambulances and police are arriving now. We have to stay a while and make our reports. Then maybe you and I can have dinner together, okay?"

"Sure, of course," Pete exclaimed, as dozens of patrol cars cordoned off the area.

§

"Yes, I know . . . it won't happen again . . ." Gabe said into his Bluetooth headset. The phone on his desk showed Granddad's photo and number.

"Don't blame yourself, Gabriel," the old man replied. "Peter is your roommate, not your prisoner. None of us knew Satori was involved until this morning. But we need a new plan to protect him."

"How does he even know about Pete? He's just a normal guy," Gabe asked.

"I'll just assume that was a rhetorical question," Granddad laughed. "But clearly Satori is afraid that someone like Peter could help us preempt his actions. You must know how powerful that knowledge is. And if Peter could be turned to help Satori, it would be devastating to everything we try to do. His premonitions can work both ways, you know."

"Just like Sheila Farness," Gabe replied. "Yes, I know how dangerous this is."

"Do you think of her often, Gabriel?"

"Not often, but from time to time. You remember that I asked her to marry me, right?"

"Of course I do. I was very happy for you both," Emmanuel said.

"And from one day to the next, it all changed," Gabe sighed. "I'm glad we never included her in the business. That would have been incredibly bad, given how things turned out. But that makes me wonder why you're so eager to get Pete into the business."

"I may be old, but I'm no old fool, Gabriel," he laughed. "Working for one of our companies and being in the business are two different things. But changing subjects, what plans do you have to protect Peter Smith?"

"I talked to Mike about that, and he's arranging for around-the-clock surveillance. You know--the kind Pete will never notice. I've also spoken with Maria, Sam, and Bob. They will let me know whenever he leaves or arrives at the building," Gabe stated. "I assume that's why you're buying Bertrand Industries, right?"

"Oscar is a good friend of the family, and he deserves to have a secure and happy retirement. Just so you know, he's staying with the company as CEO for as long as he wants. It's a good investment," Granddad noted.

"And . . . ?"

"Yes, of course, Peter is part of the overall consideration, although I'd never tell him or anyone at the company that."

"Granddad, you know that Pete might change jobs over and again. You can't go around buying every company in town. Eventually everything will be owned by you or Satori."

"Coalescing the existence of the city into the most primal battles of all," Granddad replied. "No, I have no interest in anything like that, but I know that Satori does. But buying a company that Pete decides to work for is not the way he works. Kill him and be done with it, that's his way."

"Granddad, I just got a text from Sam saying that Pete and Uncle Josh have just left the building."

"I thought they'd be dining at your place."

"You know Josh. His world view is a bit different. I'm sure he wants to slum it with Pete to make sure he remembers how most people live," Gabe said.

"Your uncle is a saint," Granddad replied. "I often wish I was more like him."

§

Sheila loved the beach, which was fortunate, as the Satori estate on Madeira was on a private beach that stretched along several hundred yards of prime real estate. She was wearing her red bikini and soaking up the local sunshine. Her first cup of coffee was sitting on a small table next to her lounge chair. Satori was right, she really did need a vacation, she thought. Three or four days here would do the trick. She loved traveling in Europe and her upcoming jobs were a perfect excuse to see as much of the continent as she could. Of course, the authorities would not be pleased by the terror her team would inflict, but that was their problem to deal with. She heard the sound of footsteps on the loose-gravel beach and turned her head to see Joao, the head butler, approaching with her cell phone on a silver platter. A bottle of tequila and a shot glass were also on the platter. "Miss, Mr. Satori has asked you to call him now," he said.

"What's the tequila for?" she asked.

"Mr. Satori said you may need it," he grinned as he picked up her coffee cup, put in on the tray and set the tray on the small table. He bowed slightly and hurried up the beach toward the broad porch facing the sea.

She took the phone and held down the number one key until it began to dial. "Master, it is me, Sheila. How may I serve you today?"

"Sheila, my dear, did Joao give you the tequila?"

"Yes, Master, but it is still morning here."

"Please drink a shot before I say more," he replied.

She quickly poured liquor into the glass until it overflowed and then swallowed it in one gulp. "The tequila is excellent, Master, but my throat is on fire."

"I've made a few serious mistakes, Sheila."

"I hope you don't include me among them, Master," she squirmed, suddenly realizing she could have just been poisoned if he said "Yes."

"No, not you, Sheila. You are my best friend. And believe me, if you were, I would not poison you like a coward in the night. My first mistake was not using better tools to eliminate the Smith fellow," he replied.

Master, I was happy to resolve the issue with the Manson brothers who failed you so utterly," she said.

"Well, we've had another failure, just hours ago. I had a fellow try to run him down in the street, but the damned Prospect family intervened," he groaned.

"Would you like me to return to New York to handle it personally?"

"Not just yet, Sheila. Your assignments in Europe are much more important to us. Since the Prospects will be watching young Mr. Smith, I've decided to sit back and see how things progress. I am very hopeful that your work on the Continent will distract them long enough for me to get to him," he explained.

"Do you think you can convince him to join us?"

"If I can separate him from the Prospects, I believe I can," he laughed. "His talents would be very useful to us."

"You are correct, Master. Advance knowledge of any Prospect family actions would be an incredible benefit to your company," she replied. "Do you need me to clean up after the botched traffic incident?"

"No, my dear. I handled that a bit differently. The driver had a heart attack at the right moment, and we moved the car after he passed out. I'm sure the police will call it a terrible tragedy. However, the Prospects are already closing a circle around Mr. Smith. That's why your tasks are more important than ever now," he said.

"I understand, Master, and will do everything I can to exceed your expectations. What else can I do for you, Master?" she asked.

"Sheila, do you ever think about Gabe Prospect and what might have been with him?" he asked.

"Master, to be honest, I do think about him from time to time, but you must realize that he is firmly in my past. I have chosen to serve you and I will always do so. Why do you ask?"

"Perhaps I'm an old fool, Sheila," he sighed. "Our working relationship has always made me happy, and I must confess I have feelings for you." Sheila was shocked. She held the phone frozen in her hand for a full minute. "Are you still there, Sheila?"

"I'm sorry, Master, but you surprised me. I am very flattered by your words and have strong feelings for you as well."

Now Bill was stunned. "Thank you, my dear. Perhaps then I can ask two more questions."

"Of course, Master."

"First, would you please call me Bill? I think Master is too formal."

"I would be honored, Bill," she giggled.

"Second, I am currently flying in your direction. Perhaps you and I can have dinner on the veranda after I arrive?"

"I will be awaiting your arrival, Bill."

Chapter 8

Joshua Prospect and Pete Smith sat at a table in the small Japanese sushi restaurant two blocks from Gabe's residence. Joshua would have preferred to take his guest to his own neighborhood to get a flavor of normal life, but did not want to take unnecessary risks with this unique man who had so bedazzled his relatives. Pete was busily tapping a text into his phone while Joshua considered the young man between sips of his green tea. Gabe told his uncle that the clientele here was mostly Japanese and their meal had turned out be excellent.

Pete set down his phone and said, "I'm sorry about that, Josh, but my cousin has been worried sick since I moved into the city. She keeps asking me how I am, over and over again."

"I think it's great to have someone who cares that much for you," Joshua replied. "You are lucky to have such a concerned cousin, Pete. And frankly, after what you've been through since you arrived, I can see her point."

"I know you're right," Pete agreed. "But accidents happen all the time."

"Pete, most folks don't have a vision of the accident about to happen to them," Joshua noted as he extracted his cell phone from his pocket. He sighed and stood up. "Sorry, Pete, I have to take this call. Don't pay the bill. It's on me and I'll be right back." He pressed the connect button and walked out of the restaurant.

Pete pressed his phone into his pocket and sipped his tea. He could see Joshua outside talking on the phone. He did not look pleased and seemed to be shouting into the microphone, which seemed counterintuitive for such a gentle man. Not wanting to intrude, he sat back and closed his eyes. He thought about Isabel and the accident and shuddered involuntarily. He opened his eyes to see a beautiful blonde woman sitting across the table from him.

"Hi, Pete," she said as she extended her hand to shake his. "My name is Sheila. My boss and I have been looking forward to meeting you."

"I'm sorry, but how do you know who I am?" he asked.

"We know all about you, and we know the Prospects will do anything they can to keep you away from us. But I think that's unfair. You're free to do whatever you want and work for anyone you want. I guarantee we can pay double what they will offer you."

"I don't understand. This doesn't make any sense," he said.

The woman stood up and moved next to him. She took his hands and pulled him to his feet, then leaned forward and pressed her lips against his. Her body was leaning into him and her perfume was saturating his mind. When at last she pulled back, she was smiling and giggling. "I like you a lot, Pete. You and I will definitely be meeting again."

Joshua had reentered the restaurant and came up behind her. "Sheila, what are you doing here?" he asked.

In what seemed like the blinking of an eye, she opened her purse, withdrew a handgun, turned and shot Joshua in the chest. Blood splattered everywhere as Joshua fell to the ground. The other customers screamed and rushed to escape the restaurant. Pete was frozen in place. Sheila turned to him and patted him on the cheek, saying, "See you soon, Pete."

"Pete. Pete!" Joshua exclaimed. Pete opened his eyes to see Joshua sitting across the table again. "Are you okay?"

He was trembling and sweating. He tried to wipe his brow but his hands were shaking too severely. "It's nothing," he stammered. "It was just another dream."

"Tell me about it now, before you forget any of the details," Joshua demanded. Even though he was always uncomfortable talking about his dreams, Joshua's tone drew every detail out of him. Pete explained the dream and Joshua listened intently and even made a few notes on a scrap of paper he pulled from his pocket. After a minute, Joshua looked up and said, "And you're sure her name was Sheila?"

"That's what she said."

"That is absolutely amazing!" Joshua replied. "First let me tell you that my family knows these people and they are real. Sheila Farness works for William Satori, who is sort of a competitor with the Prospect Enterprise."

"But why would a business competitor want to kill you? Or to hire me for that matter?"

"I can't say," he sighed.

"Because you don't know or you can't tell me?" Pete asked.

"Maybe a little of both," Joshua chuckled. "You may not believe me, but I am not part of the family business, even though I love my Dad, brothers, and sisters. I think their businesses do good work, but it's just not my style. And what Sheila said is absolutely correct. You are free to choose who to meet and who to work for, although I would ask you to exercise extreme caution if you decide to work for Satori."

"Why can't you answer my questions?"

"Did my Dad ever tell you the tale of the two doors?" Joshua asked. Pete nodded. "You have the right to make your own decisions. That opinion shouldn't be skewed by my beliefs or those of my family or Satori for that matter. You need to learn for yourself and make the choices that work for you."

"Does everyone in your family talk in code?" Pete asked.

"Everyone except my brother Luce, I'm sorry to say."

"If you don't mind, may I change the subject?"

"Of course," Joshua replied as he slipped four twenty-dollar bills into the folder holding the dinner bill.

"Well, I didn't mean to spy on you or anything, but I noticed you were screaming into your phone out there. Is anything wrong?"

Joshua sighed deeply and looked down at his lap for a full minute before he lifted his head to look at the other man and said,

"Full disclosure, right?" Pete nodded. "Have you heard of Leonard and Vincent Manson?"

"Something sounds familiar, but I'm not sure."

"Leonard was the man who tried to rob you at knifepoint on the subway when he had a heart attack." Pete's eyes opened wide and his mouth fell open. "Vincent was his brother and the cabbie who drove you into the city to Gabe's house. He died in the bomb blast you saw in your dream."

"How do you know all of that?"

"The Mansons live near my apartment in the Bronx. We were acquaintances but I wouldn't characterize us as good friends. When I heard about the deaths, I went to pay my respects to Mrs. Manson and her daughter. Rachel told me that her husband had planned to kill the person who killed Leonard if God would put him into his cab."

"And God did . . ." Pete gasped.

"No, He did not, Pete. You did not kill Leonard Manson. That's why Vincent did not try to harm you, even though you had a vision of what would have happened if he did. But I don't think his death was a random seizure either. I think Satori is behind it."

"But why?"

"That's a good question, and I can only speculate."

"Okay then, speculate," Pete pushed.

"Sheila tried to hire Leonard to take the bomb into the coffee shop. But he was stupid enough to turn her down and threaten to call the police. If he had done so, the bombing plot would have been stopped and Satori would have been ruined," Joshua explained.

"Wow! This is all very hard to believe, Josh. But it doesn't explain why you were so upset on the phone."

Joshua sighed again. "Okay, I am in charge of safeguarding Rachel and Shirley Manson since they came to see my dad. Now, they've disappeared."

"Do you think Mr. Satori is involved in that too?"

"Maybe, I don't know for certain. I left a few friends nearby to watch out for them and somehow they slipped out without being seen," Joshua replied.

"They may just have gone on vacation or to visit relatives," Pete suggested.

"I can't tell you why but it is extremely unlikely that my friends would have missed them leaving," Joshua noted. "After I drop you off at Gabe's, I've got to go visit my dad and let him know I failed. That's why I was upset. Let's go," he finished as he stood.

§

Sheila woke early, just as the first light of sunrise began to illuminate the beach in front of Satori's estate on Madeira. She lay quietly for several minutes watching Bill Satori sleep. This was a dream come true for her. Of course, Bill was much older than she, but she had devoted her entire life to the man beside her. She was satisfied to do his dirty work—anything to please him. But she did not know why she had become so slavishly devoted to him.

It had been several years ago when he ran into her in a bar in Barcelona, Spain. She was on a business trip to help her fiancé, Gabe Prospect, with the small office in that city. Gabe had given her a binder for the local manager and, given her fluency in Catalan, she was the obvious choice.

Bill Satori's face and reputation were known to her before he entered the small bar and sat several stools away from her. He was nursing a glass of whisky over ice when she rose, walked over and sat next to him. After some idle chat, he asked her about her job and she dutifully mentioned her position at the Prospect Enterprise, which immediately got Bill's undivided attention. They talked for several hours that evening, enjoying drinks and tapas. It was getting quite late when he offered to give her a ride back to her hotel. It was only four or five blocks, but it had started raining and she was happy for the lift. As the limousine traveled the last two blocks, Bill pulled out all stops. He offered her a better job at twice the base pay and a generous bonus plan. Sheila told him she would have to discuss the matter with her fiancé, kissed him on the cheek, and hurried across the sidewalk into the hotel. By the time she laid down in her bed, her mind was made up. Gabe would understand; after all, this was only business, and when they got married more income would be better than less.

But Gabe did not understand. He tried to tell her that Satori Industries was not a good company and sacrificed everything for profit and political influence. Somehow, that did not matter to her anymore. She had been entranced by the charm and power of Bill Satori and accepted his offer. Her relationship with Gabe suffered with her long absences and seeming lack of concern for him. After several months she broke the engagement and returned the diamond ring. Sheila never looked back or regretted her decision.

Sheila slipped out of bed quietly so as not to disturb Bill. She put a robe over her nightgown and went downstairs and out onto the patio overlooking the Atlantic. Within minutes, Joao came out with a steaming cup of coffee and a croissant for her. He smiled and returned to the house. She checked her e-mail on her smart phone and, seeing nothing important, set the phone down and watched a line of squalls slowly approaching from the southwest. It would be a rainy afternoon, she thought.

Ten minutes later Bill Satori left the house and crossed the patio to join her. Somehow, he had already showered and was wearing a dark blue suit. He kissed her on the forehead and sat down across from her. Joao rushed over to give his master a coffee and then hurried away. "Good morning, sweetheart, how are you today?" he asked.

"I feel great, Bill. How about you?"

"Never better, my dear. I am sorry to say that I must head to Paris later today for several meetings this afternoon and tomorrow. Can I give you a lift?"

"Of course, Bill, thank you. Are you certain you want us to travel together, given my appointments over the next several days?" she asked.

"Don't worry about it," he laughed. "The police are too stupid to figure anything out and, besides, I have many friends in high places on the Continent. Our plans are already in motion and we will not be discovered. In fact, I would like you to accelerate the plan a bit."

"Is something wrong?"

"Not yet, however, each day we let Mr. Smith stay with the Prospects, our chances of getting him on our side dwindle. If your first attack is not for three days, then that gives them seventy-two hours to themselves. If the first mission is tomorrow, we gain forty-eight of those hours back," he replied. "Also, I think you are our best asset to convert Mr. Smith; and remember I said convert, not terminate. Mr. Smith's condition is advancing rapidly, and neither he nor the Prospects know what they are dealing with, but I do."

"Of course, Bill, I will do what you ask. But what do you have in mind?"

"You must do whatever you can to convince Peter Smith to join us. Money is no object. Power is no object. Sex is no object. Do you understand, Sheila?"

"Yes, Master."

"Darling, please call me Bill," he begged. "I know it sounds like I am discounting our relationship, or whoring you out, but nothing could be further from the truth. I love you, Sheila Farness, and I hope we can be married one day soon. But I cannot underestimate the importance of this mission."

"Bill, I will do as you say, but I don't want you to be hurt if something physical happens between him and me. You must know that sex with Smith would mean nothing to me."

He took her hands in his and squeezed them gently. "I know, darling. Honestly, I would prefer it not to happen, but this man is that important to us." He stood and looked out over the ocean. Rain would arrive in less than an hour, and a cool breeze started to blow across the patio. "Sheila, if Smith remains with the Prospects, everything is lost for us. They will anticipate each action we take and preemptively stop them. If he works for us, he can be the highest paid accountant in the history of the world and doesn't even have to share his dreams with us, as long as he doesn't share them with the Prospect family."

She stood and put her arms around Bill, saying, "I will do as you wish, sweetheart. As soon as we are done on the Continent, I'll head to New York."

He kissed her lips softly. "I'm afraid there are more changes, my love. Several of my associates will fly with us from here to Paris. After the first bombing, you will leave and they will continue the jobs."

"Bill, is that a good idea?" she asked. "What if they mess up or get caught? Won't that lead back to you?"

"You are an amazingly wonderful woman, Sheila," he said. "If they mess up, I will punish them and they know that. But it is impossible for them to get caught, although I can't say any more right now."

"As long as you're certain it will be okay?" she asked. He nodded and kissed her again. "Okay, let me go shower and get ready so we can go." She turned to head back to the house.

"Sheila, one last thing," he said. She turned and walked back. "What is the list of targets again? I think I remember, but wasn't certain if I had them in the correct order."

She laughed. "Bill, you never forget anything. The list is Prague, Budapest, Amsterdam, Brussels, London, and Paris."

"I think I want to change things a bit if you don't mind, but this has to be top secret, just between you and me, okay?" She nodded. "I'd like to change Brussels to Rome and London to Lisbon. And they must be the last targets, so you have to move Paris up."

"You're the boss, sweetheart," she laughed. "Whatever you think is best."

"There's a bit more to it than that," he smirked. "First, I want two attacks per day. The entire operation must be complete in three days. Second, you cannot tell anyone until the night before each attack. Your team must be certain that the original list is still in place until the last possible minute."

"Of course we can do that, Bill. But I guess I don't understand what you're thinking."

"Think of it as a test of young Mr. Smith. If the authorities get wind of the attacks and show up in force in London and Paris, then perhaps we have a leak in our organization, or Mr. Smith has some direct mental linkage to someone in my organization. If they show up in Rome and Lisbon, either one of us is the leak, or Mr. Smith has a truly incredible gift. I just have to know which!"

"Very well, Bill. It will take a bit more coordination, but I'm sure we can pull it off."

"Sheila, I want total mayhem on the Continent before we're through. That should be enough to get the Prospects to loosen their grip on Peter Smith. It should also give you two days to get to know him better," he smiled and then began to laugh.

§

Pete was standing in the long line for security clearance at an airport he had never seen. All the signs were in a language he could not understand with English subtitles that were not quite legible either. He must be dreaming again, he realized. A young family was in line in front of him. Two cherub-faced children were playing a form of hide-and-seek around their parent's suitcases. The father was stern-faced and trying to get his wife to rein in the little ones. She spoke in a hushed tone that the children knew they could ignore for now. Soon enough Dad would use his angry voice, and they would have to stop playing, but that time had not arrived yet. He looked ahead at the line of humanity and wondered where in the world he would travel to today. He glanced at his ticket packet for information. He dreamt often of traveling by plane, but normal tickets and check-ins were not part of the dream. He would leisurely walk on board and the plane would be instantly airborne, but not in this dream. The ticket was wedged inside what should have been his passport, but it was wrong too. There was the image of a shield in the center, with what appeared to be two lions and two eagles inscribed. The only word that was readable was Ceska, but that meant nothing to him. Being a dream, he could not read either document well, but he knew the passport was not American. Things were becoming too confusing, and he thought he should wake up and end this silly dream. He glanced behind and saw an older man with only a backpack for luggage. The man was a dead ringer for Emmanuel Prospect, except his hair and beard were salt-and-pepper gray rather than gleaming white. He tried to speak to the man, who only smiled and patted him on the shoulder.

The line moved around a corner to double back. To his right, beyond the restraining line was the exit line for passengers who had checked in. Three short, muscular men were walking by and staring at him. He could feel their eyes burning into his skin. The last of the three grinned, showing his dark teeth. He extended the middle finger on his right hand and laughed as he passed by. "Now that was bizarre," he thought, shaking his head to clear the image as another passenger walked up the exit lane. Pete recognized her immediately. It was Sheila, looking exactly like he saw her in his vision at dinner last night. Her red dress clung to her sensuous curves, and she was smiling at him as she approached. She stopped next to him and touched his cheek with her hand, gently stroking his face. She leaned into him and said, "See you soon, lover boy," and then walked away. He followed her with his eyes until the man behind him caught his eye and frowned. Pete felt a blush moving up his neck and turned back to the line. That was when he noticed the two children had stopped playing. He had not heard the father's voice, but both were now sobbing softly and clinging to their mother, who had knelt down to comfort them.

That was when the first explosion occurred. The noise was overwhelming. Then the mass of people between him and the counter were flying back into him. He and the entire throng flew backward and crashed to the ground. He was buried under other people and struggled to move. There was a smell of sulfur in the air, and he could hear people screaming in pain. Black smoke blotted out almost all light, and he could feel pools of blood on the stone floor underneath him. Why was he still dreaming? It did not make any sense. People in the pile began to move, and he was finally able to get up and look around. Next to him was the father, holding his wife's lifeless body in his arms, his two dead children covered in blood at his feet. Now he could hear sirens as dozens of heavily armed police rushed into the hallway to check the damage and aid the survivors. A second explosion rocked another counter fifty yards away. More fire, more screams of agony filled the air. Pete was frozen in fear. How many more bombs are there, he wondered?

He felt a hand on his shoulder and turned to see the man who had been behind him. His face was burned and covered in blood. Pete did not understand why he was even still alive. "Peter, don't forget them," the man said, pointing to the dead children.

"I won't, Granddad," he replied.

"Look at your passport, my son," the man said.

He looked and somehow it had changed. The shield was completely different as was the wording. He could make out the word Magyar, but nothing else. "I don't understand."

"You will."

A knock at the door finally shook Pete out of his dream. He was still shaking and hearing the explosions in his mind as Maria stuck her head in and told him that breakfast would be ready in half an hour. After she closed the door, he sat on the side of the bed, holding his head in his hands. "Was this another vision, or just another stupid dream?" he said out loud.

Chapter 9

Pete walked into the kitchen to find Gabe standing at the stove with Maria, who was preparing a large pot of soup. The aromas were filling Pete's senses as he approached. The soup was dark red and full of meat and what appeared to be hominy. "So what are you two up to?" he said.

"Pete, you are in for another treat today, my man," Gabe laughed. "Maria is making pozole for us."

"Soup for breakfast?" Pete asked.

"It's very traditional. It's a pork and hominy stew, which you finish with your own selection of condiments. You are going to love it, I guarantee that!"

"Sounds good, but can we talk first, Gabe?"

"Is everything okay?"

"No. Everything is definitely not okay," Pete replied.

"Is it something I did?"

"No, and I apologize if I gave that impression," Pete said. "I've had another dream, and it's worse than the others."

"Worse than me pushing you onto a burning bed or a bomb blowing up a coffee shop?" he asked. Pete only nodded. Gabe asked Maria to keep things simmering while the two men had their talk. "Come with me, Pete," he said as they left the room.

Gabe led Pete across the living room and into his bedroom. The room was quite large with two seating areas near the two massive windows overlooking Central Park. One seating area faced a large flat-screen TV. The other was just for conversation. Gabe led Pete to a couch near the television and they both sat down. "Are we going to watch a movie?" Pete asked.

"No, maybe later, but right now we're making a secure video call to my uncle," Gabe said as he punched the buttons on a small controller. After a few seconds, the television came to life with the image of a brown-haired man sitting behind a massive desk. "Uncle Michael, thank you for taking my call."

"No problem, Gabe," the other smiled. "I take it this is your new roommate, Mr. Smith. How do you do, son? I've been looking forward to meeting you."

"I'm fine, sir," Pete replied. "It's a pleasure to meet you."

"Pete, Uncle Michael is the Chief Operating Officer of the Prospect Enterprise. He is the number two man to my granddad," Gabe reported.

"I heard you make quite the impression on my father, Pete," Michael replied. "That's not easy to do. How can I help you Gabe?"

"Pete has had another dream, and he says it's a doozy. He hasn't even told me about it yet, but I thought you should make your own assessment. Is that okay?" Gabe asked.

"You know, I don't know if this is a good idea," Pete said as he stood up. "I don't really know why your family is so interested in my dreams. It's kind of creepy."

"Pete, please sit down," Michael said firmly. Pete sat almost involuntarily. "I promise I will tell you why we are so interested in you soon. But you must trust us. Please go ahead with your story."

Pete did not want to talk. The Prospect family and their preoccupation with his dreams were unnerving. He still could not understand why he was here in this amazing penthouse apartment, paying almost no rent, and everyone was following him around. But there was something about this Uncle Michael that drew the story out of him. He recounted everything that had happened, especially focusing on the misery on the poor father's face as he watched over his destroyed family. His face had been one of utter hopelessness and abject despair. Perhaps that was why the man behind him told him not to forget them. It was not until he finished the retelling that he noticed that Uncle Michael was the man behind him in the line. He was almost positive that was true. But how could that be? Could his mind have blended the other Prospects together to create a composite? As he finished, he mentioned that coincidence as well.

To his right, Gabe sat slack-jawed, unable to force words out of his mouth. Michael sat quietly, with his two hands in front of him, in the form of a dome with all fingertips touching each other. His lips were tight and his brow was furled. After at least a minute of sitting quietly and digesting what he had heard, he smiled and said, "Thank you for telling me. I know that must have been difficult."

Pete cleared his throat and said, "I'm okay."

Gabe climbed to his feet and crossed over to a small refrigerator and withdrew two water bottles, handing one to a grateful Pete who took a long drink. "Uncle, Pete mentioned the words Ceska and Magyar. You know what that means, right?"

Michael gave an instantaneous frown to his nephew and replied, "Yes, I know. They were Czech and Hungarian passports. So far, all the news is quiet today, but I'll have some folks take a look."

"You think it was some kind of premonition or something?" Pete asked, looking startled at the thought.

"Pete, I don't know," Michael said. "You've seen a lot of strange things in your dreams, many of which have come true. I don't know why any more than you do. But we intend to find out."

"You know Satori is involved," Gabe noted.

"Yes, I have been informed," Michael replied. "I hate to say this, but at this time, there is little we can do. We will keep an eye on things, but a dream is not enough for us to shut down airports. The police would laugh their heads off."

"Uncle, that isn't good enough!" Gabe shouted. "You remember what he said about that man and his butchered family. We can't ignore that!"

"Calm down, Gabe. I will do what I can, but you have to understand that the police in Budapest and Prague are not going to take Pete's dream as evidence of a terrorist threat. They would think all of us are crazy. If we tell them, and they do nothing, and then it happens, the blame would likely come back to us. If we tell them, and they heighten security and nothing happens, we would lose all credibility."

"This whole thing sucks," Gabe said dejectedly.

"I agree wholeheartedly," Michael said. "But that's the way it is and you know it. And no matter what happens, everyone will still be okay, and you know that too."

"Now I'm confused," Pete said. "If the bombs kill that man's family and all those other people, how is everyone supposed to be okay?"

"I told you I'd tell you soon, Pete, but not now," Michael answered. "Please trust me. I may not tell you everything when you want to hear it, but I will never lie."

"Thanks for everything, Uncle, and yes, I understand what you said, and it's all true," Gabe replied. "I'm sorry if I got upset."

"I'm pissed off most of the time, Gabe, so don't worry about it. Like today, I had to get here early and missed my breakfast, and I'm pissed about that too."

"Uncle Michael, Maria is making pozole right now. You should come over," Gabe noted.

"Really, she's making pozole? You know that's my favorite. I still don't know why I let you steal her from me. I can be there in twenty minutes," Michael replied. "Pete, I look forward to meeting you in the flesh a bit later. I can tell you that I am amazed by your talents. Now I know why my dad is so infatuated by you." The screen went dark.

§

Sheila was sitting quietly with her eyes closed aboard one of Satori's private jets. Everything had gone according to plan today and the team was prepared to execute the next steps of the plan tomorrow morning. She had wanted to be there personally to make certain the execution was flawless, but Bill had been adamant. She wondered if the Smith fellow had foretold the events in Budapest and Prague. It did not matter either way though. The bombs had gone off and the global press was already blasting Al Qaeda for the attacks. Not surprisingly, and as Bill had suggested, the terrorists groups were eager to accept responsibility in order to further the sense of panic in the Western World. After two more days, they would likely change their tune. The scale of death and destruction across Europe would shock even them, and they would have to acknowledge their eager acceptance of responsibility would lead to more foreign troops on the ground in their native countries and even more rebellion within their groups. But they had chosen the door they stepped through and, like it or not, they were allied with Satori Industries forever.

"Ms. Farness, we will be arriving in New York in two hours," said the steward who was now standing next to her seat.

"Thanks, Frank. Could you refresh my drink please?" she asked. He smiled and took her glass back to the galley. News of the attacks would be hitting all the news outlets about now, she thought. Most major airports worldwide would heighten security immediately. She smiled, knowing tomorrow's attacks could not be stopped by a few hundred soldiers guarding the tarmacs of the world. All was going according to plan. Bill Satori would be proud of her again. Frank returned and set the glass of whisky down on her side table and walked away. She took a sip and swirled the liquor around in her mouth. Now it was time to focus on Peter Smith. But if he was truly clairvoyant, there was a strong likelihood that he had seen her in his dreams as well. How could she convince him that her appearance was coincidental? That was a difficult question to answer. Bill had suggested that she seduce him. Maybe it really would be that simple. She smiled again.

§

"Okay, Pete," Gabe began. "First you add oregano and lemon juice to the pozole to your taste. Then you finish with chopped onion and cilantro, radishes and cabbage. Just watch me. You'll get the hang of it quickly."

Pete watched as Gabe added condiments to his soup and stirred to blend all the ingredients well. "I thought your uncle was coming over."

"Something must have come up. Don't worry about him, he's always getting involved in new stuff," Gabe replied as he shoved a spoonful of soup into his mouth.

Pete tasted the soup, and it was every bit as wonderful as Gabe had promised. "This is really delicious, Maria. Thank you."

"*De nada*, Senor," she smiled.

The elevator doors opened and Michael strode out and hurried to the kitchen. His face was beet red, his hair was disheveled, and his suit was singed as if he had walked through an open fire. He smelled of soot and sulfur. "Damn it all!"

"Uncle Michael, what happened to you?" Gabe gasped.

He grabbed the remote and switched on the TV. "It doesn't matter which channel you pick. They're all the same," he replied as he sat down next to Gabe. Maria walked over and offered a bowl of soup and he waved her off. "Maybe later."

"We're providing continual coverage of the terrorist attacks today at the airports in Budapest, Hungary, and Prague in the Czech Republic. Only two hours ago multiple bombs were detonated in both airports. Tentative reports are that hundreds if not thousands of people have been killed or wounded. Both airports are now shut down, and security levels have been heightened across the globe," the news reporter said.

"Oh God," Pete gasped. "This can't be happening."

"Following is a translated interview with a young Czech man who was with his family at the airport in Prague when the bombs exploded," the newscaster continued. The screen switched to the exterior of the heavily damaged terminal. A local reporter was standing with the family of four who seemed unhurt, although they were covered in blood and dust from the blast.

"That's him!" Pete shouted. "That's the family from my dream. How can this be true? They died."

The father had his arms around his family. The wife and two children were sobbing and shivering in the light rain. He said, "It was the most horrible thing ever. We were headed on vacation to Paris and were waiting to check in for our flight. My kids were playing around our feet and the crowd was restless and eager to get going when the explosion hit. I was so afraid. Time seemed to slow down and I could see people flying through the air toward us. I tried to grab my children but the blast was too strong. Then I felt incredibly calm. It felt as though a man had wrapped his arms around us all, but it wasn't just a man. I thought I could feel long wings wrapped around us like a cocoon as we flew backward with the crowd. After we landed, I was desperate to hold my family, and was so happy we were all there together. None of them seemed to be hurt, but there were many, many dead people and pieces of bodies and rubble from the building. The smell of smoke and death was everywhere. I looked for the man who saved us, but could not find him. I pray to God he survived the attack."

Michael clicked off the television and sat silently.

"Thank you, Michael," Pete said. "I have no idea what you did, but thank you."

"Don't thank me Pete. Too many people were killed and injured today. I blamed myself at first. I should have listened to you. But then I realized that you did not have a premonition at all," the uncle replied.

"I don't understand, Uncle," Gabe replied. "This is exactly what Pete saw in his dream."

"Didn't you hear what the reporter said? He said it was two hours ago when the bombs exploded. Pete, what were you doing two hours ago?"

"Sleeping?" he answered.

"Exactly! You did not dream about what would happen. You were dreaming about what *was* happening," Michael explained.

"But why didn't the family die like in my dream? And why is your suit singed like you were in the blast?"

"I can't really answer that now, but I will soon," Michael replied. "I only wish there was a way for you to dream about these things before they happen. Then maybe we could take action."

"So, what do we do now, Uncle?" Gabe asked.

"Well, I for one, will have some of Maria's delicious pozole, if you don't mind," Michael replied.

Chapter 10

Gabe was hurrying down the crowded sidewalk. He had not been summoned to the Prospect Enterprise home office in years, and he liked that just fine. Shortly after Uncle Michael left the apartment, Gabe's dad had called to invite him to a meeting of the senior executive team. Gabe had been pouring over the daily figures as usual when he took the call. Everyone at the home office was going crazy following the explosions in Eastern Europe. Even though Al Qaeda had eagerly taken credit, Pete's dream contradicted that. The details in his dream had been too incontrovertible to ignore. Gabe felt the mass of pedestrians pushing by him as he was buffeted from side to side. He was used to pushing and shoving, but this was different. It seemed like a wave of humanity was pushing him back, delaying his progress as though trying to make him later than usual. After several minutes of nearly no progress, he pushed his way to the wall of the nearest building and put his back to it to allow the mass to pass by.

"Hey there, Gabe, how are you?" said a voice causing him to turn his head to the left. It was Sheila, standing with her back to the wall as well. "What a mob, right?" she smiled.

"Sheila, what are you doing here?" he asked, dumbfounded by her sudden appearance.

"Where did you think I was, Prague?" she laughed. "I thought you'd be happy to see me here. Guess not."

Gabe leaned into her and kissed her on the cheek. "I'm sorry, Sheila. Things are crazy today. First the terrorist attacks and now this crowd."

"I know. I can't believe how brazen those Al Qaeda bastards are. I sure hope they catch them this time," she said.

"You think it was really them?"

"What do you think, Gabe?"

"I don't know. I was on my way to the home office for a meeting with my granddad on that subject exactly," he replied.

"You think it was Bill, don't you?" she frowned. "I think that's totally unfair. Why would he do such a thing?"

"That's what I'd like to know too. Why did you do it, Sheila?"

Sheila looked stunned for a moment. The look quickly changed to seething hatred. She stood inches from his face, poked him in the chest with her index finger and said, "You should watch your mouth with such allegations, buddy boy. Bill and I have friends in this town." As she spoke, he noticed that six short, muscular men had formed a semicircle around them to push back the crowd of passersby.

"So now it's Bill and not Master, huh?" he replied. "You two must be getting pretty chummy. I'm happy for you, Sheila."

"So, Gabe, I'm on my way to meet your new roommate, if you don't mind," she noted.

"I don't think that's a good idea, Sheila."

"I couldn't care less about what you think, Gabe," she replied, speaking slowly to emphasize each word as it passed her lips. "It's the two doors, remember. Even your new roommate gets to make his own decisions. Satori Industries has a lot more to offer him than you do."

"I could tell Sam and Bob not to let you in," he said.

"And my friends here could kill them and not regret it," she replied, and then laughed. "Honestly, Gabe, no one is going to kill anyone, but I am going to meet Peter Smith. You just have to deal with that."

"You are right on that, Sheila. Pete can make his own decisions, but so you know, he has already met you in his visions, and none of those experiences were positive. You will probably scare the crap out of him."

"That is my problem and I can handle it. By the way, I'd appreciate it if you'd call Bob and tell him to let me in. It will be simpler that way, don't you think?" she asked.

"Okay, no problem. If this is going to resolve into whatever Pete decides, there's no sense letting it drag out. Once I get out of this crowd, I'll make the call," he replied.

She leaned in and kissed his lips. "Thanks, Gabe. My friends and I will leave you now. Say 'Hi' to Granddad for me." She winked at him and walked away down the sidewalk, lost almost immediately in the large crowd.

Gabe wiped the sweat from his brow and noticed his hands were trembling. He took two deep breaths and began to move up the sidewalk again. The crowd had thinned, and he quickly completed the last two blocks to the tall glass-clad building and stepped inside. He fumbled with his phone as he sent a text to Bob about Sheila's visit.

"Mr. Prospect, are you all right?" asked the man behind the large marble desk in the lobby.

"Yeah, I'm fine, Jack," he replied.

"Your grandfather has been calling me every couple minutes to see if you are here yet. I think you'd better get going."

Gabe rushed to the waiting elevator and selected the top floor. He was still trembling and panting for breath when the doors opened on the eightieth floor. He turned to his right and followed the long corridor into the C-level suites. At the end of the corridor, he pulled open the door to find his granddad and six uncles sitting at the long glass table. They could tell immediately that something was not right and stood at their chairs. "Gabe, what is wrong?" Emmanuel asked.

"I ran into Sheila on the way here. I'm sorry I'm late," he replied as he filled a glass with ice water and then drank deeply. "She's on her way to my place to meet Pete."

"That was not unexpected," Uncle Michael said. "But I must say I'm a bit surprised she isn't still in Europe for the next events."

"Clearly, Satori has decided that turning Pete is a higher priority," Uncle Gabriel noted. "That means they are very concerned that he could provide insights into their operations."

"Yes, but so far his insights are concurrent with the events," Emmanuel said. "That doesn't do us any good."

"I disagree," Michael said. "Pete saw the attacks as they happened. He saw Sheila and the others who left the explosives behind. Normally, it could have been just a dream. But now that Sheila is here already to contact him, we know conclusively that they were behind the attacks."

"Okay, let's say we know Al Qaeda did not launch these attacks, and we know Satori did," another uncle argued. "But we can't stop anything without premonition."

"Simon is right," Emmanuel said. "But why did he do it? He has no business interests in Eastern Europe."

"I can't believe you asked that question, Dad," Michael said.

"I'm sorry. You are right, Michael. I think what I meant is why did he get personally involved in this? There are many others who would happily walk through that door to commit these atrocities. Why did he act personally?" the older man replied.

"Excuse me for interrupting, but Pete has had premonitions before," Gabe noted. "We also know that Pete had this dream while sleeping, but we do not know he had it at the moment of the attacks. He could have dreamt it over and again until he woke up. When he has had waking visions, they have been in advance of the activity."

"That's an excellent point, son," Uncle Luce remarked and then turned to face his father. "Dad, Pete's talents are growing by the day. He needs training to hone his skills. He needs to learn how to wake from his dreams when he first gets them, and then report to us."

"If we get that chance," Emmanuel replied. "Sheila can be very convincing, and we must remember that Pete is a young and ambitious man."

"Do you really think Satori can turn him?" Luce asked.

"No. It takes something inside a person to make them choose that door. Pete seems like an intelligent and reasonable young man. However, Satori does not have to turn him."

"Granddad is right," Gabe replied. "Satori can give him millions in salary and a big penthouse in the city with hot and cold running women to fulfill his fantasies. I doubt he cares about Pete's visions one bit. He only cares that Pete doesn't share his visions with us. What do we do now, Granddad?"

"There's not much we can do at this moment, Gabe," Emmanuel sighed. "Let's hold hands and give thanks and pray that Peter Smith chooses well."

§

Pete was stuffed. He had never had pozole before and gorged himself with a second bowl. He thought about taking a nap, but had only been awake a few hours, so he decided to watch a little television. He was tired of the news of the bomb blasts and the interview with the Czech man and his family. He clicked through the channels hoping to find a movie or something else entertaining to watch. He thought about walking around the neighborhood, but Gabe had made him promise to wait for him to return. After his nightmare and the discussion with Uncle Michael, he felt no desire to put himself in danger just yet. He leaned back into the soft couch and felt his drowsiness taking over. He clicked the remote again and noticed a movie about an airplane trip which caught his attention. He sat back to see what was happening.

The movie seemed very familiar and reminded him of many romantic comedies he had seen where silly scenes were filmed on airplanes. He watched for a while but soon had trouble keeping his eyes open. He strained to keep watching, but his weariness was winning the battle for his eyes. There was a scream and his eyes opened wide. The airplane seemed different somehow. Rather than a set made to look like an aircraft, usually being too big and plush, it now looked like a real airplane, with people pushed together on too-small seats on rows too close together.

A small girl in a window seat was screaming. Her mother was trying to console her, but was speaking in a language he did not understand, which he thought was doubly odd. The flight attendant was in the aisle next to the mother and child, trying to reassure them everything was fine. The plane shuddered and the attendant struggled to keep her feet. It shuddered again and the attendant fell to the floor. Two more attendants rushed to her aid. The people on the plane were clearly distressed, and the pilot's announcements did not calm anyone down. Tears poured down the little girl's face as her mother caressed her hair. Then the mother screamed, and it was a blood-curdling scream. The attendant followed her eyes out the window where a hideous face was plastered against the glass. It had long fangs and dark-red skin. It seemed to be laughing at them. The people in adjoining rows began to scream as well.

The creature on the wing then turned and walked down the wing. It was very large, at least ten feet tall with long black talons on its feet, which cut into the metal wing leaving small gashes. It turned back toward the window and laughed again, and then let go and was blown back away from the jet. The people on the other side began to scream as another giant creature jumped off the other wing. The flight attendant rushed forward and began speaking to the cockpit crew over the intercom.

The passengers frantically looked out their windows for the monsters but could not see anything. Two minutes passed and the people began to calm down. Perhaps it had been mass hysteria and they would be landing safely soon. Pete tried to wake up but did not really know if he was dreaming or if this was still the movie. Suddenly, the two giant creatures shot ahead of the plane. The scene turned to the cockpit where the two pilots first saw the creatures as they flew faster than the jet. Their wings were the color of blood, and the creatures looked like giant bats with almost human faces. When the creatures were almost far enough ahead to disappear from view, they stopped, turned, and dived back toward the plane. The pilots took evasive maneuvers, diving to avoid them. The creatures pulled their wings tight against their bodies and slammed into the engines, which exploded. The plane lost all power and began to plummet downward. Everyone was screaming and praying for salvation. The pilot made a desperate mayday call to the tower.

For some unknown reason, the plane stopped falling and leveled off. The passengers erupted into cheers. The pilots were dumbfounded. They had no power, but the plane was flying. That was not possible. The scene cut to the plane's exterior where the two monsters had landed on the top of the plane and dug their talons into the metal. They flapped their wings as fast as they could and soon the plane was accelerating again, but dropping altitude precipitously. It was headed toward a massive airport terminal unlike anything Pete had ever seen. When the plane was two hundred yards away, the monsters released it and flew away. That's when Pete noticed something familiar. Far in the distance, appearing between the two winged beasts, the Eiffel Tower stood proudly over the city of Paris. Seconds later, the crippled airliner crashed into the terminal at Charles de Gaulle Airport and exploded.

Pete opened his eyes and gasped for breath. He was sweating and shaking violently. What had happened, he wondered. Was that another vision? He prayed it was a stupid dream.

"Hi there," Sheila said. "I hope I didn't wake you."

"What? You shouldn't be here," he squeaked, still trying to cope with the explosion and death in his mind.

"Gabe said it would be okay if I met you, Peter." She stood up and offered her hand. "I'm Sheila Farness. It's good to meet you finally."

"Why are you here?" he asked while limply shaking her hand. "I think I'd like to be alone right now."

She smiled and sat next to him, casually putting her hand on his knee. "Are you okay? You seem kind of upset."

He coughed and wheezed. "No, I'm okay. It was just a stupid dream."

She squeezed his knee. "Why don't you tell me about it?"

"I don't think that would be a good idea," he replied, finally gaining composure after his nightmare.

"Okay, have it your way," she frowned. "I just wanted to get to know you, Pete. I represent Satori Industries, and we've heard good things about you. I'd like you to consider working for us."

"So you can hear my dreams first, right?"

She laughed, and her laugh was very contagious. He had calmed down enough to sit back now and consider the beautiful woman sitting next to him. It was no wonder Gabe had been so attracted to her. "Frankly, Pete, Bill Satori and I do not give a damn about your dreams. We are interested in reality, period. You keep your dreams to yourself. I guarantee that no one in our company will ever ask you about them. We want your brain and your hard work, and we are prepared to pay exceedingly well for them."

"Why? I'm just out of college with almost no experience. What do have I to offer?"

"Pete, I like you a lot. Bill has authorized me to offer you ten million a year in salary with a one-million-dollar signing bonus. You will also get a company-paid penthouse here in Manhattan. How does that sound?" Sheila said.

"That sounds amazing, but it still doesn't make any sense," he replied. "There has to be a catch for that much money."

"There's no catch, but there is one condition," she said. "As you should know, the Prospect Enterprise and Satori Industries are direct competitors around the globe. As such, it would not be acceptable for you to continue to be acquainted with their family. It's strictly business. If you want to be buddies with Gabe or Mike or whoever, there are those in Satori Industries who might think you are a corporate spy. How long have you known the Prospect family?"

"A few days only, since I came into town looking for a room to rent," he said.

"See, it's no big deal then," she smiled. "There are millions of people in New York, and we would only ask you to stay away from a handful so we can be confident you are not giving away our corporate secrets. Companies around the world do the same thing every day and it's totally legal."

"What job would I do for your firm?" Pete quizzed.

"You would be working closely with me," she cooed as she pressed her body closer to his. "Would you like that?"

"You are a beautiful woman, Sheila," Pete replied.

She blushed slightly and kissed his lips. Then she stood and opened her purse, removing a business card. "Here is my number. Call me when you decide. I recommend waiting a day or two to think about it. Bill will go crazy worrying and probably double the signing bonus and offer a higher salary. You might as well get as much as you can. I'll show myself out." She bent down and kissed his forehead and then turned and walked to the elevator where the doors were already open as if waiting for her. She gave him a little wave as the doors closed.

Pete was dizzy and almost stumbled as he stood up. He pulled his cell phone from his pocket and dialed his cousin's number. After six rings, the call went to voice mail. He considered telling her about his dream and Sheila's visit, but then thought better and just disconnected. He sat back on the couch and held his head in his hands. "What am I going to do?" he said out loud. "I must be going nuts!" The house telephone began to ring. He remembered Gabe's warning not to use or answer the phones, so he sat back and tried to clear his mind. This is what he came to New York for, he argued. He could work for Bill Satori and make ten million dollars a year! But what about the dreams? Too many of them were coming true now. What if Bill Satori and Sheila Farness were really behind the bombing in the city and the airport attacks in Europe? What kind of people would do such a thing? He was so lost in thought that he did not notice the phone had stopped ringing.

Maria came in from the kitchen with a cordless phone in her hand. She walked over to Pete, saying, "The phone is for you, Mr. Pete," as she handed him the device. He took it and said a soft hello.

"Hello, Peter. This is Emmanuel Prospect. How are you doing?"

"I've had better days, Granddad."

"Whatever is wrong, son?"

"I had another dream, but I'm sure this one is just that. It was too surreal to be real," Pete noted.

"Please tell me about it, Peter, and don't leave out any details."

Without a second thought, Pete recounted the entire dream, emphasizing the improbability of giant flying creatures destroying an airplane. Most of Pete's dreams had been realistic, almost like news-station footage. This dream was different. There was no such thing as a giant, ten-foot bat with a human face and fangs. Pete told him how he thought he might be losing his mind, fearful that his dreams would become more and more delusional until he was truly insane. He also recounted his meeting with Sheila and her job offer. By the time he had finished talking he had calmed down and felt better for the release of tension and anxiety. "So you see, Granddad, it was just a nightmare. None of that can be true, can it?"

"Wow! You've had quite a day, Peter. First of all, I sincerely doubt that you are losing your mind. We've all had crazy dreams. That doesn't mean the incident will not occur though. Sometimes our minds cannot comprehend how a disaster could occur, and so our brains invent a mechanism to make it all work out," Emmanuel replied.

"You think someone will crash a plane into the Paris airport?"

"When exactly did you have this dream?"

"It had to be less than one hour ago, Granddad," he answered.

"The good news is that nothing like that has happened yet," the old man replied. "I'd like to believe it will never happen, but your last dreams came true, exactly as you foretold them. We need to take your dream very seriously. Is there anything else you remember, son?"

Pete pondered the question for a moment and then remembered. "Yes, as a matter of fact. I could hear the passengers talking, but it wasn't French. I took two years of French in college. I'm not fluent or anything, but the language seemed more Germanic, like German, Dutch, or some Scandinavian dialect. What do you think that means?"

"I don't know, son, but perhaps it's a clue to the origin of the flight. Charles de Gaulle is one of the busiest airports in the world with planes from dozens of countries landing there."

"I was thinking it might be a clue to another target," Pete said. "Like today when there were two attacks."

"Hmm. That's a good point. Okay, Pete, I think that's enough for now. I'll have some of my people check it all out."

"Granddad, thanks for listening to me. I feel a lot better now that I got that off my chest."

"Peter, please feel free to call me anytime. I'll make sure Gabe gives you my direct number. By the way, what will you do about the Satori offer? It is quite generous," Emmanuel asked.

"It's a lot of money. But there is something about Sheila that bothers me a lot. And I don't mean just the dreams I've had about her either. Do you understand that?"

"Yes, I do. There is so much that you do not know yet. I wish I could tell you more, but now is not the proper time. My job offer still stands, Peter. While I can't be as generous as Bill Satori, I can offer you something better than money," Emmanuel noted.

"And what is that?"

"The opportunity to make a difference in the world, Peter Smith. Take care and I will talk to you again soon."

Chapter 11

Pete tossed and turned for hours before falling asleep. When rest finally arrived, it was immediately invaded by another dream. Four giant red bat-like creatures pounded the air with their leathery wings high above the clouds over Lake Geneva. On a signal from the lead monster, two peeled off and headed directly north while the others kept their northwesterly line of flight. Both planes would be in visible range within ten minutes and they knew exactly what to do when they spotted them. Narga had to adjust his plans just hours ago when she called him with the change of attack and target, which pissed him off. He knew better than to quibble with that woman right now. He knew that his master would tire of the bitch soon enough and come to his senses. His best friend Barsat flew off his right wing, which made him very happy. At least he was with his friends this day and did not have to assume the shape of the weakling humans. They had served the master forever, it seemed, and were happy to fulfill any of his demands. Teaching the humans today's lesson would help cement their dominance of the world. "We're almost there, Barsat!"

"Yes, brother, I know. I see an airplane ahead. Is that the one?"

"No. That appears to be a domestic plane. Can't you see the Air France logo?"

"Ah, yes, I can see that now. How much farther before we find the KLM jet?"

"It won't be long now, brother," Narga laughed. They flew on, flapping their wings as fast as they could.

"I'm feeling very strange, brother," Barsat cried. "I feel as though we are being watched." He stopped flapping his wings and slowed to a stop, turning around to look for intruders.

"Don't stop now, you fool!" Narga shouted. "We will miss our chance. I think I see the jet now! Hurry up!"

Barsat began to flap his wings and chased after the other. The jet was close now, already making its initial approach to the massive airport just ahead of them. As he closed in on his brother, a brilliant flash of white light shot down and struck Narga, dragging him downward toward to the ground. Barsat began to chase after his brother as a second flash of light knocked him out of the sky. The two monsters tumbled downward out of control. A minute later, both smashed into the ground and laid groaning in pain and panting for breath. Narga tried to stand and collapsed back onto the ground. "What happened?" he moaned. Barsat had managed to sit up and was staring over his brother's shoulder with widened eyes. Narga spun around to see two men standing before them. "Who the heck are you, and how did you do that?"`

Michael and Gabriel walked toward the two beasts laughing. "I think you already know the answer to that question," Michael said. "You have been two very bad boys today. Don't worry; your other two friends have been taken care of as well. There will be no terrorist attacks today."

"My master will take care of you and your family!" Narga argued. "You have no right to stop us from our destiny."

"We both know that isn't true, Narga," Gabriel noted. "We've been at this for a very long time. What we don't understand is why you are attacking these airports and airplanes. Killing all these people isn't going to win you any fans. This isn't Satori's style, if you know what I mean."

"We follow orders, just like you two," Barsat said. "It is not our job to question his wisdom."

"So, what do we do now?" Narga asked. "It's not like we could achieve anything by fighting."

"I suggest you two go see your master and tell him you've failed," Michael said. "Once he has beaten you, perhaps you'll see the light and come back to us."

"Don't count on it," Narga said as he and Barsat dissolved into red smoke and disappeared.

Pete opened his eyes and laughed. He had a dream with a happy ending! He could not remember the last time that had happened. Perhaps the two planes were saved! All he knew was he had to find out now. He jumped out of bed and flung open the drapes. It was still very dark. He activated his phone and saw it was only 4:30 a.m. He sighed and walked out of the bedroom to discover that Uncle Michael was sitting quietly in the darkened room, sipping a glass of whisky. As Pete approached, Michael noticed him and smiled. "It's pretty early for you, Pete. Are you okay?

Still smiling, Pete walked over and sat next to the other man. Michael looked very tired, as though he had really battled the monsters in his dream. "I'm fine, but you look worn out. Was it really you in my dream? What kind of monsters were you and Gabriel fighting?"

Michael sipped the last of his drink and set the glass on the coffee table, then turned to Pete and said, "So, you had another dream. Why don't you tell me about it?"

"But it was real and you were in it. I don't understand. Are you telling me that you and Gabriel didn't stop the monsters attempting to down those airliners?"

Michael chuckled softly to himself. "Pete, all I can tell you is that no airplanes will crash over Europe today. My father wanted to thank you personally for telling him about your dream yesterday."

Pete jumped to his feet. His euphoria about the happy dream had disappeared, to be replaced by contempt for the man on the couch. "You know, Michael, I think I've had it with the Prospect family. No one tells me anything. First, everyone wants me to tell them about my dreams. Now, you're ignoring everything I said." He turned and headed back toward his room.

Michael stood and called after him, "Pete, I'm sorry. Please don't walk away from me." Pete stopped walking but did not turn around. "Okay, your telling my father about your dream did help us stop the attacks on the two planes. You had a premonition, and we used that information to stop it from happening."

Pete turned around and replied, "Okay. Go on."

"You have to understand that this situation is complicated. No one on earth believes that there are ten-foot bat-like monsters flying around. You said that my brother and I stopped them. How would we do that? We're both living in the city and the attacks were thousands of miles away. That isn't physically possible," Michael argued.

"But I remember what I saw. I don't know how you did it, but you did."

"Perhaps your vision was allegorical? Let's say that Gabriel and I did play a part in stopping the attacks. Maybe your mind created a story line that matched the previous dream. If you dreamt monsters downed the planes, then you might dream that we knocked them out of the sky."

"Most of my dreams have been realistic. Why would my mind start making up stories like that?" Pete asked.

Michael walked over to Pete and put his hand on his shoulder. "Let's try not to over-think any of this. Pete, you have an incredible ability to foresee the future. Your dreams have saved many lives today. I sincerely hope you continue to tell us about your visions so we can help even more people. If you start doubting your dreams because they become unbelievable or magical, then you might discount the real tragedy that is about to occur."

Pete sighed and looked down. "Michael, I hear what you're saying and will do my best. I'm just afraid I'm losing my mind, bit by bit. So, you're telling me there were no monsters?"

"What I said was that no one on Earth believes such creatures exist." Michael then smiled, turned and walked into the waiting elevator car, leaving Pete standing alone in the open living room.

§

Pete woke to the chirping of his cell phone. He found himself on the couch with the phone vibrating on the coffee table next to him. Michael's empty glass still sat on the table next to his phone. He pressed the connect button and put the phone to his ear, saying, "Hello?"

"Is this Peter Smith?" the male voice said.

"Yes, I'm Pete Smith. Who is calling please?"

"I'm sorry to call so early, Mr. Smith, but I'm in Europe today so it's early afternoon here. My name is Bill Satori. I think you have met my VP, Sheila Farness."

Pete sat up and replied, "Yes, sir, I met her just yesterday. Thank you for the incredible job offer, Mr. Satori."

"You are quite welcome, son. By the way, have you had time to consider that offer?"

"I'm still thinking about it, sir. I just don't understand why you'd pay me so much. I'm just out of college. Did you know that?"

"Yes, I am aware of your background. Mr. Smith, I am a businessman with many operations globally, and I need young ambitious folks to help us expand. As you may know, the Prospect Enterprise is our major competitor; and frankly, I want to deny them the recruits they are seeking. It's just one way I am trying to beat them in the marketplace. Since you're a young buck, you probably don't know how cut-throat and sneaky real business is."

"I'm sure you're right, Mr. Satori."

"I must say that I'm surprised you didn't jump at Sheila's offer. A million-dollar signing bonus is quite generous. You only have to stay ninety days in order to make it permanent. At the base salary she quoted, you'd earn another two and a half million in that three months. And still you aren't certain? Please explain that to me, son."

"I think you misunderstand, Mr. Satori," Pete said. "I just met Sheila yesterday. It's been less than twenty-four hours. I haven't even had the chance to discuss this with my family yet."

"Hmm. I wasn't aware you were married."

"No, I'm not. I meant my parents, sir."

"Ah, okay. I'm glad to hear that. At Satori Industries, we ask our new executives to work long hours and travel extensively for at least a few years. That can be very difficult on young families."

"That's not a problem for me, sir," Pete replied.

"Pete, let's be frank, shall we?" Bill started. "I don't like the Prospect family and they don't like me. Our professional relationship will always be difficult as we vie for the same customers. Sheila tells me that you could provide my company with a strategic advantage against them, and that's worth a lot to me."

"What if she's wrong, sir? As I've said, I'm a young guy out of college with little experience."

"Let's look at that, Pete. Let's say you start for me on Monday and I fire you Monday afternoon. According to the employment agreement, you'd be able to keep the signing bonus and half-a-day's pay. That's still a million dollars. Now if you're even an average talent, say you survive here six months before being fired. Now you've been paid six million dollars and are out on the street. Neither of those options is bad in my opinion."

"You are absolutely right, sir."

"Okay, Pete, you go ahead and have a chat with your family. I'll call you again tomorrow at this time and you can give me your decision. Is that acceptable to you?" Bill noted.

"That will be perfect, Mr. Satori."

"Thank you, son. Goodbye," Bill said as he disconnected Pete's line. "How did I do, sweetheart?"

"You were perfect, darling," Sheila said. "I think you convinced him."

"I think I should have doubled the offer and made him accept right now," Bill argued. "Now the Prospects have another day to convince him to stay there."

"Why didn't you do that?"

"When he said he needed to talk to his family, I felt certain he would not decide today. He's still holding on to his mother's apron strings," he replied.

"I think it will still work out. You are offering the money. So far, what have the Prospects offered him?"

"That's a good question, dear. I'm sure our offer is better though, or he would have just blown us off. But there is still a risk he will walk away from them and us. This high pressure selling might be too much for a farm boy like him. We need other options!"

"I would be happy to kill him if you want."

Bill sighed. "We tried that once and it didn't work. If we fail again, he will fall into the hands of the Prospect family and all will be lost," Bill replied.

"I won't fail, Master."

"You don't understand, Sheila. You're just like Narga and Barsat. Something big is happening and killing Peter Smith isn't going to happen. Other forces are putting visions in his head that will stop every attempt on his life," he noted. "No, we need a plan where he is unharmed, but safely away from the Prospects, even if he isn't with us."

"That might be difficult."

"I already have a plan and Narga and Barsat are here waiting for me to give them their new orders. I'll fill you in on the details later. I love you, Sheila," Bill said, and then hung up his phone.

"You're not going to punish us, Master?" Barsat asked. He and the other monster had morphed into human form and sat on a couch in front of Bill Satori's desk.

Bill laughed out loud, and then stood and walked over to his bar, quickly filling three glasses of whisky. He offered a glass to each man and took one for himself. "Here's to our success, my children." After drinking, he sat back down and considered the men in front of him. "I know you did not fulfill your mission with the airplanes and think you failed. But you actually succeeded. You have proven conclusively that Peter Smith has precognition. And you have proven that the Prospects can use that skill to stop us. Before now, all of that was theoretical."

"I'm confused, Father," Narga said.

"Think about it. We have been battling the Prospects for a very long time. We do what we do and they do what they do. We try to stop them and they try to stop us. That is the nature of our existence. It's a status quo, if you will. Neither has the advantage," Bill continued. "Now, Peter Smith comes to town. Here is the one man on Earth who can change the balance of power. He knows exactly what we will do before we do. He can help them to stop everything. If he works for the Prospects, we are all doomed."

"Then we must kill him as the woman said!" Narga shouted.

"Weren't you listening to me? If Pete has advanced warning about every attempt on his life, he will just change his plans and not be where he would have been. If he tells the Prospects about an attempt on his life, they will jump in and save him. We can't kill him! And I insist that we do not try to kill him!" Bill exclaimed.

"Then what should we do, Master?" Barsat asked.

"You are my children and I love and trust you," Bill said warmly. "I am going to give you an endowment and you will start a new company in a new city. Conveniently, you will reach out to Peter Smith and offer him a job far away. He will be grateful to escape both Satori Industries and the Prospect Enterprise. You will be his friends and protectors. Your company will grow and you will all earn a lot of money. Even though you and your company will no longer be part of Satori Industries, I will help you succeed. All you have to do is enjoy life and make certain Mr. Smith enjoys his."

"That doesn't sound like anything we are good at, Master," Narga argued.

"This is the most important job in our organization. Only with Peter Smith out of the way can the old status quo be reestablished. The Prospects will have lost their advantage and you will be saving all of us. Learn to like Peter. Help him be happy. Save all of us! I am counting on you."

§

After his discussion with Uncle Michael, Pete Smith could not sleep and realized that he had had enough of the city. He jammed some clothes and toiletries into his small duffel bag, took the elevator down to the ground floor and walked out onto the sidewalks of New York. The air smelled fresh and clean as though a brief shower had just passed. After a few moments, he realized it was his mood that had changed, not the weather. For days, he had been caught in the strangeness of the Prospect Enterprise. He felt that family was pulling him in and he was beginning to lose his individuality in their embrace. Now he had to deal with Satori too. None of this was what he had planned when he took the flight from O'Hare to JFK. Leaving Iowa behind was his ticket to finding himself and making a future, not for succumbing to the Prospects or Satori.

He entered Grand Central Station and headed for the nearest ticket kiosk. He felt elated. Now he was back in control of his destiny! Screw them all, he thought. When it was his turn at the machine, he purchased a ticket on the next train to Tarrytown and rushed toward the platform. He had just ten minutes before the departure time and did not want to spend even one more minute in the city. Within two minutes, he was sitting on the train, grinning like an idiot. He had done it! He had escaped the tight embrace of the Prospects! Gabe had warned him time and again not to leave the building without him, but here he was, free at last. When the train lurched forward, he pulled his phone from his pocket and dialed his cousin. "Hi, Alice, it's Pete."

"Hi, cousin, what's going on?" she replied.

"I hope it's okay if I can stay at your place for a few days," he said.

"Of course you're always welcome here, but is everything okay, Pete?"

"Yes, I'm fine and everything is better than fine," he began. "I just felt smothered by the Prospect family. They're nice, but I was beginning to feel like a prisoner in that condo."

"But what about the job at Bertrand Industries?"

"I don't start until Monday, so I still have the weekend to decide what I want to do," Pete replied. "Alice, I really don't think I have the stamina for New York anymore. Things are just too crazy right now. Did I tell you the Prospect Enterprise bought Bertrand?"

"No, you didn't. But there are other companies in the city. You should be able to get a job just about anywhere."

"Thanks for the vote of confidence, but I feel like the Prospects will follow me wherever I go."

"Pete, that doesn't make any sense. Why would they care so much about you?" she asked.

"I have no idea, and that's why it bothers me so much," he replied. "I also wanted to tell you that their biggest competitor, Satori Industries, has offered me ten million a year with a million-dollar signing bonus. What do you think about that?"

"No way! I don't believe you!" she exclaimed.

"I didn't believe it either, but Bill Satori called me himself just a little while ago. Now I have his and Emmanuel Prospect's personal cell numbers in my phone. This shit is really happening and I don't know why. It doesn't make any sense," he complained.

"Please calm down, Pete. When will your train arrive? I'll pick you up myself."

"It should be about an hour. I'll call you when I arrive. Thanks for listening, Alice," he said softly.

"See you then, Pete." The line disconnected. Letting all of his frustrations out wore him down. He closed his eyes and within seconds he was fast asleep.

"Fifty million dollars!" shouted a voice waking Pete minutes later. Two men were sitting on the bench across the aisle from him and were in deep conversation.

"Shush!" one of the men said. "We don't want everyone on this damned train to think we're loaded, Winston."

"I'm sorry, Sloan," Winston replied. "When you said we should come pitch our business plan to your dad, I had no idea he would fund us. I thought the whole trip was a waste of time."

"I remember your incessant whining, Winston. Now you'll have to eat crow. Of course, with our bankroll, you can eat it with caviar if you want!" The two men laughed.

"Thanks for taking a couple days to go visit my old college buddy," Winston noted. "I haven't seen Phil Nation in years, not since he married Alice."

The color drained out of Pete's face. He turned to face the two men and cleared his throat. "Excuse me, but did you just mention Phil and Alice Nation?"

Wilson glared at him and said, "What's it to you, pal?"

"Alice is my first cousin."

"Really?" Winston said. Pete nodded. "You must be Pete Smith! Phil told me that one of his wife's cousins was looking for work in the city. Sloan's dad is a big shot in the city and he thought we might help his friend find a job, but that was weeks ago. We actually live in San Diego."

"Wow! That must be nice!" Pete replied. "I can't imagine year-round gorgeous weather and beaches. I'm from Iowa myself."

"Well, San Diego is pretty nice, but I wouldn't say the weather is perfect. We've got our rainy season. Then there's the May gray to deal with, not to mention wildfires and earthquakes. But I suffer them gladly rather than dealing with long, cold winters here," Sloan said. "Did you ever find a job, Pete?"

Pete blushed. "Well, actually, I have three job offers right now. But I'm beginning to think New York is too big for me."

"Wow! Three offers, that's amazing," Winston said. "I'd be happy with one."

Sloan slapped Winston on the knee. "Not anymore, pal. With my dad's help, we are starting a new business, right?"

Winston smiled and said, "That's right, buddy. No more working for the man for us! Hey, Pete, what's your background? We're going to need good people too."

Sloan frowned, saying, "Winston, we can't beat big city wages just yet."

"I just got my finance degree from the University of Iowa," Pete said. "And thanks for thinking of me. As I said, I'm ready to leave New York already. I always thought I could find a small company here and help them grow. But so far, it's only the big companies that want me, and I'd feel stifled in one of them. I know we just met, so please don't feel any obligation to consider me, though. I'm sure there are lots of better qualified people in San Diego."

"So where are you headed today, Pete?" Sloan asked.

"I just had to get out of Manhattan," he sighed. "I'm going to stay with Phil and Alice for a couple of days and then decide what I really want to do."

"Well, I sure hope Phil told his wife that we were coming for a few days too," Winston replied. "Do they have room for everyone?"

"It will be pretty tight, I'm afraid," Pete said. "Alice is picking me up at the Tarrytown train station. We can talk to her about it then, okay?"

Chapter 12

Pete ended up sleeping on the couch. But that did not bother him at all. At least he was out of the Prospects' grasp. He knew Satori would be calling him in the morning and was rehearsing his speech rejecting the job offer. He still could not believe he was turning down ten million dollars. Perhaps if Bill Satori knew the role he played in Pete's nightmares, he might understand. The entire visit to New York had been a disaster. Not only had he almost been robbed and run down, his dreams and the daily events were too outrageous. Life was not supposed to be like that. He wondered how other New Yorkers dealt with the constant barrage. Perhaps they were made of sterner stuff than he.

It didn't matter what any of them thought. Pete's life and those of Phil and Alice were about to change forever. It had been an amazing dinner. After just a few hours of conversation, he felt like he had known Winston and Sloan all of his life. He had always been friendly with Phil, but they never really bonded as brothers until last night. Now they would all be moving to San Diego to help start a new business! All the pressure on Pete's shoulders had been lifted and he felt young again, confident that his dreams would fade away and be forgotten like everyone else forgets their dreams. Soon he was asleep.

An odd sound caused him to open his eyes, but he was no longer in his cousin's home. He was lying on a broad sandy beach. Gentle waves rolled up the sand toward him. The icy cold water caused him to shiver. He stood up and walked up the beach to avoid the next waves. A large hotel sat on the sand. It was a beautiful structure with white walls and a red roof. He had never seen anything like it, except perhaps in a movie. Halfway between him and the hotel, Uncle Joshua sat on the sand smiling back at him. Pete was not surprised that the Prospects had enlisted Josh for this job; but he was surprised that he accepted it. Pete walked up to the man and sat beside him on the sand. "I can't believe you signed up to do this, Josh!"

"What in the world are you talking about, Peter?" Josh laughed. "This is your dream, not mine. Why am I here?"

"I have no idea, Josh. But I never thought you'd be the one to make me go back to Manhattan."

"Frankly, I'm glad you're out of there," Joshua replied. "Not everybody can stand up to my dad and say 'No.' You must have been really pissed off to give up all of that, not to mention the ten-million-dollar salary from Satori."

"How did you know about that?" Pete asked. Joshua only frowned at him. "Oh, yeah, this is my dream, right? Okay, what did you want to tell me?"

Joshua put his hand on Pete's shoulder and smiled. "Pete, doesn't it strike you as odd that you randomly run into two guys on a train and next thing you know you're moving cross country? You need to make sure you think this out and know who you're dealing with."

Pete laughed. "You know, with what has happened to me since I took the subway into the city, this just seemed typical."

Joshua replied, "Well, perhaps that's a clue for you to consider. What happened in the city wasn't random and neither was meeting Sloan and Winston. You are being lead down a path toward . . ."

"Two doors, right?"

"Yes, as a matter of fact. You are headed for two doors. I want you to choose the correct one."

"How am I supposed to know which one is the right one?" Pete asked.

"You remember the guy who left the bomb in the coffee shop?" Pete nodded. "Well, I don't know the story of his life, but when he chose to leave the bomb in the crowded restaurant, he knew what would happen. At that moment, he chose poorly and many people were killed and injured," Joshua explained. "You will make many choices as you live your life. Many will be choices between good and evil, although most will only be minor sins. None of them will be the last set of doors. At some point you will encounter those last doors and you will know which is right and which is wrong. That is the moment your destiny is linked to. If you choose poorly, that will be it. You will be lost forever."

"You are such a jerk, Josh!" said a voice behind them. Both turned their heads to see Sheila Farness standing just behind them in a very small red bikini. "You had your five minutes; now get out of here so Pete and I can chat." Joshua disappeared and she grabbed Pete by the arm and pulled him to his feet. She started walking up the beach toward a large patio and he followed her. They climbed up the stairs and sat at a small table. A waiter appeared and set a pitcher of gin and tonic on their table and left them with two glasses. Sheila poured until both glasses were full and raised her glass in a toast. "Here's to what could have been, lover boy!"

After sipping the drink, Pete asked, "What is going on here? Why are you in my dream?"

"First of all, Mr. Satori is not happy that you are turning down his offer, but he is a fair man and is quite happy you've deserted the Prospects too," she replied.

"It was all too much for me, Sheila. I'm just an ordinary guy. I was never worth ten million dollars a year. It was just crazy," Pete rambled.

She put a finger up to his lips to stop him from talking. "I know, but it would have been fun." She stood and began to massage his shoulders. "Pete, you have to know that the Prospect family is totally full of crap. They'd have you believe there is a god out there watching every step we take. Look at me! I've done lots of shit and I'm rich and happy." She pulled him to his feet and put one arm around his shoulders, waving the other across the horizon. "This is reality, Pete. Each of us chooses to do what we want. We succeed or fail because of our skill and fortitude, not because some deity helps or hinders us."

A massive cloud bank was forming over the ocean. The clouds roiled and lightning danced across the sky. "Emmanuel Prospect would have you believe that a god would make the oceans boil!" The ocean began to boil and froth. "He wants you to believe that fire will consume evil people." The hotel and nearby buildings exploded in flames. Plumes of black smoke·filled the air and the smell of sulfur was overbearing. "He would have you believe that demons live among us and the dead will rise from their graves!"

Dozens of people walking along the beach began to twitch and squirm. Their bodies turned red and contorted until they were ten feet tall with giant leathery wings. Skeletons rose out of the sand and started to walk toward them. As they walked, sinew, muscle, and skin grew on their bodies. The red monsters attacked the humans, striking them and biting off chunks of skin and limbs. The people screamed at Pete to help them, but he was frozen in fear.

Sheila turned Pete to see his face. She smiled sweetly and kissed his lips. When he opened his eyes, everything was back to normal. A cool sea breeze caressed his face. "See, Pete, none of that is true. It's the stuff of legends, movies, and dreams. You and I are real. You get to decide what success you want. Don't believe everything people tell you. You are in charge of your life." She kissed him again.

He woke up soaked in sweat on the couch. Alice was tapping his shoulder. "Pete, it's your turn in the bathroom."

§

Bill Satori contemplated the face of his brother on the video screen. It had been so long since he had talked to Emmanuel Prospect that neither could remember. They were raised together and shared the same great responsibility until Bill had thought better and left home forever. Bill knew his brother was better suited to that role than he. Bill also knew what people were really like. He was never fooled by the misconception of innate human decency.

People wanted power, plain and simple, and many would do whatever it takes to achieve that end. So, it worked for the people and for Bill Satori as well. He would give them the opportunity to achieve power and then he would share in the rewards. Somehow, neither his father nor brother could see what was so obvious to him. They were fools, he thought. "Manny, it's been a long time," he said at last. "Frankly, I'm surprised you'd stoop to calling me."

"Bill, let me be clear. I want you to leave Peter Smith alone. If you interfere in his life, you and your ilk will pay a heavy price," Emmanuel replied.

Bill smiled and chuckled under his breath. He had not spoken to his brother in years, and the first thing out of his mouth was a threat. "So much for brotherly love, I suppose. I can tell you that Mr. Smith has rejected my very kind job offer and is leaving the city. I recommend that we both stay out of his life, dear brother."

"Although it pains me, I agree that is the best option for us. We will both let Peter live his own life and not attempt to convince him to partner with either of us. Is that agreeable?" Emmanuel asked.

"Of course, I agree completely, Manny."

"You have to know that I will be keeping an eye on him though. You have never been the most trustworthy person in our family."

"It pains me to hear you say that, dear brother," Bill laughed. "But I suppose your lack of trust in me is to be expected."

Emmanuel sat looking at his brother for a couple of minutes, just considering their past together and the long separation that led up to today. "Bill, you know I have to ask this. Why don't you come home and give up that life? You can change."

Bill laughed again. "I could say the same to you, Manny. No, I like things just the way they are now, especially now that Peter Smith is no longer around."

Emmanuel smiled and said, "Yes, I bet you do like that. But I have faith that he will come back to the Prospect Enterprise soon."

"Or he may come to Satori Industries."

Emmanuel frowned and raised one eyebrow. "I certainly doubt that!"

"We shall see. We shall see. Goodbye, brother," Bill said and hung up the phone. "Old fool!"

"Do you think he knows?" Sheila asked. She was sitting on a couch in Satori's office, wearing a red sundress and high heels.

"No. If he had any notion of what's going on, he would not have called at all," Bill replied. "But he will find out and sooner than we'd like." He stood and walked around the desk and stood in front of the woman, holding out his hands to take hers. He pulled her to her feet and kissed her lightly on the lips. He stepped back and grabbed her by the throat and began to strangle her. "You stupid bitch! Why did you put yourself in Peter's dream again? Are you trying to give him to the Prospects? What were you thinking?" He released her and pushed her down onto the couch and turned around. He heard a click and spun around to see her aiming a pistol at him. He laughed. "What? You're going to shoot me now?"

"I did not put myself in his dream, Master!" she exclaimed. "I swear on my life I did not do it!"

He looked down at the floor, and then looked up smiling. "Sheila, I'm sorry. You have to understand what I've seen. Who else would do something like that? Not the Prospects, of course."

Her voice quavered and she hurriedly put the gun back in her purse. "I don't know Master, perhaps one of your agents? None of them like me very much. The contempt is written all over their faces."

"That's an interesting thought," he laughed. "None of them or either of us would win any awards for honesty and integrity. Darling, please forgive me for being rash. I should have given you the benefit of the doubt rather than jumping to silly conclusions."

"Bill, I was so scared. I really thought you were going to kill me," she replied.

He sat next to her on the couch and caressed her knee. "I swear on my life that I will never kill you, Sheila. If I did that, you'd be lost to me forever. That is the last thing I want, I can assure you of that!"

"I don't understand Bill."

"Sheila, all things in time. After we are wed, I will welcome you fully into my family, and then you will know everything. You'll never be afraid again, my dearest," he said. "In the meantime, I would like you to keep an eye on Narga and Barsat. I have a feeling they will screw up their new assignment. But don't get too close, we don't want Peter Smith to see you, okay?"

§

Pete, Phil, Sloan, and Winston were sitting in the living room of the Nation home, drinking coffee and making plans for their upcoming business start-up in San Diego. Alice had left after breakfast to run errands around town, especially to buy more food to feed the army suddenly camped in her home. "So guys, Winston and I are flying to California on Monday to get things going. My dad's attorney is putting together the incorporation papers and finding a real estate agent to help us find a site. When can you all come out so we can get started in earnest?"

Phil started to speak just as the doorbell rang. "I'll get that," he said and stood up, walking to the door.

"I think I can leave anytime, Sloan," Pete began. "I just have some stuff still in the city and need to pick it up. If I can do that today or tomorrow, I can leave Monday too, if I can get a flight."

"If you can leave Monday, you can go with us. My dad is loaning us one of his private jets for the trip, so space is no problem," Sloan bragged.

"Wow! That's so cool," Pete replied. He noticed that Phil had returned to the room with Joshua Prospect. "Josh, what's going on?" He stood and walked over to the other man and shook his hand. "This is a big surprise." He turned to the others and said, "This is Joshua Prospect, a good friend of mine."

Perhaps Pete had not seen the look on the faces of Sloan and Winston, but Joshua did see. When they had first seen him enter, looks of abject terror flashed across their reddened faces. Now they were trying very hard to look calm. He smiled and waved at the two sitting on the couch. "Good to meet everyone." He turned to face Peter. "I have your stuff outside with Sam. When he heard you were leaving, Gabe asked Maria to pack up everything."

"Thank you, I guess," Pete said.

"I wish you all the best, Pete," he replied, putting his hand on Pete's shoulder. "Be sure and check to see that we got everything. You still have our cell numbers, right?" The other nodded. "Good, if anything's missing, just call any of us. By the way, my dad insisted on giving you a check. It's just some walking around money while you're getting set up in San Diego. You have to keep it or he'll get insulted, okay?"

"Okay, but I wish he hadn't."

"Pete, all that any of us want is for you to be happy," Joshua stated. He turned to the others and said, "That's what we all want, right?" Sloan and Winston smiled with their mouths, but their eyes were cold and angry.

"Well, I don't want to impede this brain-storming session, so I'll be on my way," Joshua continued. "Pete, why don't you come help Sam and me bring in the rest of your stuff." They walked out of the room.

"You guys don't like Josh Prospect very much, do you?" Phil asked.

"What makes you think that?" Sloan growled.

"Geez, never mind," Phil said as the others returned and set Peter's belongings in a corner of the room.

"Thanks again Sam and Josh," Pete said. "Give my regards to the whole family."

"You're welcome," Joshua replied. "Take care. I hope you and your colleagues are very successful. We'll be keeping an eye on you all, and can hopefully throw a few orders your way, once you're up and running." He turned to face Sloan and Winston, saying, "Tell your father I said 'Hello,'" and then he and Sam left the house.

"What is it with you two and Josh Prospect?" Phil asked again.

"He and his family are a bunch of pompous jerks!" Sloan sneered.

"Calm down partner," Winston cautioned, "Remember, we're leaving all of the intrigue behind us here. Phil and Pete, please forgive Sloan, he tried to sell stuff to the Prospect Enterprise some time back and they ignored him. Just a bad taste in his mouth, that's all."

"Yeah, just a bad taste," Sloan noted. "But screw the Prospects, boys, we have a lot of work to do."

Chapter 13

Two nights without a bad dream was not quite a miracle, but Pete would settle for that. He could have had bad dreams, but simply forgot them upon waking, like normal people do, and that would be fine, he thought. Now he was sitting on the private jet, fifty thousand feet over America's heartland, headed to a new life on the West Coast. Phil would come out in a week, although Sloan had to promise to send him back if Alice experienced any issues with her pregnancy. Sloan and Winston were huddled together at a small worktable close to the rear of the jet, while Pete was sitting close to the cockpit at their request. He understood that the partners of a new business needed time to make their plans. He had only known the men for three days, so it was not unusual that he was not in their inner circle. Cindy, the flight attendant approached his seat and gave him a fresh glass of soda. "Can I get you anything else, Pete?" she asked in her sweet southern accent.

"No, I'm good," he replied. "Thanks, Cindy." She smiled and walked back to the galley. He slouched down in his seat and closed his eyes. Soon, he had drifted off to sleep. Almost immediately, he began to choke and opened his eyes to see the cabin filling with black smoke. He looked around but no one else seemed to be on board. He unbuckled his seatbelt and rushed to the cockpit, flinging the door open. What he saw contradicted reality, so he knew he must be dreaming. A huge red beast was sitting in the pilot's chair, smoking a large cigar. Hearing the door open, it turned and smiled at Pete, baring its black dagger-like teeth. "What's going on?"

"Have a seat, Peter," the monster said. It grabbed him by the arm and pushed him into the other seat. "Buckle yourself in."

Pete was too stunned to do anything other than what the beast asked. "What did you do to the pilots and Sloan and Winston?"

"Hey, this is your dream, Pete. But don't worry about them, they're right out there," the beast said, pointing out the windscreen.

All around the plane, hundreds of massive red-winged monsters flew in formation around the jet. When he looked closely, he thought the closest monster had a face similar to Sloan. He shook his head in disbelief, and tried to pinch himself awake. The beast pilot laughed. "That never works, Pete. You're sleeping. You're not really pinching anything except in your mind."

"What am I supposed to do now?" he asked.

An incredulous look flashed across the beast's face. "Like I said, this is your dream, do whatever you want." The beast turned to look out the windscreen. "How did you get in here anyway?"

"Through the door of course; how else would I get in here?" Pete scoffed.

"Well, you might try another door," the beast laughed mockingly.

Pete fumbled with the safety harness but none of the buckles would come loose. He strained and tugged on them to no effect. Seeing his troubles, the beast reached over and sliced through the belts with his razor-like claws, and smiled, saying, "You know Pete, I am beginning to really like you."

Pete pulled himself to his feet and walked out of the cockpit, slamming the door behind him. The smoke was blindingly thick in the cabin now, and he was choking for breath. The stench of sulfur filled and burned his lungs. He hurried down the corridor until he ran into a second door that looked exactly like the cockpit door, which did not make any sense at all. Perhaps he had turned himself around. Taking a chance, he opened the door and rushed in, closing it behind him. Logic had gone out the window again. He was still in the main cabin, at the back by the galley. He turned quickly to see there was no door behind him. There was no smoke in the cabin. The air was cool and fresh, but there was still no one else on board. As he walked forward, he called out to Cindy, Sloan, and Winston, but there was no reply. He put his hand on the handle for the cockpit door and thought about opening it, still terrified that the monster would be flying. He was not waking up, so without other options, he opened the door and stepped in.

"Hi, Peter, it's good to see you again," Emmanuel Prospect said from the copilot seat. "I'm glad you are dreaming about me. Please take a seat."

Pete sat down and buckled his harness and then turned to the other and asked, "Did you make this dream, Granddad?"

"No, I did not. First, I don't believe you're dreaming at all. This is a vision that you chose to see at this time."

"What was that monster in the other cockpit?

Emmanuel smiled and replied, "I have no idea, Pete. I've just been sitting here. This is your dream, after all. Do you want to tell me about it?"

"Not really, but there were two doors: one leading to the monster and the other to you. Do you think that means something?"

"Your mind probably constructed the dream from my favorite story," Emmanuel noted. "Thanks for remembering it. If there was a monster and me, perhaps you were experimenting with the idea of good versus evil."

"Granddad, do you think I stepped through the wrong door when I decided to move to San Diego?"

"Of course not! You're a free man. You can live anywhere you want and work for anyone you want. That is why I asked you to sit in the pilot's seat. You're the captain of your life, not me, and not some monster. You'll know when you make the big decision. You'll know the consequences and make a conscious choice. Moving to San Diego is making a choice for sure, but it is not deliberately choosing evil," the old man said.

"I don't know what to do, Granddad," Pete said. "I'm beginning to believe this move is a bad idea."

"It's way too early for that kind of conclusion, Peter. Try to have some fun. Enjoy your life, son. If you ever decide to come and work for me, just let me know."

"Oh, and thanks again for the gift, but fifty thousand dollars is a lot of money, Granddad."

"You already thanked me. But can I ask you one more favor?" Pete nodded. "If you ever have one of those dreams or visions like the terrorist attacks, please call me. Hopefully, we can save some lives," Emmanuel asked.

"I'll let you know, but I haven't had such a dream in several days," Pete said. "Perhaps my nightmares will end soon."

Emmanuel patted him on the shoulder, "If that's what you want, I hope so too."

Pete opened his eyes to see Cindy patting him on the shoulder. "Pete, could you please bring up your seat back? We're getting ready to land."

§

Bill Satori was pacing back and forth in front of the fireplace in his New York penthouse. When Narga and Barsat told him that Joshua Prospect had seen them and learned of their plans, he knew a drastic change of plans was in order. He glanced at Sheila, who was sitting in an armchair casually sipping her glass of wine. As he admired her long legs, he wondered if he should ask her to kill Peter Smith and end this fiasco once and for all. There would be repercussions from the Prospects, but that was already a foregone conclusion now that Peter was tied to his organization. He smiled slightly remembering how Emmanuel had told him he was not trustworthy. "Sheila, it's not a good night for me. Perhaps you should take a jet to San Diego now and I'll talk to you tomorrow."

She stood and walked over to him, putting her arms around his neck. "Bill, I know what you're thinking, but I don't think it's a good idea to kill Peter."

He pulled back in shock. "Are you starting to read my mind now?"

"No, not at all. That was the first thing I thought of as well. But after thinking some more, while it would reestablish the status quo, I think we would be robbing ourselves of his talent unnecessarily." She took his hands in hers. "I think Peter can be convinced to work for you."

Bill laughed out loud, but stopped quickly when he noticed the look of anger on her face. "Peter is not going to work for me. He's not the type."

"Bill, please listen. Pete is freaking out from all his horrible dreams about bombings and plane crashes. I know I can ratchet that fear down and convince him that his dreams are only dreams and any similarity to real events is coincidental only."

He stared into her eyes and only sensed honesty. "I don't know, Sheila. How exactly will you do that?"

"I'm not sure yet, but if I can separate him from the Prospects and your agents, I think there's a chance. It might take a while and I'll be in deep cover. No one can know where we are. And please don't have Narga and Barsat, or any of the others watching over me. If Pete gets any notion of what's going on, he'll bolt to the Prospects," she explained.

"I still think it would be easier just to kill him and be done with it."

Sheila caressed his cheek with her hand. "Sweetheart, please let me try. If there is even a remote chance he can be on our side, it's worth it, don't you think?"

He turned to face the fireplace. The flames had died down but the embers were glowing red hot. "I'll miss you, darling. How long do you think this will take?"

"I don't know that either. But you can keep an eye on us."

"And what if you fail?"

She opened her purse and removed her pistol. "Then I'll blow his head off."

"That's my girl."

§

Pete woke early since his body clock was still on Eastern Standard Time. He climbed out of the bed and walked over to the window, pulling open the curtains. The Pacific Ocean stretched out to the horizon beyond the broad sandy beach. Several people were walking along the beach while a small crowd had already gathered on the patio for breakfast. Sloan had booked rooms for everyone at the Hotel Del Coronado for two weeks. They thought that would give them enough time to find a business location. Since they were paying, Pete was more than happy to hang out at this historical hotel. He took a quick shower and pulled on short pants and a tee shirt and went out to explore. His first goal was to put his feet in the Pacific Ocean. The entire time he had been in New York, he never made it to the Atlantic, which had been a shame. He was not about to miss his chance to step in the Pacific.

He walked away from the hotel toward the water's edge as a small wave rolled up the sand and washed over his feet. The water was like ice, and that was somehow familiar. He spun around and the image of the massive hotel brought a look of terror to his face. This is the same hotel he had seen in his dream! He shook his head to clear the memory of that awful recollection. A second wave of cold water shocked him back to reality and he hurried away from the ocean. There was no one sitting on the beach, and definitely Joshua Prospect was nowhere to be seen. He began to calm down. It was chilly today, and no bikinis were in sight either. He decided he worried too much and walked up onto the balcony to have breakfast. He noticed Sloan and Winston smiling and waving at him, so he walked over and joined them. "Did you sleep well, Pete?" Winston asked.

"Yes I did, and you know, I don't remember any dreams. That's great for me," he replied.

"By the way, this breakfast is a buffet, so just go help yourself. We'll order coffee for you if you like." Sloan offered.

"That would be great, thanks." Pete rose and walked over to the buffet table and filled his plate with scrambled eggs, sausage, hash browns, and toast and then returned to join his business partners. His hot coffee was waiting when he arrived.

"Pete, we're heading out a bit later to look at some locations," Winston opened. "Would you like to join us?"

"Sure, that would be great!" he exclaimed. "I love getting into all the details."

"Since you're our finance guy, we also need to share the business plans and start working on budgets and the like," Sloan continued. "We'll need business bank accounts, credit cards, and the whole nine yards, so there's lots to do."

"I'm ready to put my degree to work, Sloan. Thanks again for the opportunity."

"Oh no!" Sloan groaned.

"What did I say?" Pete asked.

"Oh no!" Winston sighed. Both men now held their heads in their hands, shaking them from side to side.

"You two miserable pieces of crap!" shouted a woman's voice behind Pete. He strained his neck to see Sheila Farness standing directly behind him. "I'm glad I found you, Pete," she said as she put her hands on his shoulders and then took a seat next to him.

"What is going on, Sheila?" Pete asked. "I already turned down Mr. Satori's offer."

"That's what you think," she said. "These two sacks of garbage work for Satori. When I found out what he was doing to you, I knew I had to stop them."

"What?" He looked at the other two men and asked, "Is this true? Are you part of Satori's gang?" Both men nodded sheepishly. He turned to Sheila and asked, "But why do you care? You're part of his team too. He told me himself!"

"I used to be part of his team, Pete," she replied, squeezing his knee with one hand. "Satori does lots of stuff that stinks. He knew you wouldn't take the ten million, but would stop at nothing to get his hands on you, so he used these buffoons to trick you. How much were they going to pay you?"

"We talked about fifty thousand to start."

"See what I mean? Satori wants to keep you from the Prospects, just to piss them off. You turn him down cold. So he creates a new fake company to hire you and saves virtually all of the salary. It made me so mad that I quit! 'Screw you, Bill Satori,' I said right to his face."

"I'm not sure I can understand what's going on here," Pete sighed. "How can I believe you?"

"Why do you ask such a question? I only met you once. I'm not a devil or anything. Besides, ask the moron twins over there. I'm sure the word is out by now."

"Sheila is right. Mr. Satori sent out an e-mail today stating that Sheila was no longer connected to Satori Industries and that we should all avoid any contact with her. He was really pissed off," Winston acknowledged.

"So now I have no job and am two thousand miles from my family," Pete groaned.

"Pete, you can go back to New York and still get the ten million," Sloan said. "Once Mr. Satori hears about what happened here, I'm sure he might even raise that offer."

"I wouldn't recommend that Peter," Sheila said. "Now you and I both know he can't be trusted."

"Sheila, you've always been an insufferable bitch," Sloan snarled. "You know we are going to report all of this to Mr. Satori. He will not be happy."

"Screw you and screw Satori," she replied. "I don't give a damn about any of you." She grabbed Pete's arm and pulled him up to his feet. "Let's get away from these jerks, Pete."

Sloan stood up and said, "Pete, please don't go. We'll work something out, okay? Money is no object."

Sheila was pulling him away, but he turned to face the two and replied, "Please give me some time to sort this out, okay?" He turned back to Sheila and said, "Where are you taking me?"

"Back inside. You need to get your stuff and check out. I've got a beach house north of here. You can stay with me a few days," she said without turning to look at him.

Chapter 14

Gabe Prospect stared at his computer screen. He simply could not believe what he was reading. One of the major stories on the WSJ website said that Sheila Farness had left Satori Industries. Was this a ruse or was she perhaps coming to her senses, he wondered. His heart fluttered for an instant when the image of her in bed with him flashed across his mind. It had been years, yet there was still a place for her in his heart. It bothered him to think she might still have an effect on him after she so heartlessly dumped him. He read the words again and again, "Sheila Farness has left Satori Industries to pursue other interests." Clearly that was code for being fired, but why now?

"Don't believe a word of it!" a voice said from behind him. He turned to see his father standing two feet away. He jumped to his feet and hugged Luce. "You know this is a contrived story, son."

"How can we be sure?" Gabe asked.

"If Sheila wanted to change and stay alive, she would have sneaked over to our building and told one of us about it," Luce argued. "With her position, you can't just pursue other interests."

"But maybe . . ."

Luce put his hands on his son's shoulders. "Son, I'm sorry if this is tugging on your emotions, but you have to face reality. As your grandfather would say, she had already stepped through that one wrong door and can never return."

Gabe sighed and sat back on his chair. "You're right, Dad. I know you're right, but damn, this sucks. Why would they do something like this?"

"Well, as I see it, there could be several answers, and more than one could be served by this announcement," Luce began. "The most obvious conclusion is that this is cover for her to get close to Peter Smith. He doesn't know Satori as we do. He might have suspicions, but nothing more. If he believes that Sheila has left Satori, he might learn to trust and even have feelings for her."

"That's not good."

"You are right, it is definitely not good," Luce agreed. "Second, you know that your uncle ran into Narga and Barsat in Pete's cousin's house?" He nodded. "Since those two were uncovered, it would only be a matter of time before Pete learned they were working for Satori and the whole new company adventure was a fraud. To Pete, she's now the hero who saved him from them."

"And then there's me . . ."

"Yes, that is another possibility. Satori loves to make you suffer. You are a Prospect after all. Sheila has chosen him over you, and this article will hurt you. It has, hasn't it?" Gabe nodded and put his head down. "Well, now that you know, you can forget about it and her." He put his arm around Gabe's shoulders. "Son, I'm worried about you. Ever since you broke up with Sheila, you've been stuck here looking at numbers all day, every day. You need to move on and find someone new."

"Dad, I'm not the type to go to clubs all the time. And I don't dare consider the extended family! You know what they all think about us!"

"It's a damned shame too," Luce agreed. "But that's how it is, and that's not going to change."

"You know, that was one of the things I like most about Pete. I figured he and I could hang out and meet women together. It would have been more natural to have a wingman when I go out. So what do you want me to do, Dad?"

"Go on vacation," Luce replied. "I already cleared it with my dad, so you're on vacation as of right now. Take as much time as you want."

"Vacation? Traveling alone is no fun. Where would I go anyway?"

"I don't know, Gabe. Why not try San Diego?" Luce said as he turned and walked back to the elevator.

§

After Pete and Sheila arrived at her La Jolla beach house, she showed him to a guest room where he unloaded all of his possessions. When that job was complete, the two went for a stroll along the beach. Pete was still not convinced that Sheila was on his side. From what he had gleaned from conversations with the Prospect family, she was a close confidant of Bill Satori, and it was highly unlikely she would quit for a young man like him. On the other hand, he knew little about the Prospect Enterprise other than what they had told him themselves. With his only experience being a few days as Gabe's roommate, he did not know what to believe anymore; and Sheila Farness was a beautiful woman who had lots of money. Also, her hospitality could not be denied. She told him he could stay here as long as he wanted, although she would have to leave from time to time to find a new job.

Half a mile down the beach from her home, they walked away from the beach toward a small restaurant. She took his hand in hers and led him inside and to a small table near the bar. She ordered two margaritas from the waiter and an appetizer sampler plate. He watched her reviewing e-mail on her smart phone while considering the curve of her cheeks and those startling blue eyes.

"Anything important, Sheila?" he asked at last.

She smiled and set her phone down, picking up her drink instead. "No, nothing at all, Pete. Here, let's toast to our mutual future success." After sipping her drink, she sat back and smiled again. "Pete, how are you doing? I know the incident with Sloan and Winston must be bothering you."

"Actually, that's the one thing that doesn't bother me at all," Pete chuckled. "The whole thing happened way too fast, and I'm surprised my brother-in-law or I didn't figure it out before. Life just isn't that easy."

"Well, it bothered me plenty," she snapped. "I know it probably doesn't make sense to you that I'd quit my job because of this, but it was just the last straw. I hardly know you, but I've known plenty of others who have been hoodwinked by Bill Satori. At some point, a person has to stand up and say 'Enough!' I guess you were that point for me."

"Sheila, I don't want to be an inconvenience to you," he replied. "I mean, I really appreciate what you've done for me, but I don't intend to be your long-term houseguest."

She frowned and took a gulp of her margarita and then reached across the table to hold both of his hands. "Pete, you are no inconvenience. I've worked for Satori for a long time and have made plenty of money. I have several houses and massive investment accounts. If I chose to, I could retire now and live very comfortably for the rest of my life." She released his hands and dropped her head. "I do think about that, probably more than I should."

The waiter returned and set the platter of food in the center of their table, smiled and left. Sheila took a potato skin and bit it. "You think you might retire? But you're so young!" Pete noted.

"Pete, I'm not married and I've had little time to form or build any relationships since I've worked for Satori. I've spent my youth flying around the world doing his business. At some point a woman has to decide if that's what is really important."

"Sheila, if this is out of line, just tell me to shut up, okay? What happened between you and Gabe Prospect?"

She coughed. "Wow! I didn't see that coming!"

"I'm sorry," Pete apologized.

"No, that's okay," she replied, reaching out to hold his right hand. "Gabe is a great guy. Unfortunately, when I met him I was a lot like you. I was young and just out of college. My mind was full of ideas about finding my place and building a successful career. Pete, I had to choose between my feelings for him and my future and career. You probably know the Prospects and Satori hate each other. My career potential was great with Satori and just so-so with the Prospects. At that point in my life, I chose career. Gabe couldn't deal with that, and his family eventually forced our split." She sipped her drink and continued, "Why the interest in my relationship with Gabe?"

"I don't know for sure. I like Gabe and I didn't want to cause him any more pain," Pete said as he caressed her hand with his thumb. "Do you think there's still a chance for you two?"

She pulled her hand away and replied, "No. I'm afraid that's a door that's closed forever now."

Pete leaned back as a look of disbelief passed across his face. "Why is it always doors with everyone? Do you guys practice this?"

"What are you talking about, Pete?"

"The Two Doors."

"Oh, no! Not Granddad's favorite story? Pete, I just meant that the split with Gabe was not friendly, and there is no way we'll get back together. I'm not a philosopher like Emmanuel Prospect," she noted.

"I'm sorry, Sheila. It's just that doors seem to be all the Prospects want to talk about."

She smiled and began, "Well, they aren't here and we are. Let's just forget about that family and enjoy our drinks, okay?"

"You're right. Now more talk about the 'you-know-who' family."

"Pete, I get the feeling that you really like me, or am I just crazy?"

He took her hands in his and replied, "What's not to like, Sheila? You're beautiful, very smart, sexy, articulate, and rich!" She only smiled.

§

A tiny glimmer of light squeezed through the small slit in the window, casting a dim light on Rachel Manson. She was chained to a concrete wall by her hands, and her body hung limply. Her breath was slow and weak and her eyes were open but not really focused on anything. Her clothes were in shreds and her body was caked in mud, blood, and sweat. How long had it been, she wondered, and where was Shirley? She had not seen her daughter since the men came for her hours ago. "God protect her," she whispered. She struggled to remember what happened to them. They were home, right where they told Emmanuel Prospect they wanted to be. A team of four guards from the Prospect Enterprise were watching over things: two outside and a personal guard near each woman.

Rachel had been walking up the stairs. At least that's how she remembered it now. Each time she woke in the cell, her memory seemed a bit improved. She remembered the guard had told her a silly joke as he followed her up the stairs. She was laughing and almost stumbled. Lance took her arm to steady her so she would not fall and helped her to the top of the stairs. She remembered thanking him and then walking into the bedroom and closing the door so she could change. Then there was the hint of a smell, something like smoke and sulfur, which seemed quite odd. She turned to see a massive red beast smiling at her with long black fangs. Before she could scream or even take a breath, the beast grabbed her and they were gone. Perhaps she had passed out. What happened next? She was not clear on that. There was a clang on the door and she looked up. The latch turned and a short angry man walked in with Shirley and threw her to the floor. Then he un-cuffed Rachel and allowed her to collapse onto the floor as well. He laughed angrily and walked out of the room, locking the door behind him.

Rachel pulled herself to her knees and crawled over to her daughter. Shirley was lying on her stomach. Her tattered dress was torn where she had been whipped. The sores oozed blood. Rachel turned her over and held her daughter in her arms. Shirley groaned from the pain in her back. "Baby, what did they do to you?"

"Mom, why are they doing this to us? What did we do?"

"I don't know, sweetheart, but I know it has to do with Satori again," Rachel sighed.

"But what about the guards in our house? It had to be them. Who else could have gotten through?"

"Tell me what you remember about that night, baby," Rachel begged.

"Timothy and I were playing chess," Shirley began. "We were having such a good time that I'd almost forgotten what happened to Dad and Uncle Lenny. I had to go pee, so I got up and went to the bathroom. Just as I closed the door, it seemed I was flying through the air. I assumed that Timothy had set off a bomb or something."

"Flying through the air? I remember that too!" Rachel exclaimed.

"Something was holding onto me, but I was too afraid to look up at it." She held out her arms. "I remember looking at my arms and there were these red feet with long black talons holding me." She looked up at her mother. "I thought I'd lost my mind. Then I passed out and ended up in here with you."

"Maybe it wasn't the Prospects, baby."

"I think they're all evil, Mom, but remember what Satori did to Dad and Uncle Lenny?" Rachel replied. "If it was them, why are we even alive? Wouldn't they have just killed us too?"

"Your daughter makes an excellent point," said an unfamiliar voice. They had not heard the door being unlocked or opened, but there was a giant red beast standing in the cell now.

"What do you want from us?" Rachel said, trying to cover Shirley's body with her own.

The beast sat on one of the two cots in the small cell and smiled. "Mrs. Manson, your brother-in-law threatened my business and your husband endangered my plans. No one can survive after doing that to me."

"Then go ahead and kill us too," Rachel begged. "We have nothing left."

"While you did endanger my business by talking to my dear brother, since you are women, you may yet serve a purpose in my organization," the beast said.

"Go to hell!"

"Oh, I'm so scared," he laughed. "Boys, come on in!" Two giant winged monsters came through the door, grabbed the women, and chained them back to the wall. He stood and walked up to the women, running his hands up and down their torsos. "You must understand that my species needs to procreate too. My sons need to expand our race, and due to your current situation, I think you will make adequate incubators for their progeny."

"Stay away from my daughter or I'll kill you!" Rachel screamed. Both women began to scream for help.

"Shout all you like," the beast said. "There is no one to hear you in this place." He turned to the winged monsters and said, "Please be gentle with them, boys. We will need them for a long time." He laughed uproariously and walked out the door, closing it behind him.

Chapter 15

Pete sat up in bed, his heart pounding and every muscle tensed. The dream was burning in his mind and the smell of sulfur and sweat clogged his nose. He glanced at Sheila lying next to him and was suddenly repulsed by her. She had not been in his dream, but his gut told him she was somehow connected. He pulled on his clothes, grabbed his phone and computer and ran out of the house. I can get new clothes, he thought. Now he had to go someplace else. He ran for several blocks, south, he thought. He had never been to San Diego, so he did not know where he was going, but he had to be as far away from Sheila Farness as he could.

He came upon a small park along the beach and sat under a shade tree, panting to catch his breath. Who were those monsters, and why were they about to rape those poor women, he wondered. It was too surreal to actually be happening. He remembered the monsters from his dreams about the airplane attack over France and the private jet ride here. Now they were back again and did not seem to be allegorical at all. Those creatures had beaten those poor women and were now going to impregnate them. "What did Michael say?" he asked. "I think I remember him saying that no one on earth believes they exist. That's not the same as saying they don't!" he shouted. A woman by the shore was staring at him. She gathered her two young children and left the park quickly. Good, he thought. She would call the police and he would end up in jail, far from both families. He leaned back against the tree and looked at his phone. He pressed the key to bring up his contact list and scrolled down, and then pressed the connect button.

"Joshua Prospect," said a familiar voice.

"Uncle Joshua, it's Peter Smith. I need to see you," he replied.

"What's wrong, Pete?"

"It was another dream, but worse that the rest."

"Tell me about it, Peter." Joshua asked.

"It was like in a prison cell. There were two women who had been beaten and chained to a wall. Then there were these monsters in the cell with them. I remember them being dark red and huge. The room was filled with smoked and smelled of sulfur. It was awful, Josh!"

"Pete, this is very important. Do you remember if you heard the women's names?"

"No, I never heard their names, but I think it was Rachel and Shirley Manson."

"Why do you say that?"

Pete sighed, and continued, "The younger woman mentioned Dad and Uncle Lenny twice."

"Where exactly are you, Pete?"

"I'm in La Jolla, California, I think. I'm at a tiny ocean-side park called La Jolla Hermosa Park," he replied. "What are we going to do?"

"Pete, as luck would have it, Gabe and I are in the area. You sit tight and we'll be there in ten minutes at most. Is there anything else I should know?" Joshua asked.

He sighed again and held his head in his hands. "I think the monsters were going to rape those women." There was silence on the line. "And Josh, please don't tell Gabe, but I slept with Sheila Farness last night. She invited me to stay at her place."

"Okay, Pete. Don't worry, we'll be there. Does she know you left?"

"No, I woke up from the dream suddenly. When I looked at her, I felt sick. What have I done? I'm sorry, Uncle Joshua."

"Pete, we're in Gabe's car now, so don't worry. But you might want to find somewhere to hide until we get there. She might come looking for you. Bye," Josh said as he closed the connection.

Pete looked around. There was nowhere to hide. As he continued to look, a red Mercedes convertible pulled up and Sheila got out, holding a pistol in her right hand. "Kiss and run, huh, lover-boy!" she shouted at him. "You've got a lot of nerve, Peter."

She walked up to him and began to poke him in the chest with the barrel of her gun. "You did it, didn't you? You called the damned Prospects again and told them about another dream."

"Sheila, I don't know what you're talking about," he cried. "I just wanted some fresh air."

She laughed out loud. "So, you leave me in bed, grab your phone and computer and run five blocks just to get some air? Please, you can lie better than that! Tell me what you told the Prospects or I'll kill you where you stand, Pete!"

Pete was backing away and Sheila kept approaching. She had a look of loathing hatred on her face, and her lips were pressed together in a tight line. Then she stopped and her expression began to soften. "Okay, Pete, I'm sorry. Forget the stupid dream and just get in my car and all's forgiven."

An older woman's voice shouted from across the street, "I'll call 911, so you'd better get out of here!" Sheila spun around and fired three shots toward the woman who was standing by her front door. Thankfully, she was not hit and dived back in her house and locked the door.

When she turned around again, Pete had managed to back up another ten feet. "Pete, I didn't aim at the old bitch. She's fine. Now get in my car!"

"I don't think that's a good idea, Sheila."

Her expression turned to anger again. She rushed over to Pete and struck him across the head with her pistol, knocking him to the ground where he crashed onto the soft sand. She cocked the gun and aimed at his head. Just then, she could hear the first sounds of a siren approaching. "I guess it's your lucky day, Pete. I'll see you later." She slipped the pistol into her purse and ran over to her car. Seconds later she was gone.

An SUV pulled up and Joshua jumped out. He ran over to Pete and helped him to his feet. "Come on Pete, we have to get out of here," he said as he pulled Pete along. He pushed him into the rear seat and slammed the door and then climbed into the front seat.

Gabe drove away as fast as he could. Joshua turned to look at Pete who was holding his head. "I guess Sheila found you first. Are you going to be okay? Please let me take a look at your head."

"She shot at a woman across the street! We need to go check on her," Pete argued.

"No one was injured but you, and we have to get you out of here," Gabe said.

"How do you know that?"

"It's okay, Pete. We know," Joshua said as he put his hand against the wound on Pete's head. "How's that?"

"The pain is gone! What did you do?"

"Pete, there's no time. We have to find out where Rachel and Shirley are, and I need you to help," Joshua said.

"Josh, I had a dream. I don't know anything other than it was a dark cell," Pete replied. "How can I help?"

"Pete, I'm going to hold your head in my hands for a moment. You will probably fall asleep when I do, but that's okay. We will make sure you are safe. I need you to trust me," Joshua begged.

Pete's mind was reeling and he had no idea what to think. Then he remembered his other meetings with Joshua. If there was one person in the Prospect family who could be trusted, it was this man. "I trust you, Josh."

Gabe pulled the car over to the curb, so Josh could unbuckle his seatbelt and turn around fully. He smiled at Pete and said, "You'll be fine, and thanks for calling me." Pete smiled as Joshua put his hands on either side of Peter's head. Pete's expression turned to one of horror as his dream began to replay in excruciating slow motion. He began to see details he never imagined while he was asleep. It was overwhelming his mind such that he thought his head would explode. That was when he passed out. Joshua eased Peter down to a reclining position on the back seat, and then turned around to face Gabe.

"Well?" Gabe asked.

"I know the place well, but I'll need your dad's help," Joshua said, "and maybe your Uncle Michael too."

"Good luck," Gabe said as Joshua disappeared from the car. He threw the car in gear and drove down the street.

§

The giant red beast walked down the bare concrete corridor from the cell laughing. He turned left down another corridor and opened a door. Bill Satori walked into his office in Manhattan. He was chuckling as he sat at his desk. "Well, the Manson family may still be useful to us," he said to himself. He spun around in his chair and took a whisky bottle off his credenza and filled a small glass. He turned around to check his e-mail and found Emmanuel Prospect sitting on one of the couches by the windows. "Manny, this is a surprise. What can I do for you today?"

"Your perverse mind sickens me, brother," the other said. "You will pay for what you've done!"

"I haven't done anything, dear brother," Bill smiled. "I've been here all day, just ask my assistant." He picked up his phone handset. "Shall I call her in?"

"Save me your petty lies, Bill. We already know what is happening and some of my sons will take care of it. You have failed again."

"What on Earth are you talking about, Manny? I think you must be losing your sanity. What exactly do you think I've done?" Bill asked.

"Peter Smith has come back to us, Bill. He is safely in our hands again." The color drained from Satori's face, and he stared at his brother without blinking. "Not only that, he has had a dream and told us about it."

"It's interesting that you believe in dreams now, Manny. Perhaps you should see a doctor?"

"Isn't it odd that you'd pick that location for the assault on the Manson women?" Emmanuel asked.

"There's been an assault? How terrible, but who are these Manson women you speak of?"

"You might want to ask Narga and Barsat about that. They should be getting unwanted visitors any second now," Emmanuel laughed. "You're such a fool!"

"You keep your bastard children away from my family!" Bill shouted as he stood up and waved an accusatory finger at his brother. "You have no right to interfere. I'm leaving." He walked around the desk and grabbed the doorknob, which had become intensely cold, so cold in fact that Bill Satori groaned and contorted in pain, unable to release the knob. After a few more seconds, he was frozen solid.

Emmanuel stood next to his brother and whispered in his ear, "You'll thaw out in an hour or so, brother. Now that Peter Smith is on my side, your evil games are at an end."

§

"Why should you get the young one, Narga?" Barsat argued. "You're not my boss."

"I may not be your boss, but you are a follower, not a leader, Barsat. I'll tell you what: Next time you get your pick first, how about that?" Narga said as he ran his hands over Shirley's body.

The two women had stopped shouting and were trembling with fear as tears poured out of their eyes. "You don't have to do this!" Rachel begged. "Please don't do this!"

Barsat pressed his lips to hers and wrapped his arms around her body. "Woman, you should be honored to bear my children. You will win immortality and be feared and loved."

Narga was fondling Shirley and rubbing his body against hers. "I'm sorry, Mom," she cried.

The room was suddenly filled with intense white light, causing the beasts and the women to close their eyes tightly. Narga and Barsat stumbled backward, covering their eyes with their hands and groaning in pain. As the light began to subside, they turned to see that the brightness was pouring from a long sword held high by Uncle Michael. Joshua was standing on his left. "Barsat and Narga, I wish I could slice you both in tiny pieces for what you've attempted to do," Michael said.

"Do what you want, but it won't do any good!" Narga shouted. "How did you find us in this place?"

"There was a vision . . ."

Barsat looked at Narga and said, "I knew it. That damned bitch failed, and Peter Smith escaped. Perhaps now our father will understand her uselessness."

"Shut up!" Narga replied and then turned to the two Prospects. "Okay, I guess now we leave and call it a day."

"You wish it were that easy," Joshua said. "You have violated sacred ground by bringing these women here. You must be punished."

Narga laughed and pointed to himself and Barsat. "Look at us, fool, don't we look punished enough already? And what can you do?"

Joshua only smiled as the door opened again and a figure cloaked in a black hooded robe entered the room. The temperature soared and the women and monsters began to sweat profusely. Fires started spontaneously in each corner of the room, and the flames licked up the walls and across the ceiling. The cloaked figure touched Joshua on the sleeve and pointed to the women. Michael and Joshua unchained the women and carried them out of the room. Narga and Barsat were panting for breath in the thickening black smoke.

The cloaked figure removed the hood, revealing himself to be Luce Prospect. When the monsters saw his face, they shrieked in fear. Luce extended his right arm and made a downward motion, and the two beasts fell to their knees. "Please don't do this, Master. We used to be your friends, don't you remember?" Narga begged.

"I'm sorry, but when you left me to join your father, you knew you could never return here and, yet, here you are," Luce said. "How dare you defile this place with your crimes and perversion?"

"We only came because our father told us to, Master. We never would have come here otherwise, I swear," Barsat cried. "Have mercy!"

"Then you can thank him for this later," Luce replied. "I take no pleasure in this, but you know the rules. You must pay for this violation before you can leave this place." The two monsters were crying and wringing their hands as Luce stepped between them and placed an index finger in the center of each of their foreheads.

They screamed in pain and writhed on the floor, but could not break the connection to Luce. Their arms and legs flailed without direction. Both monsters lost control of their bodies and foamed at the mouth as blood seeped out of their eyes and ears. A few tears formed in Luce's eyes and a look of terrible sadness filled his face. After two minutes, he removed his fingers and walked out of the room. As he closed the door, the fires extinguished and the smoke cleared. Both monsters were passed out on the floor.

Luce joined the others outside the door. "We're done here," he said. "I hate having to do that. Why don't one of you trade jobs with me?"

"Luce, you are a noble man and my dearest brother, but I am grateful each day that cup was not handed to me," Michael said.

Joshua put his hand on Luce's shoulder and said, "Why don't you and Michael take the ladies somewhere safe? Bill will be here soon to see me. But give me a second with them first." He walked over to where Rachel and Shirley were sitting and sat next to Rachel on the floor.

"What happened in there, Josh?" Shirley asked. "The screaming was terrible."

"I know, but Narga and Barsat needed to pay for their crime," he replied. "Don't worry, we did not kill them."

"You should have killed them for what they almost did to us!" Rachel shouted. "What kind of monsters are they?"

"I can't really say any more right now," Joshua replied. "But we can talk later if you like. Right now, my brothers are going to take you back to your house. I've asked two of my female cousins to join the team. Please do not go anywhere without them. Even in the bathroom, have one of the women there. They won't watch, but it's critically important that someone is with you at all times."

"That's okay with me," Rachel said. "After what just happened, I don't want to take any chances with something like this again. In fact, if you know a safer place, I think I can stay away from home for a while."

"Perfect! My nephew Gabe has a great place in Manhattan that is absolutely safe and has plenty of room. I'll come by tonight for dinner with you, okay?"

Rachel leaned over and kissed Joshua on the cheek and said, "Thank you for saving us, Josh. And I'm looking forward to your explanation about those monsters later."

Joshua stood up and said, "Sure. That's fine. I'll be there." Then he leaned over and touched each woman's head and they fell asleep. He walked back to his brothers.

"I assume you erased the memory of this place," Michael said.

"No, but I softened it a bit," Joshua smiled. "They'll remember being in a cell and being attacked, but it will be by human men and not the beasts. You two better get out of here now. My guest is about to arrive." Joshua was standing in the corridor alone.

"What are you doing here?" said a voice behind him. He turned to see Bill Satori standing ten feet away, rubbing his right hand and still shivering.

"I was waiting for you," Joshua smiled. "Shall we go?" The corridor was empty again.

§

The barren desert stretched to the horizon in every direction. The sky was cloudless and the temperature was over one hundred degrees. Only a few scrub bushes and random patches of boulders baked in the relentless glare. Bill and Joshua were walking across a salt flat, and the surface crunched under their feet. "You remember this place, Bill?"

The old man chuckled and replied, "How could I ever forget? It was the place of my greatest failure." They kept walking in silence for several minutes until they came upon two small boulders underneath a Saguaro cactus, providing a bit of shade. Bill grunted as he sat on the stone. Joshua sat on the other stone facing him. "Joshua, I must apologize for picking that location. Frankly, I'm not certain why I did that."

"Perhaps you were hoping to be stopped?"

The old man laughed. "Why would I want to be stopped? That makes no sense."

"But still you brought them there. You had to know that we would find you," Joshua said.

"Actually, no I didn't. If Peter Smith would have stayed in bed with Sheila, my sons would have finished their encounters quickly and none of your ilk would have found out. Now my sons have been tortured and it's my fault."

Joshua frowned, saying, "Torture is a difficult word, Bill. I prefer to say they have been instructed about their error and have made atonement."

Bill laughed again. "You have a way with words, Joshua. You always have since the time we met here first. That was so long ago. But the level of pain my sons endured is torture, and you have to acknowledge that."

"Bill, you have never atoned for what you have done, so you cannot know what it is like and make such a judgment," Joshua began. "You and your friends cause death and misery around the world all the time. Those women would have been forced to bear offspring like Narga and Barsat for years to come. Their lives would have been destroyed and their humanity lost forever. Your sons were exposed to the evil of their lives and intentions. There was no physical pain, only forced recognition of their perversion."

"Why are we here, anyway?"

"This place defines our relationship, Uncle. From the first time we met here and you tried to convince me to join your family, this place has been where we meet. To me, it defines the vast emptiness in a man's soul who chooses your family. To pick your side, his spirit must be devoid of compassion and love. All the joy of his life must have been drained away in order to be with you voluntarily. What do you think?"

Bill chuckled under his breath. "Of course you would see it that way and pardon me for disagreeing. Still, I have a feeling there is something else you want to add."

"When I came here that first time, I wanted to free myself of the distractions of life and focus my entire mind on what was really important," Joshua noted. "I hoped to be as close as a man can get to the disembodied spirit. I hoped I would see the plain truth clearly without the cloudy goggles of existence."

"I can agree with that view, nephew," Bill said. "I think it is only our vision of what a man will see that is different. You think a man will see that there is warm and fuzzy good all around and embrace love and self-sacrifice for the betterment of all." He laughed. "What a load of hogwash! What a man will see is that no one cares for him and his success is entirely in his own hands. If a man falls to his knees and clasps his hands together, the Prospects are not going to pay his salary, feed him, and keep his wife from cheating with his best friend. Life is hard. People have to do what they can to succeed and keep others from taking everything away. Some are lucky. They end up with good jobs and lots of lovers and cash. Most are not. They struggle daily to get enough to eat. Life gives them crap, and they do what they must to survive."

"Like bombing coffee shops to get surveillance equipment orders?"

Bill frowned at the other. "Whatever they have to do! I'm leaving!" He stood and began to walk away across the salt.

Joshua jumped up and began to follow him again. "Uncle, stay away from the Mansons and Peter Smith!"

Bill turned and rushed up to Joshua, shoving him with both hands. The younger man fell to the ground. "Listen to me, Junior. This world of yours is full of crime, hate, and death. This is not some idealistic Prospect experience for most people, so spare me your sanctimonious drivel. Your family can keep doing what they do and we'll do what we do. That is the nature of the world and you know it." He turned around and continued walking.

"Uncle, I meant what I said!"

Bill stopped and turned around again, but did not approach. He shouted, "Joshua, you have always been fair with me so I'll do you a favor. I will spare the older Manson woman. But I will have the younger one, and I will kill Peter Smith. You and your family can fight me, but I swear I will defeat you!" He turned into a dust devil and raced away.

"Well, that didn't go very well," Joshua said out loud.

Chapter 16

Pete woke on a couch in the living room of Gabe's Manhattan apartment. He sat up to see who was around, but the room was empty. He stood and walked over to a picture window overlooking Central Park. The sun was shining now, but a large bank of intensely dark clouds was approaching quickly. The cloud formations were massive with anvils reaching forty or fifty thousand feet into the sky. It reminded him of the super cells that would form in the Midwest, bringing tornadoes, hail, and torrential rain. Even through the thick plate glass, he could hear the wind beginning to howl. Pete walked into the kitchen to look for Maria, but she was nowhere to be found. For a brief second, he wondered if this was the beginning of another horrible dream. He prepared a pot of coffee and poured a cup, and then added half-and-half and sweetener to his liking. Sitting at the dinette table, sipping his coffee, he could see small raindrops start to splash against the windows.

After a few minutes, a young woman walked into the kitchen. At first, she was startled to see Pete sitting at the table. Then she smiled meekly at him. "Hi," she said.

He stood and walked over to her, extending his right hand. "Hi, Shirley, my name is Pete Smith."

She pulled her hand back quickly. "How do you know my name?"

"That's a bit complicated. Can I get you a cup of coffee?" he asked.

She nodded and sat at the table. "What do you mean by 'It's complicated,' Pete?"

He set a cup of coffee in front of her and retrieved the creamer and sweeteners and then gave her a napkin and spoon and sat across from her at the table. "I guess you could say I tipped off Gabe and Joshua about your capture."

She smiled and said, "Wow! Thank you for saving us, but how did you know where we were?"

"Pete's a psychic," Gabe said as he walked into the room. "He had a vision and told us about it." He poured himself a cup and joined the other two. "Thanks again for calling Uncle Josh, Pete," he said as he patted him on the shoulder.

Shirley smiled and said, "So Pete, do you work for the Psychic Hotline or something?"

"No, and I wouldn't call myself a psychic anyway. Thanks for the label, Gabe."

"Hey, I was helping you out, man, but I agree that wasn't the best word to describe your unique talent. I guess the better word is prophet," Gabe said. Shirley sat expressionless and stunned, not knowing what to believe.

"I don't think you're making things any better, Gabe," Pete replied.

"Pete, I'm not trying to make things better. I'm just telling the truth."

"So, Pete is a prophet, huh?" Shirley gasped at last. "A real prophet, that's hard to believe. Where's your robe and white beard?"

"Okay, enough of this kind of talk," Pete said. "Shirley, I have dreams. But unlike most people, a lot of my dreams have been coming true. I don't know why, but I'm not some religious ascetic or anything. For Christ's sake, I just graduated from business school."

"Well, I don't know what to believe, Pete. But if your dream helped save my mom and me from those monsters, I can never thank you enough," Shirley said as she reached across the table and squeezed his hand. "I've never been more frightened in my life!" She turned to Gabe and asked, "What time is Joshua coming for dinner? I want to find out what else he's learned about those men who attacked us."

"Men?" Pete asked.

"Yes, men, Pete," Gabe replied. "Well, Shirley, Josh doesn't really believe in schedules and deadlines, and that's probably why he's not in the family business. I imagine he'll call before he heads over, but if you're hungry, I can ask Maria to make something for you. Don't wait for Josh or you might starve to death."

Shirley stood up and replied, "No, that's okay. I just wanted to tell my mom. I'm not hungry at all. I think I'll go see how she's doing. See you both later." She walked out of the room.

Pete leaned over to Gabe and complained, "Those were not men, Gabe. What's going on here?"

"Hush, keep it down Pete. No sense scaring Shirley and her mother," Gabe said. "Now, were you ever in the cell with them?"

Pete looked stunned. Gabe already knew that he saw what he saw in a dream. "So, you're telling me I imagined the monsters and it was just three guys?"

"Pete, please listen to me. I don't know what you saw in your dream. Remember that you talked to Josh and not me. Neither you nor I were ever in the cell with the women and whoever attacked them. After we got back here, I had a call from my dad and he told me the women will remember men. That's it. You have to understand that this is a delicate situation, and whether men or monsters attacked those women, it is still a terrible crime."

Pete sat back and considered the words of Gabe Prospect. Once again, there had been no denial or affirmation of anything. It was more rhetoric designed to obfuscate the subject. "Okay, I think I'm starting to get it. No one in your family will confirm or deny anything about the attackers. And I agree it's easier to move forward if they were people and not some kind of demons."

"I couldn't have said it better myself."

"But what were they?" Pete begged. Gabe only laughed.

§

Rain and sleet poured down onto the city. Lightning crackled and broke the darkness with flashes that stretched across the sky. Thunder rumbled down the steel canyons of Manhattan along with near hurricane force winds that pushed dumpsters and benches around like flotsam on an angry sea. The few people foolish enough to be on the streets fought their umbrellas, and more often than not the umbrellas won, taking wing and soaring up into the air, leaving their owners to dash for cover from the relentless downpour. All flights were delayed at the area airports until the bulk of the storm passed to the east and over the ocean. Lights flickered in many residential areas as the inches of rain continued to mount. Joshua Prospect was watching the scene from the other side of the glass wall in his nephew's apartment. Shirley and Rachel Manson flanked him, mesmerized by the enormity of the weather.

Across the room, Gabe and Pete sat watching the latest weather reports on television. The storm had apparently stalled over the city, and no one knew when it was likely to weaken or continue its voyage across the sky. Low-lying areas were already reporting flash flooding and power was failing in other districts. "Looks kind of like Armageddon, doesn't it?" Pete asked.

"Don't even joke about that," Gabe said. "It's just a storm, man."

Joshua and the women came over and joined them on the couch. Joshua and Rachel sat with Gabe and Shirley with Pete. "Gabe, thank you again for dinner," Rachel said. "Maria is just a great cook, almost as good as I am."

"I may hold you to that some day, Rachel," he replied. "Maybe when Maria goes on vacation, you can take over for her."

"I don't know if you can afford me," she laughed and then turned to Joshua and asked, "So what is the status of those three men? Are they in jail or what?"

Joshua cleared his throat and said, "I guess we have to leave that up to the police, Rachel. For all I know, they may have let them go."

"We're both ready to go to the station and file our complaints," Shirley said. "Those bastards deserve severe punishment, and especially their father who was whoring us out to them."

"I'm certain justice will be done," Gabe said.

Shirley put her hand on Pete's knee and asked, "Tell us more about your dreams, Pete." He was staring straight ahead and did not respond. "Pete, are you okay?"

Pete let out a long, low groan. All color had drained from his face and his hands were trembling. "Pete, what's wrong?" Joshua asked.

"Maybe he's having a fit or something," Rachel noted.

"There's no time," Pete said. "They're almost here."

"Who are you talking about?" Rachel asked. Pete did not answer but extended his hand toward the windows where Joshua had been watching the storm approach. Everyone except Pete and Joshua jumped up and rushed over to the windows to see what might be happening. The sky was black and heavy raindrops splashed against the glass, but nothing else was visible in the inky blackness of night.

Joshua moved and sat with Pete and put his hands against his head. The images flashed through Joshua's mind, and he began to tremble as well. After a few seconds, he was able to stutter, "Gabe, situation."

A massive discharge of lightning filled the sky with light and dozens of individual bolts shot across the heavens. In the light of the blast, a huge flock of large birds could be seen coming in their direction. Gabe was struggling to pull his phone from his pocket. He dropped the phone just as the power went out in the building, plunging the group into still darkness.

Pete shook himself out of the vision and grabbed his own phone. He brought up the contact list, selected one and pressed the send. A second flash of lightning lit up the flock of birds again, although they were quite close now and definitely not birds. Pete pressed the connect button again and waited. Perhaps the cell network was down as well, he wondered.

A third flash of lightning exploded across the sky and revealed the giant bat-like monsters to be less than one hundred feet from the building. There had to be hundreds of them now. "Hello?" said a voice on the phone.

"Granddad, it's Pete. We have a situation," he said as the monsters landed on the walls of the building and began to smash at the glass.

"Oh, God, I remember them now," Rachel cried. Shirley screamed.

The windows began to crack under the attack, and the monsters rushed into the room, smashing the furniture and throwing everything around. Gabe jumped in front of Rachel to protect her. A monster slapped him across the chest, knocking him across the room where he crashed into a wall and remained still. The monster put his arms around Rachel and said, "Too bad, you would have been a good mother for my children." He carried her over to the door to Pete's room and threw her inside and then crushed the doorknob to seal her inside.

Joshua stood between the beasts and Pete and Shirley, looking defiant. "You bastards cannot succeed. You've gone far enough!" Narga grabbed Joshua and threw him out the broken windows, and he tumbled downward out of sight.

Narga walked up to the last two and signaled his brothers to stop their attack. "So, Pete, it's good to see you again. My father asked me to kill you, but I think I'll take you both with us. If he wants you dead, he can do it himself."

"What in God's name is going on here?" Pete asked.

Narga replied, "God has nothing to do with this, human." He and the others began to laugh. "Okay, boys, let's get out of here before their reinforcements arrive." He grabbed Shirley and flew out into the dark sky.

Barsat grabbed Pete by the waist. "You should have kept the job with us, Pete. Then you could have had a comfortable life. Too bad you chose the wrong door!" He and the other monsters flew away.

In less than a minute, the room filled with brilliant white light. As it faded, several dozen men were standing in the room. Uncle Michael rushed over to Gabe who was knocked unconscious. Uncle Simon heard screaming from Gabe's room and ripped the door off its hinges. Rachel rushed out and threw her arms around him. She was crying and gasping for air. A second bright light filled the room, and she turned to see Uncle Gabriel flying in through the broken windows carrying Joshua in his arms. He set him down on a sofa and touched his forehead. Joshua's entire body was broken after falling so many stories to the pavement below. Rachel rushed over and got on her knees, gently caressing Joshua's forehead. "You have to save him!" she shouted to Gabriel.

"Please be calm, sister," he replied. "Joshua will not die this night."

The elevator car opened and Emmanuel Prospect entered the room, hurrying over to Joshua who was not moving or breathing. "My poor boy," he sighed as he saw the mangled body in front of him.

"Mr. Prospect, can you help him?" Rachel begged.

Emmanuel touched her cheek with his hand and replied, "Joshua will be fine. Please be at peace." He bent down and kissed Joshua on his cheeks and forehead. Then he took his son's hands in his and said, "Time to rise, my son."

Joshua opened his eyes and sat up. He looked completely normal again, as though he had just awakened from a bad dream, even though his clothing was torn and soaked in blood. "I'm sorry we failed, Father," he moaned.

Emmanuel sat on the couch next to his son and motioned for Rachel to sit next to him as well. He draped his arms around their shoulders and said, "You did not fail, Joshua. We do not control the course of time. This was the time for this event to occur."

Rachel was crying and shaking, but managed to squeak out, "But what about Shirley and Pete? Those monsters must have taken them!"

Emmanuel stroked her hair and replied, "They are both okay for now. Unfortunately, we must let the course of events proceed and pray we are able to save them."

"But you said this was a safe place!" she shouted. "Now she's gone!"

"Rachel, please have faith," the old man begged. "We will do everything we can to save her."

"Father, it may be too late to save Peter," Michael said.

Emmanuel looked up at his son and replied, "I know. I hope Peter remains strong until we can rescue him. You know where they are, don't you?"

Michael nodded and lowered his head.

§

Pete woke up in his bed in Gabe's apartment. The memory of the monsters breaking in and attacking them surged through his mind, causing him to sit straight up, his muscles tensed and heart racing. Had it been a dream, he wondered. He climbed out of bed and walked over to the door and opened it a crack. The apartment looked completely normal. It had been a dream, he realized. Feeling overwhelmed with relief, he crawled back into bed and considered calling a psychiatrist to find out if he was insane. He shrugged it off and fell back asleep. His sleep was dreamless, which was a blessing after what he had been through. The faint smell of smoke woke him seemingly hours later. He blearily opened his eyes to see Gabe sitting on a chair at the foot of his bed, smiling and chuckling to himself.

"Gabe, what are you doing in here? What about the privacy rule?" he asked.

Gabe just sat smiling.

"Are you deaf, Gabe? Get out of here!"

"Don't you dare order me around, you piece of garbage!" Gabe shouted. "I know what you did with Sheila, you bastard. You knew I had feelings for her and you slept with her anyway! Don't you have a soul, man?"

Pete sat up and replied, "I'm sorry, Gabe. It was a terrible mistake."

Gabe stood up and walked over to where Pete was sitting on the edge of the bed. He grabbed Pete by the neck and pulled him off the bed and above his head. "You picked the wrong man to screw around with, Peter Smith."

Pete was gasping for air and pulling on Gabe's hands, but to no avail. He began to feel as though he might pass out or be strangled to death. The walls of the room burst into flames. Orange fingers of fire climbed the walls, consuming the wallpaper as they passed. The flames licked across the ceiling until the entire room was a ball of fire. Gabe began to laugh.

"Gabe, stop it," Pete squeaked.

"Go to hell, Pete," Gabe said as he threw him down onto the bed. The ceiling above the bed collapsed on top of him. Pete screamed in pain as the fire ran across his skin and consumed his pajamas. The floor collapsed and Pete and the burning bed fell into a shaft of fire. He screamed again and passed out.

Pete felt totally separated from his body. Perhaps this is what death felt like, he thought. He was no longer on fire and seemed okay, although he was floating in absolute blackness. After a moment, he tried to feel his body, and everything seemed normal, although his eyes were useless in the blackness. After what seemed like several minutes, he began to notice a soft sound far away. He strained to hear it, but it seemed like a mumble. He focused his mind on the sound and it started to get louder, although still unintelligible. He tried to move in the direction of the sound, but it seemed to come from every direction. He concentrated his mind on the sound, trying to exclude everything else in order to understand what the voice was saying. Finally, he heard it.

"Pete! For God's sake, wake up!" Shirley shouted.

He opened his eyes to find Shirley ten feet away, chained to a wall. She appeared to be wearing a hospital gown. She struggled to move and was straining to get closer to him. "Shirley, where are we?"

"How would I know?" she asked. "What is this place?"

Pete was chained to the wall opposite Shirley. He, too, was wearing a hospital gown which was open in back. The wall felt like ice against his shoulders and buttocks. The room was a hallway that seemed impossibly long in both directions, and chains were placed every few feet along both facing walls. Skeletons were suspended from many of the sets of chains. The walls, ceiling, and floor were white, although there were dark stains under many of the chains. There were no light fixtures, but bright light seemed to emanate from the ceiling, casting a medicinal glare on all surfaces. "I wonder where we are," he said at last. "How long have we been here?"

"I've been here for hours, but you just appeared a few minutes ago," she explained. "Where were you?"

"I don't really know," he said. "It was surreal. I was back in my bed and Gabe came in and tried to burn me alive. Shirley, I don't know what's real anymore. My dreams and reality are blending together, and I think I'm losing my mind. Please tell me where we were the last time you remember."

"We were in Gabe's apartment during the storm, and the red monsters broke in. They threw Joshua out the window and then took us."

"That wasn't a dream?"

"Not unless I'm dreaming this too," Shirley laughed. "What do you think they want from us?"

"I'm afraid it's nothing good. One of the beasts told me I was to be killed, but he would let his father do it. And I'm really sorry, but I think you already know what they want you for." She began to cry.

Far down the corridor, three dark red beasts approached. As they became closer, Pete recognized them from his dreams. The one in front had been the pilot of the private jet. He and the others had been in the cell with Shirley. She recognized them as well and began to scream and struggle against the chains. "Help me, Pete, please?"

"I'll try, Shirley. I guarantee that I'll try my best," he replied. She stopped screaming and dropped her head. Teardrops fell onto the floor beneath her feet.

The lead beast signaled for the other two to stop and continued until he stood between the two people. He turned to Shirley and stroked her cheek gently. "I'm sorry, child. I will not harm you and we will not impregnate you. I am afraid my rivalry with my brother has caused you to be here."

"Please let us go," she begged. "If you want us to stay away from the Prospects, we swear we will. Just let us go."

"I doubt that is possible now, child. No human has ever left this place alive, although in your case, I sincerely wish you could," the beast replied.

"Please release her, Mr. Satori," Pete urged.

The beast spun around and grabbed Pete by the throat, pinning his head to the wall. "Hello, Peter Smith. I must admit I was upset when Narga did not kill you in Gabriel Prospect's apartment. Of course, after I recalled how he suffered at the hands of Luce Prospect, I softened. Then I realized the opportunity I have with you now," Bill said as he released his grip on Pete's throat. "Now you can no longer help them with your visions. Now you can help me!"

"Why would I do that if I'm dead already?"

Satori laughed and his two sons began to laugh as well. "You're not dead, Peter. You are still very much alive," Bill said as he ran his claw down Peter's arm and a trail of blood oozed out and dripped onto the floor. Peter was thrashing about on the chains but could not escape the monsters. "What I said is that no human has ever left here alive, although I admit it is quite rare to have living guests. Generally, they are altruists or valiant soldiers attempting to cure the evils of the world. You two are a bit of a conundrum."

"It was you, not Gabe Prospect, in that last vision I had," Pete said. "He would never do that to me."

"That is true, Peter," Bill acknowledged. "But Gabe and I have Sheila Farness in common. He may not care that you slept with her, but I do. Although in fairness, I did suggest that she do so."

"What are you talking about?"

"Peter, Sheila works for me, and I intend to make her my wife," Bill said. "I told her to try to separate you from the Prospects even if she had to become your lover." He thumped Peter on the chest, causing more wounds to open and more blood to ooze down his gown. "But I am still a man! I can be as jealous as the next. I wanted her to convert you, but she is still my woman!"

"You are a man?" Shirley gasped.

He turned to her and smiled. "Yes, my dear, my sons and I are human, although it may be more correct to say we are of humanity."

"I'm so confused," she said.

"Don't worry about it, Shirley. We will have plenty of time to discuss it, but later." He passed his hand over her face and she fell asleep. "Narga, move the woman to a secure private room. Make sure she has a decent bed and everything she needs there and is not disturbed."

"Yes, Master," the winged beast replied.

Bill turned to face Peter again and smiled. "As for you, Peter Smith, I have something else in mind. I would like you to work for me."

"Never!"

Bill laughed. "Please, that is not how it works here. You and I will take a little trip and I will teach you the true nature of existence." He took Peter's hands and both disappeared.

§

Joshua was sitting in his neighborhood coffee shop, holding his morning coffee in his hands for warmth. There was a tinge of autumn in the air today, and the chill had seeped into his bones on the two-block stroll from the Manson home. He had left Rachel there with four of his best guards who had been advised never to take their eyes off of her. The brazen attack on Gabe's apartment had been witnessed by hundreds of ordinary people and the newspapers were full of cell phone photographs of the carnage and destruction. Joshua could not believe that Satori would risk such exposure. People were terrified that the giant monsters would return and destroy more homes and lives. All the Prospects could hope for was the short attention span of the public. Within a week or two some other crisis would arise and people would stop talking about the incident, happy to focus on something else and let this fade into memory.

There was a man sitting at the next table, hidden behind his newspaper. On the front page, Joshua could see his own picture as he plummeted from the broken window-wall toward the concrete below. He shuddered when he remembered that moment and turned away. Thankfully, the picture was quite fuzzy and the face of the falling man was not clearly visible. He took another sip of his coffee as the man closed his paper, folded it and set it on the table. Joshua was stunned. The man at the next table was Barsat, who smiled and held his index finger against his lips. He rose and pulled his chair over to Joshua's table and sat down. He leaned toward Joshua and whispered, "Hello, Joshua. I see you're no worse for the wear."

"What do you want, Barsat?"

"My father needs your help," Barsat replied.

"My help? That doesn't make any sense. You guys are holding all the cards," Joshua argued.

Barsat cleared his throat, sipped his coffee and continued, "Your father upset him so much that he took the Manson woman just to prove a point. Now, he wants to release her, but you understand that is a problem."

"I thought he wanted your brothers to impregnate her."

"Please keep your voice down," Barsat whispered. "That was before he got his hands on Peter Smith. He just changed his mind. But no living person has ever left the place they are now. Certainly you know that!"

"And Satori thinks I can help her escape?" Joshua asked.

"It's not an escape, and you have left there alive before. We all remember that. My father thought you could take her away with you," Barsat noted. "Do you think that would work?"

"It would probably work, but why didn't he just ask my dad to help her? He could do it in an instant."

Barsat chuckled under his breath. "You know their relationship is too broken now. They can barely stand to be in the same room without killing each other. My father would have to admit he was wrong and beg your dad for help. Do you really see that happening?"

"No, I guess not," Joshua admitted. "But I will have to ask my father for permission. If he says okay, I'll come and get her right away, but no tricks, okay?"

"No tricks, I swear," Barsat replied.

"What about Peter? Is he okay?" Joshua asked.

"He and my father are taking a little trip. My father is trying to convince him to join our team."

"And if he refuses?"

"Then he dies," Barsat said coldly. "That's why they're on a trip, so no one in your family can find him and try to rescue him."

"Barsat, may I ask you a question?" Joshua asked. "You have to know that the attack on Gabe's apartment was seen by many witnesses. Why would your father risk such a blatant transgression? We have always worked behind the scenes."

"Joshua, I agree the attack was stupid. I never would have done something like that; however, my father is convinced that Peter Smith is the most severe danger to him. As long as Peter is not under our control, he can prevent us from doing anything, or at least allow you to prevent anything. Pete's existence is an abomination to us," Barsat replied.

"I understand that, but that attack may change everything!" Joshua exclaimed. "Now people around the globe will have their eyes opened to reality. The calm of the last thousand years may be swept away by ever-escalating warfare. We agreed to the rules of interaction and now they are out the window."

"Coalescing the existence of the world into the most primal battles of all," Barsat said. "That is exactly what my father wants. The idea of hiding behind the scenes and allowing these Beings to find their own way is revolting to him. He wants them to see reality and chose their sides."

"What do you want, Barsat?"

"Gee, no one ever asked my opinion before," he smiled and thought for a moment. "I think I have to agree with my father. We have been playing this game for too long, and neither has really gained any advantage. While people have improved their lot, they don't seem to be growing closer to either of us. In fact, many don't believe we exist at all."

Joshua frowned and said, "This is their planet, not ours."

"That's where you are wrong, Joshua," Barsat replied. "These humans created my family. We are as closely related to them as their children. In many ways, we are their children."

Joshua sighed and dropped his head. "I feel sorry for them, that's all."

Barsat rose and patted Joshua on the shoulder. "Don't let it get to you. You and I are pawns to move wherever our fathers point us. Please don't forget Shirley. She'll be thrilled to see you." He walked out of the coffee shop, turned right and disappeared down the sidewalk.

Chapter 17

Pete and Bill were standing on a beach. Tall stands of strange-looking ferns and other jungle vegetation pressed up to the sand. Several islands could be seen across the water, which lapped up at their feet. On one distant island, a small volcano belched clouds of soot and gas into the cloudy sky. Bill released Pete's hands and began walking down the beach and Pete hurried to catch up to him. "What is this place, Bill?"

Satori, now in human form, stopped and turned to face the other. "This is not a place you'd ever recognize, son. In fact, none of these islands exist anymore. I'd say we're somewhere in the Utah desert of your time." He turned back around and continued walking.

"In my time? What does that mean?" Pete asked, but Bill did not acknowledge him. He decided he had no option but to follow the older man and starting walking. An odd shadow passed over his head, and he looked up to see a Pteranodon flying overhead. He stood frozen and slack-jawed at the living dinosaur fifty feet over his head. The creature turned and started to dive toward him and he began to run toward the trees, but the beast was closing in on him quickly. He was still thirty feet from the trees when he heard a screech and fell to the ground. Satori had reverted to beast form and was wrestling with the dinosaur in the air. After ten seconds or so, the Pteranodon thought better and flew away. Satori landed next to Pete and sat in the sand laughing. "Did you really take us back in time?" Pete panted as he sat up on the beach.

"Oh man, you should have seen the look on your face when you were running from that thing!" Satori laughed, holding his sides. "I guess you never know how fast you can run until you find out you're on the menu."

"Why are we here, Bill?"

"I chose this place to ask you to be open-minded, Peter," Satori answered. "Back in the place of atonement you said you'd never work for me. Well, that is your choice, but I can tell you if you still feel that way, I will leave you here."

"What?"

"Peter, you are on a journey to discover the true nature of existence, life, and death. If you agree to continue, we will leave now. If you are absolutely certain that you can never work for me, even if that means sitting on the sidelines, making millions and doing anything you want, except talking to the Prospects, then why should I enable you to help them?" he asked.

"You'd leave me here to die, stranded in prehistory?"

"Everybody dies, Peter, and I'm not asking you to choose to work for me now. All I want is for you to go with me willingly and watch and listen to what I have to say. You can make your decision much later, okay?" Satori said, extending his hand.

"I guess I don't have much choice," Pete replied as he shook the beast's hand.

Satori laughed again. "Look at it this way, my boy. The Prospects haven't found you here, although they might someday, if the wild animals don't eat you first. If you keep going with me, they may intervene on your behalf. Now take my hands and we'll leave this place. I never cared for dinosaurs." Pete took his hands and they disappeared as a small group of raptors strolled out of the jungle near where they sat. As the animals smelled the sand, the Pteranodon swooped down, grabbed one in its jaws and flew away.

§

"Joshua, there has to be another way," Narga argued. The two were standing in a hallway that stretched out to infinity in both directions.

"My father says it's the only way," Joshua replied. "You have to do it or he cannot help us."

"My father said she was not to be harmed!"

Joshua put his hand on the man's shoulder and said, "I'm sorry, but there is no other way. If Satori wants her to live on Earth again, it must be done. My father has already forgiven you for this. We all know she is here because of your father and not you. There will be no punishment from him or your father."

Narga's head dropped and tears welled in his eyes. "Promise you will forgive me, Joshua." The other nodded. Narga turned to the wall, where a door began to appear. When it was in place, Joshua patted him on the shoulder and Narga walked through the door.

Shirley Manson was sleeping on the large bed. The white bedcovers were pulled up to her neck and a smile moved across her lips. As Narga walked across the room, he morphed into the red beast and spread his wings. When he reached the bed, Shirley opened her eyes. "What do you want?"

Narga pulled the long dagger from a scabbard on his back and looked at her. "I'm sorry, but it has to be this way." He raised the blade over his head.

"Your father said no one would harm me," she screamed. Narga plunged the blade into her chest, over and again. She tried to scream but blood poured from her mouth. Narga slit her throat and threw the blade onto the ground. The bed was soaked in bright red blood. Shirley gasped a final breath and died.

Narga looked down at his arms and hands covered in her blood. He turned and walked over to the door and walked through. "It is done, Joshua," he murmured.

"I wish it could have been different, brother," Joshua sighed. "But it is over now and I thank you."

"Will she remember what I did?" Narga asked.

"I don't know, but I will tell her why you did this if she asks. I swear it," Joshua replied. Narga only sighed and walked away down the corridor. Joshua walked into the room and went over to the bed. He picked Shirley's body up in his arms and both disappeared.

§

Bill and Pete were walking down a narrow, but strangely familiar sidewalk. They crested a small hill to see Pete's hometown just ahead of them. On the opposite side of the road, a large cornfield stretched over several hills. The sidewalk was lined with a fence, with a cemetery on the other side. "Why are we here, Bill?" Satori did not answer but walked through the gate and into the graveyard. Pete had escaped the dinosaur island and was close to his own time now, so he knew he should just follow orders and rushed to catch up to the other man.

Satori had stopped at a small grave marker and was placing a bouquet of flowers on the ground. Pete joined him and looked at the stone. It said "Peter Smith, Beloved Son, 1990 to 2014." Pete felt faint and sat on the ground, holding his head with both hands and trying to understand what he was seeing.

Bill bent down and patted him on the head. "Peter, as I said on the jungle island, everybody dies. But this is not the only reality, my son. The future is unwritten and neither the Prospects nor my family know what is going to happen."

"But it's 2014 right now?" he gasped.

"This is a possible future if you choose not to work for me," Bill explained. "As I told you more than once, if you decide not to be on my team, I will try to kill you. I cannot risk you helping the Prospects, but be assured they may save you from me." He pulled Pete to his feet and pointed to the stone, which was dissolving. Soon a massive stone began to form in its place. "If the Prospects protect you, this is another possibility."

Pete read what he saw on the new stone, "Peter Smith, Beloved Father and Grandfather, 1990 to 2081." He strained to read his wife's name but it was a blur. "Why can't I read her name?"

"Pete, this is a possible future, and there may be almost infinite possibilities as you make choices at every crossroads in your life. If you saw a name, you might think it is someone you know and pursue her. Keep your options open, you're a young man," Bill replied. He put his arm around Peter and the cemetery began to blur and change. Gravestones flew around and the ground moved and shook. Giant skyscrapers grew on the ground and the cemetery became massive. When it stopped changing, a steady rain poured down on them.

"We're back in New York!" Pete exclaimed. "Can I go now?" Satori frowned and pointed to a giant mausoleum in front of them. The building was black marble with figures of angels and demons dancing across fields of wheat and corn, with the skyline of the city in the background. A large bronze plaque said, "Peter Smith, Beloved Father and Grandfather, 1990 to 2088." The woman's name was not legible again. "I don't understand, Bill. What future is this?"

"This is a possible future where you work for me," Bill smiled. "But now tell me about the similarities and differences among the things you've seen so far."

"Can we get out of this rain first?"

Bill smiled and touched Peter's shoulder. They were sitting at a small table in the bar of an elegant restaurant. Both were completely dry and wearing tuxedoes. A waitress walked over and set glasses of whisky in front of them and walked away. Bill took a sip of his drink and said, "I hope this is better. No go ahead and answer my questions."

Pete sat back and swirled the liquor around in his glass and began, "Well, the obvious similarity is I'm dead in all of them."

"Everybody dies."

"And it seems my least viable solution is to turn you down cold. In that reality, I never get married or have a family," he continued. "In the other two, I seem to live a long life, so that's good." He took a drink from his glass.

"Well, as I said, there are an infinite number of futures for you and everyone else," Bill acknowledged. "Every minute of every day, you make decisions that affect your future. I only showed you three, but could have shown millions if we wanted to take the time. But the gravestones did not say how you died. You could have been in a coma for decades in either of those lives. You could choose to be my friend and be hit by an out-of-control car the next morning. You could be killed by a jealous husband or by your own wife if you choose to be a philanderer. You see what I mean?"

"I think I'm losing track of the point, Bill."

Satori laughed out loud. "Life is about choices, Peter! By some random chance, you have this odd ability to foretell the future, but that is more curse than blessing. We never would have met if you did not have it. Gabe Prospect wouldn't have offered a room for rent if you were just another guy. Frankly, you'd probably be just another schmuck working himself to death for forty years to pay for his family. Now you have the opportunity to use that talent to have a better life!"

"By becoming like you?"

"Hey, that's an interesting thought, but I think you're just being cynical. The Prospects are probably making you think you can change the world by helping them stop evil. That is a lie! Peter, I did not create evil. It is part of every person. Good and evil are two sides of the same coin. Truth be known, it was the evil incarnate in your fellow humans that created me," Satori said. He waved to the waitress to bring another round. "I am not the spawn of the Creator like the Prospects and the essence inside of you. Mankind created me by the sheer mass of the evil inside of men."

Over Satori's shoulder, Pete noticed Emmanuel Prospect entering the restaurant. He fought it, but his joy flooded over him at the prospect of being saved. Before he could move to stand, Satori grabbed his hands and both men disappeared.

Emmanuel held the door open for Joshua and the two Manson women. The hostess led them to the same table in the bar and collected the empty glasses. The waitress came over and said, "Where are the two guys who were just here?"

"I'm sorry, but the hostess just sat us here," Joshua said. "I didn't see anyone."

"Just add their bill to mine," Emmanuel smiled. "I saw them and know them well. They must have just forgotten to pay." The waitress took their order and walked away.

"Mr. Prospect, thank you again for saving me from that place," Shirley said.

"Please just call me Granddad, everybody does," he smiled. "Do you remember how you escaped?"

"Not really. I was asleep in a bed and the next thing I knew, Joshua was setting me down on the couch in my mother's house."

"That's great!" he replied.

"Dad, who were the men sitting here?" Joshua asked. Emmanuel winked.

§

Peter and Satori were sitting on the side of a massive mountain, far above the tree line. The peak of the mountain was just a hundred feet or so above them. At the base of the mountain, rolling hills stretched out several miles before giving way to a vast salt flat and desert. Pete could see the waves of heat escaping from the desert below. Even though they were high up the mountain, he felt warm and content. "What is this place, Bill?"

"Sorry to steal you away from your drink, but I could not allow Manny to rescue you there. Our journey is just beginning," he replied as he stood. "This mountain and the land around it have only been seen by two living humans, one of whom is you. Think of this as a metaphor for human existence. The desert below is the place where Joshua and I first met long ago. It symbolizes the emptiness inside every person as they search for fulfillment. Joshua refused to work for me, and as part of the Prospect family, I was powerless to destroy him." He reached down and patted Pete on the head. "You will not be so lucky. Now get up and follow me." Pete climbed to his feet and followed Satori as he walked along the side of the mountain. The mountainside became steeper as they progressed, ultimately ending at a large cliff broken only by a narrow rock ledge. Satori turned around and said, "You probably shouldn't look down." He started to walk along the ledge.

Peter was on an imaginary mountain, about to walk along a narrow ledge on a cliff that fell thousands of feet straight down. "Wouldn't it be easier to go to the summit, Bill?"

"This is the only way, Peter. Get moving!" Peter eased his left foot onto the ledge. He faced the rock wall and tried to grab hold of any creases or cracks in the stone. His desperate need to check the ledge for loose stones or breaks made him look downward. The cliff was vertical and seemed to drop forever until it disappeared into a cloudbank far below. His heart was pounding and his hands were aching as they clung to the stones. After what seemed like a lifetime there on the cliff, he heard Satori laughing. He looked to his right to see him standing on a grassy slope just ten feet away from him. Bill extended his hand and Pete hurried as much as he could. Bill grabbed his arm and pulled him onto the grass where he collapsed to the ground, gasping for air. His fists were clenched tight with cramps, and his legs were wobbling. Bill sat next to him and put his arm around Peter's shoulders. "Pete, you're taking this way too seriously. Do you think I'd let you fall to your death here?"

"What's the purpose of the cliff then?" he gasped. "Why didn't we just go to the top of the mountain? Is this just more metaphors?"

"Look around, Peter!" Satori exclaimed. The desert at the base of the mountain was gone. A wide plain at the base was filled with dense forests and wide plains. Hundreds or even thousands of marble temples dotted the landscape. Clusters of villages surrounded the larger temples and a constant line of people made their way to and from each temple. Ornately manicured gardens surrounded each temple and wispy clouds floated through the blue sky. "Pretty disgusting, isn't it?"

"I think it's beautiful," Pete argued. "It's so idyllic, almost like a dream of heaven."

"It seems dreamlike to you because that's exactly what it is, Peter. This is your dream of what Heaven on Earth would be like. But it isn't real. This is what the Prospects want you to believe life would be like without me. Don't you believe it!" Satori snarled.

"Why do you say that?"

"Peter, I already explained that to you. My family did not create evil. The evil in your soul and those of every other person created us! With or without us, humans will always fight within themselves. If my brother was able to kill me, another will replace me. As long as the kernel of evil exists in each man, I will be here. Now let's get up and go. There's lots more to see," Satori said as he stood. He grabbed Peter by the arms and pulled him to his feet.

Peter followed Satori, but kept looking at the beautiful scene below. Was this really an impossibility, he wondered. Images from his last view of internet news sites snapped him out of his revelry. Perhaps there was not enough good in people for this future. With no other options, he followed Bill around the side of the mountain. After ten minutes, they reached a wall of rock that blocked their way. There was no ledge to take this time. Bill walked over to a bush against the rock and pulled it aside, revealing a narrow cave entrance. He motioned for Peter to follow him and crawled into the cave on his hands and knees.

The surface of the floor was rough sandstone that grated at his hands and knees. There were rock outcrops that tore at his clothes. The cave became narrower by the minute. After ten minutes, it was pitch black and he had to crawl on his stomach, pulling himself along with his hands and kicking with his feet. He continued onward, hopeful that Bill Satori was really still in front of him. A few minutes later, he saw a faint light ahead and heard the sound of running water. He hurried ahead and found Bill sitting in a larger cavern where a stream ran through the rock and disappeared over a cliff at the opening of the cave. Sunlight poured through the opening, providing enough light to find a place next to Bill to sit. Satori was dipping his hands into the stream and using the water to wash his face and hands.

"This is quite the journey, Bill!" Pete exclaimed. "What do we do now, cross the creek?"

Bill chuckled and said, "You only wish it were that easy." He put his hand on Peter's shoulder. "Pete, I already told you I would not harm you here, right?" He nodded. "Well, it might be helpful for you to suspend your belief system right about now." He stood up and pulled Pete to his feet.

"What do you mean?" Pete asked. Without saying a word, Satori grabbed him and threw him into the stream. Pete grasped for rocks or anything to hold on to, but the current pulled him along. He was struggling to reach the surface for a breath, but was being tumbled around in the rapidly moving water. In an instant, he flew out the opening of the cave and was falling downward with the waterfall. This was it, he thought. Dark clouds filled the valley far below where he would die when he hit the ground. He screamed and passed out from sheer terror.

§

Emmanuel Prospect sat at the head of the conference table, holding his head in his hands. The leaders of the Prospect Enterprise sat facing him. Each was wearing a bright silver chest plate and helmet. Long war blades were slung on the backs of their chairs. Michael and Gabriel were sitting on either side of their father, exchanging worried glances. "It cannot be coming to this," he said.

Luce was sitting at the far end of the table. He squirmed uneasily in his chair and said, "Father, there are still other options, in spite of the escalation by Satori."

"None of them are very good," Emmanuel replied.

Gabe, who was sitting on a side chair on the far side of the room interjected, "If I may, we have been tracking public opinion on the attack. It's only been a few days and the hit rate has already dropped fifty percent. At that rate, the incident will fade into memory in less than two weeks."

"Assuming there are no more attacks," Gabriel countered.

"I see no reason for Satori to act now. He has Peter Smith," Gabe replied.

"As I said, there are no good options," Emmanuel reiterated. "If Peter works for Satori, our old status quo may be salvaged, but at what cost to Peter?"

"It will be his choice, Father," Michael said.

"And if we can save him and he works for us, the end is near. Nothing will stop Satori from bringing about the final conflict," Emmanuel noted.

"Granddad, Pete may have already foreseen that," Gabe said

"What?"

"The night of the attack, Pete looked at the approaching storm and compared it to that battle," Gabe replied.

"That means nothing!" Michael said. "People use that word to describe natural events all the time."

"Still, it was Peter Smith, so we need to lend some credence to it," Emmanuel said. "Gabe, you know Peter best. What do you think we should do?"

"I think we should tell Satori that he can have him." All the others gasped in shock. "It's really the only way to avoid the conflict."

Joshua, who had been sitting next to Gabe, stood and began to pace back and forth. "I agree that Gabe's solution is the best way to avoid conflict, but I would never accept that. Don't you see? We're all just pawns in this game. Pete must make his own decision, and even if that leads to the end of the world, that is what must happen. Why are we here anyway? We don't control humanity, we nurture it. If humanity chooses war once again, we cannot stop them. We are here to keep Satori and his ilk in check. We are here to stop others from twisting the minds of people. We serve them, not the other way around."

Michael stood and walked over to Joshua, putting his arm around his brother's shoulders. "Joshua is right. If the war comes, we must be prepared. I have already begun to build our army. If Satori's legions attack, we must fight back. If the world is destroyed, it will have been due to the conscious choices of people."

"Let us pray it does not come to that," Emmanuel sighed.

§

Pete woke on a straw mattress on the dirt floor of a mud hut. He examined his body and could find no evidence of injury from his fall. His torn tuxedo had been replaced by a rough tunic and leather thongs. A small fire burned in the center of the hut and the smoke rose up and through an opening in the center of the thatched roof. He sat on the side of the bed and wondered where he was now. A large red hand with black claws for nails pushed the door open and motioned for him to come out. Reluctantly, he rose and walked out of the hut. Satori stood before him in his monster avatar form. The ground was covered with dirt and rocks and dozens of mud huts to the horizon. The sky was red and full of black clouds that seemed to rain mud onto the ground. Just past the horizon, several volcanoes spewed black clouds of dust into the air. In the opposite direction, a stone cliff rose straight up and through the clouds. "Where are we now, Bill?"

"Come with me," the beast said as it turned and walked away. Pete hurried to follow. They walked over several hills, but the view never changed. From time to time, a person would emerge from a hut looking totally bewildered. One of the flying beasts would grab them and fly off in the direction they were now headed. Ten minutes later, they crested a hill and could see the massive opening to a cave. Black smoke poured out of the cave, and the sounds of screams and crying filled the air. Bill started to climb down toward the cave opening, and then he stopped and turned around. "Peter, this place also doesn't exist, except in your mind, so don't be afraid, okay?" Pete nodded and Satori continued down and into the cavern. They walked for hours across the rocks and stones covering the floor. Pete heard a woman screaming and looked up to see a flying beast carrying a woman in its talons. She screamed to Pete for help as they disappeared deeper into the tunnel.

The tunnel ended in a massive cave that had to be miles across and at least half a mile in height. Satori sat on a large stone and motioned for Pete to join him. Large pools of lava covered the floor. Another winged beast flew in with a man in his talons. It flew over a lava lagoon and dropped the screaming man who fell into the magma. He screamed for a fraction of a second before his body was consumed by the liquid stone. Pete flinched and looked the other way. Satori laughed out loud. "This is pretty ridiculous, isn't it?"

"This is horrible! We are in Hell, aren't we?" Pete asked.

"Pete, come on, none of this is real!" Satori bellowed. "Look over there."

At the edge of a lava lake, a human skeleton was pulling itself from the magma. It glowed red-hot as it emerged and collapsed on the solid ground. The skeleton cooled quickly and soon muscle and sinew began to grow over the bones, followed quickly by organs and skin. Soon the man he had seen fall into the lava was lying there panting for breath. The man stood and looked around for an escape route. Seeing the way toward the cave entrance, he began to run. After about one hundred feet, a winged beast landed in his path and cut him in half with a long sword. The beast then grabbed the two parts and tossed them back into the lava and flew away. Satori was laughing and gasping for breath. "This isn't funny, Bill. How can you do that to them?"

Satori grabbed his hands. Now Peter and the human Satori were sitting on the mountainside again. The valley below was obscured with clouds. "Peter, you weren't listening. Both of the places you have just seen are not real. People made them up to represent idealistic views of good and evil. Think about it, man! If I'm the Devil and I make people do awful things, why would I punish them? It doesn't make any sense. They are my friends!"

"But . . ."

"No buts, Peter," Satori said as he stood and pulled Pete to his feet. He waved his arm across the horizon and the clouds disappeared. "This is what's real, Peter Smith!"

Every place that Peter had ever seen seemed to be compressed into that one wide valley. He could see his hometown and his father's hardware store. The Pentacrest in Iowa City was pressed close by. New York City filled the right side of the valley. The more he focused the more detail he could see. He saw Gabe's apartment building and his parent's home. His mother and father were sitting in the back yard sipping a glass of wine at the end of the day. The streets of New York were crowded with people rushing this way and that. Taxicabs filled the avenues. He saw Isabel Garcia sitting at her desk in Bertrand Industries typing an e-mail. Airplanes filled the skies moving in every direction. Trains crossed the country bringing goods to market. "Wow! This is unbelievable. But this is just an illusion too."

"Well, I guess it's obvious that I can't squeeze planet Earth into this valley, but everything you are seeing is real. Thankfully, you haven't traveled the world or it would have been much more difficult," Satori replied.

"So, you're telling me that Heaven and Hell are illusions and that life is what's real. But what happens after we die? Aren't we judged for what we have done?"

"I'll let you talk to my brother about that," Satori said. "He would probably not approve of my answer. I can tell you that your Creator is infinitely loving and forgiving. While you may pay a price for the things you do, there is no such thing as eternal punishment. Even someone as bad as me cannot conceive of that!"

"You're going to let me go now?"

"I'll send you home soon, but there is one other thing you must see," Satori began. "When my sons attacked Gabe Prospect's apartment, I escalated the conflict between us. There may be no coming back from the brink now, no matter what you decide to do. However, if you choose to be with the Prospects, I can almost guarantee there will be a global war that will destroy your world." Instantly they were sitting in the bar again in tuxedoes. The waitress came by and glowered at them. "I'm sorry, my dear, but I was called away on urgent business. I believe my brother paid the tab, but here, please take this and get us a couple of drinks," he said as he pushed a thousand dollar bill into her hand. Her eyes opened wide and she kissed him on the cheek and hurried back to the bar to get their drinks. "Peter, I thought about showing you a potential outcome of that conflict, but then it hit me that you can probably see it much clearer than me." The waitress dropped off the drinks and then kissed both men and rushed away. "I guess I made her day."

Pete chuckled and said, "If I help the Prospects, you'll destroy the world and you'll try to kill me." The other man nodded and smiled. "And if I help you, I'm damned. Those aren't great options, Bill."

Bill took a long drink and considered the young man across the table. "Pete, honestly, I don't care about your dreams. I only want you not to tell them. The battle may still come, but it won't be your fault. Pete, think about it. You come to work at Satori Industries. I will give you a penthouse that makes Gabe's look like a tenement. I'll pay you twenty million a year. If you want to work, I have many divisions that need smart, young men. If you want to run around and enjoy the money, that's good too. All I ask is that you do not give the Prospects any information about your dreams."

"Twenty million?"

"Is thirty better?" Bill laughed. "Pete, the money is no object. Think of this offer as a way to stop a global war that will destroy most of humanity." He stopped and stared over Pete's shoulder. "It would seem our rides have come for us. Think about it Pete. Call me anytime with any questions." He leaned over and whispered, "Think of what you can do for your family with that much money. I'll even give you a hundred million signing bonus if you want." He patted Peter on the cheek and stood, motioning for him to stand as well.

He stood and turned to see Sheila Farness and Gabe Prospect walking toward them. Sheila caressed Pete's cheek with her hand and then kissed Bill passionately. Gabe put his hand on Pete's shoulder. "Are you doing okay, pal?" he asked.

"I'm fine now, Gabe," Pete said.

"You two stay and have a nice dinner on me," Bill said. He pulled a wad of hundred dollar bills from his pocket and pushed it into Pete's left hand and shook his right. "We'll talk soon, Mr. Smith. It's good to see you too, Gabe." Bill and Sheila walked out of the bar and climbed into a waiting limousine, which sped away.

"Gabe, what happened to Shirley?" Pete asked.

"She's fine now. She's at her home with Joshua and her mother."

"What about your apartment?"

"It's a good as new, maybe even better," Gabe said. "I'm starving, let's eat."

Chapter 18

Pete woke with a start and found himself lying in a muddy pit. He was wearing a military uniform of some kind but could not recognize any of the insignia. He noticed several bullet holes on his shirt, which were soaking wet with blood. He pulled open his shirt and saw gaping holes on his body, but did not feel any pain. He stood up slowly and picked up the rifle that had been lying on the dirt next to him. The air was thick with smoke and the smell of gunpowder. He climbed up the side of the pit slowly until he could see what was happening around him. It was deathly quiet and the sun was just rising to the east. As the first beams of light hit his eyes, he saw thousands of bodies all around him. The soldiers had died horrific deaths. Many were missing limbs or heads. Their bodies were shredded by machine gun fire. Several were still locked in their final fight with soldiers wearing different uniforms, with all of the victims stabbed or shot multiple times. Toward the west, a line of destroyed tanks sat burning. Hoping the edge of the battlefield was in that direction, he turned and began to walk toward the fires.

Clouds of flies swarmed the area, laying their eggs in the dead bodies. They bit him everywhere, and he swatted them away from his face as he stepped around and over the fallen. After twenty minutes, he passed the burning metal hulks. But the carnage did not end there. Slightly rolling hills continued to the horizon, and the view never changed. Mud and death was everywhere. How could this happen, he wondered. He kept walking. After two hours, the fly swarms seemed to dissipate and he could quicken his pace. Another hour later and he reached a forest and the end of the battlefield.

He could hear birds chirping in the trees and the warmth of the sun gave him new strength. The quiet of the field of battle was gone. Bees buzzed and birds sang. He knew he was still dreaming, but the war images seemed to already be fading. He came along a gentle stream flowing through the forest and stopped. He pulled off his clothes and stepped into the water. It was cold but very refreshing. As the water rose to his chest, he felt an odd tingling and looked down. The water was healing his wounds. Within seconds, he was whole again and wondered how a creek could do such a thing. He climbed out on the opposite bank and noticed a white tunic and leather sandals on the grass. He slipped them on and looked back to where he had come from. Somehow, a fog bank had descended, and the other side of the river was obscured. "Thank God for that!" he shouted. He turned and walked up the bank and back into the forest. After ten minutes more the trees gave way to a grassy glade with a small pond and a marble temple. Several deer had been sipping water but stopped when they sensed his arrival. They turned to watch him, but did not scatter as he walked slowly forward. He was ten feet from the animals when he felt something had changed and spun around.

A massive stag was emerging from the forest at the same spot he had just come from. It was ten feet high at the withers and its antlers were gigantic. It walked toward Pete and he began to move away from the other deer. The stag moved slowly and deliberately. Pete stopped near the front of the temple and waited. The buck came up to him, smiled and motioned with its head for Pete to go into the temple. Pete turned and walked up the ten marble steps and into the small temple. It was a simple place, with columns supporting the domed roof. It was circular and perhaps twenty feet in diameter. The center of the dome was open to allow light into the structure. Directly under the opening was a marble throne. Pete walked around the interior looking for any writing or pictograms about what was to happen here. Finding none, he decided he would sit on the throne. As he sat, a feeling of warmth and safety poured through him. He felt as safe as in his mother's arms, although he could still see the deer and the forest outside. His weariness overcame him and he fell asleep.

Pete opened his eyes to see he was flying. A big smile crossed his face since flying dreams were his favorite. The air was sweet and full of fluffy clouds which he adored flying through. After a few minutes of joy, the air became hot and smoky. The clouds were replaced with black smoke and he gasped for air. Looking down, he saw the carnage of the battlefield where he had awoken. He could see the burning tanks and even the blood-stained ground where he had been. He squeezed his eyes closed so as not to see more. His eyes flew open against his will to reveal the city of New York ablaze and destroyed. Most of the skyscrapers had been smashed, and out of control fires burned out to the horizon. He tried to close his eyes but could only blink. Each time his eyes opened again, there was another city on fire and smashed. He saw Paris, London, Madrid, Rome, Moscow, Beijing, Sao Paulo, and dozens more. Everything was destroyed. He struggled to wake up but nothing seemed to work. He was crying and moaning in despair at the end of the world.

Pete woke again in a small cot in a concrete room. Hundreds of other cots were jammed into the room, most with someone trying to sleep. There were no windows and only one small fixture to provide light. He sat on the bed and looked around, but did not recognize anyone. He was wearing black trousers and a black shirt with some kind of emblems on the shoulders. He rose from the cot and headed for the open door and stepped out. He was in a large cavern. Dozens of similar concrete structures filled the area. He heard some talking to his left and headed in that direction. The next building was a cafeteria where hundreds of people were sitting, eating, and talking. The crowd was wearing various colored uniforms, and each color group seemed to stick together. He went through the food line and walked toward a section where everyone wore black. As he approached, Isabel Garcia, the HR Director for Bertrand Industries, stood and waved to him. He hurried over and sat next to her.

Isabel put her arms around his neck and kissed him on the lips. "How are you today, darling?" she said.

"I'm okay, I guess," he said. "What is this place?"

Everyone at the table laughed. "You're such a kidder, Pete. Eat your breakfast. We've got lots of work to do."

As he shoved the first forkful of eggs into his mouth, explosions rocked the room. People jumped from their seats and grabbed their weapons, running for the door. The sound of machine gun fire and screaming filled the air. Suddenly Pete was standing with an automatic rifle in his hands. A group of soldiers in blood red body armor surged into the room, firing at everyone. Pete leveled his rifle and fired, killing two of the attackers. More attackers entered the room, mowing down the others with withering blasts of gunfire. Pete dived for the floor as the bullets zipped by his head. Isabel was lying dead on the floor next to him. A grenade landed next to him and he closed his eyes.

Pete sat straight up and bed, wheezing for air and soaked in sweat. His heart was pounding in his chest. He realized he was back in his bed in Gabe's apartment and had just been dreaming. There was a knock at the door, and Maria's voice said, "Breakfast is ready, Mr. Peter."

"Okay, thanks, I'll be right out," he said as he fell back on the bed, each detail of his nightmare tearing through his mind.

§

Ten minutes later, Pete left his room and was surprised to see Emmanuel and Joshua at the breakfast table with Gabe. He shook hands with each and sat down. Maria offered him a plate of food and a cup of coffee and then left the room, closing the door behind her. "I'm glad you're okay," Emmanuel said, touching Peter on the shoulder.

"I'm not sure what happened that night, Granddad," he replied. "Everything seems like a dream since the attack here, but looking around, there's no evidence that anything ever happened. How is that possible?"

The Prospects exchanged concerned glances. "It did happen," Joshua said. "You have to imagine the hysteria if evidence of such an attack were still around. With our resources, it was relatively easy to get the repairs done quickly."

"I don't know. Somehow it seems more logical that I've been imagining everything. My dreams used to bother me, but now it's like I'm in a dream all the time."

"Do you think you're dreaming now, Peter?" Emmanuel asked.

Pete looked at each of the men and the plate of food in front of him. He took a forkful of eggs and chewed it. "Well, the food seems real enough, but my dreams are so vivid now that I can't be absolutely sure."

"Do you want to tell us about the dreams, Peter?" the old man asked. "Perhaps we can help you."

Pete stood and began to pace back and forth; his mind racing as he thought about what Bill Satori had told him about the end of the world and the vision of that. He stopped and stared at Emmanuel, trying to get a hint of what he was thinking. He sighed heavily and said, "Is the end of the world coming, Granddad?"

"Perhaps."

Pete felt faint and returned to his chair and sat down. "Okay. If I go to work for Satori, is there less chance it will happen?"

"Probably, but we cannot be certain of that," Emmanuel replied.

"I cannot be responsible for the end of the world!" Pete shouted. "You're forcing me to go to work for that bastard. This is too much pressure. I'm just one man."

Emmanuel glanced at the other two, who quickly stood and walked out of the room. He rose and moved to the chair next to Pete and put his hand on his shoulder. "Peter, you will not be responsible for the end of the world, no matter what my brother told you. You have to understand that neither he and his kind nor my family and I can build and lead armies of humans into battle. We can influence and help, but men will do what they choose to do."

"Granddad, you just told me there was less of a chance of war if I work for Satori. That means working for him can help stop the death and destruction."

"Peter, you have to understand that the end of the world is exactly what my brother wants. He has grown weary of the back and forth game that is our existence," Emmanuel explained. "He is also angry because he is losing."

"I don't know how you can say that, Granddad. There is war, famine, and pestilence everywhere in the world. Murder and terror attacks happen all the time. The cities are full of violence and crime."

Emmanuel smiled and continued, "Such is the nature of existence, my boy. But if you look into the past, things were much worse. Slavery, persecution, and genocide used to be the norm and not horrible aberrations. Most people died as children due to rampant disease and lack of sanitation. As people have progressed, life has become easier, healthier, and longer. If you could have lived for the last thousand years, you would know what I say is true."

"I just don't know what to believe, think, or do."

"Peter, we've already discussed the two doors. As long as you do not choose a life of evil, then everything will be okay," Emmanuel noted.

"So, I should forget Satori?"

"I didn't say that," Emmanuel frowned. "Enjoy your life. Take Satori's money if you like. As long as you don't become evil, there's nothing wrong with that."

"But what if I have a dream and telling you will help save a life? Satori said I can have no contact with you."

"Everybody dies, Peter Smith. However, if that happens, you will have two doors to choose. Having a dream and not acting on it is not a sin. Everyone has dreams and most forget them immediately. Although they may not know or believe it, many of their dreams are visions too. Since they don't remember, they cannot be held accountable. If they did act and their dreams were false, they would be considered lunatics and shunned by their friends," the old man said.

"Granddad, please just tell me what to do!" Peter begged.

"Peter, please tell me one thing first. Tell me about your dream last night. You don't need to be detailed, but overall, what was it about?"

"The end of the world."

Emmanuel looked stunned for an instant, but then smiled again. "You can do whatever you want, but if you want my opinion, I say go to work for Satori. I imagine he'll give you lots of money and won't even want you to do any work."

"I can't believe you just said that."

"Peter my boy, the world will end eventually, whether that is this week or four billion years in the future when the sun becomes a nova. You can't control that, so don't worry about it. Enjoy your life, Peter Smith. That is all I want you to do. In your life you will make many choices and I hope one brings you back to us. But either way, I hope you have a long and happy life," the elder Prospect concluded. He patted Peter on the head and walked out of the kitchen.

§

Bill Satori stood by the office window overlooking the skyline of New York, holding a cup of coffee in his left hand. He watched the people far below rushing from building to building and smiled—knowing what they did not know—about him and about the future of this great metropolis. He glanced back at Sheila sitting on one of his couches, legs crossed in a short skirt, thumbing through a magazine. For a second, he imagined himself walking over to her and ripping the heart from her chest while she begged for mercy. He smiled and turned back to the window. No, he thought, there is still much use for such a lovely woman. "Mr. Satori," said his assistant's voice over the speaker. He walked back to his desk and sat down, grabbing the phone receiver and holding it up to his ear. "Sir, there is a Mr. Joshua Prospect and Mr. Peter Smith to see you," Gladys said. "Shall I send them away?"

Bill laughed out loud, startling Sheila who dropped the magazine onto her lap and looked up at him. "No, by all means, send them in, Gladys!" he exclaimed as he winked at Sheila. The door opened and the two men entered the huge office and started walking toward the desk. Satori rose and strode to meet them halfway. "This is a real surprise," he said extending his hand to greet them. "What's this all about, Joshua?"

"I'm on bodyguard duty today, Uncle," he said as he shook Bill's hand. "Peter wanted to come see you."

"Please, both of you sit down," Bill said, waving his arm toward two side chairs in front of his desk. "Can I get you some water or coffee or anything?"

"No, thank you, Mr. Satori," Pete said as he took his seat. "And I hope I'm not taking too much of your valuable time."

Bill sat behind his desk and took another sip of coffee. He considered the two men, realizing that Joshua's presence likely meant Pete would stay with the Prospects. Why else would he need a bodyguard in this place? "So, what's up, Pete? Tell me what's on your mind."

Pete coughed and sat up straight. "To be frank, I've decided not to come to work for you."

A flush of red began to move up Bill's neck and onto his face, which was twisting into a frown. "That is unfortunate."

"But there's more to it, sir," Pete interjected. "I'm not going to stay with the Prospect Enterprise either."

Bill sat back in stunned silence for a full minute, until at last he said, "I don't understand, Pete."

Pete looked back at Sheila and then at Satori again. "Does she need to be here, sir?"

Bill looked at her and said, "Sheila, get out and take Joshua with you." She stood and walked over to Joshua and put her hand on his shoulder.

"I don't think I should leave Pete alone here," Joshua said.

"I promise I won't harm Peter, okay?"

"What do you think?" Joshua said to Pete.

"You'd better go. I'll be all right." Reluctantly, Joshua rose and walked out of the room with the woman, who followed him out and closed the door.

Bill rose from his desk and walked over to a bar, where he filled two glasses with ice and whisky. He came back and set a glass in front of Pete. "I know it's early, but I have a feeling we'll be needing this." He tapped his glass against the other and returned to his seat across the wide desk. "I'm all ears."

"This whole thing is a terrible mistake," Pete said. "I can't allow the end of the world to be my fault. Even Granddad, I mean Emmanuel Prospect, thinks it might be coming."

Bill laughed and took a sip of his drink. "Pete, my boy, this world has always been on the precipice of the end of time. When it comes, it will be due to the regular folks, not Manny or me."

"All I know is that both you and Emmanuel have told me there is a greater risk of global war if I keep telling the Prospects about my dreams."

"I suppose that is true. Those were my words. But if helping the Prospects raises the risks, why not work for me and lower them?" Bill argued.

"I just can't, Mr. Satori. It seems evil or wrong on so many levels. But what I will do is leave the city and go into hiding. Maybe I'll find a job back in Iowa or some other place somewhere where no one has ever heard of either of you," Pete explained.

Satori laughed. "I'm afraid everyone's heard of us!"

"You know what I mean. But I do need to ask a favor or two to make it work."

Satori sneered and slapped his hands on the desk. "Like what?"

"Obviously, I would like you not to kill me. Also, I would like you to actively work to prevent the end of the world."

"Anything else, Mr. Smith?"

"Bill, I just want to be left alone. I promise I won't tell my dreams to anyone, not the Prospects and not even my own mother," he concluded.

Satori stood and walked around the desk, taking a seat in the chair next to Pete. He put his hand on Pete's shoulder and said, "You know, my brother and I have been very unfair to you. How will I know if you keep your side of the bargain?"

"I think you'll know, Bill," Pete chuckled.

"That is true. Okay, I think that is a fair compromise and you have my word that no one on my side will attempt to harm you in any way, as long as you comply with your promise."

"Thank you Mr. Satori. And I'm sorry for taking so much time," Pete replied as he stood up.

Bill rose and shook hands with the other. "Peter, I will talk to my brother and suggest we both fund a small nest egg for you. You can take a vacation or do whatever will make you happier. When you decide your first destination, please call me and I will arrange a private jet if you like."

"You are very generous, sir."

Bill smiled and replied, "I guess you know this outcome is the same as working for me. I told you that I'd pay you to do nothing."

"Yes, I know, but this just feels better because I'm not being forced to pick sides. Goodbye, sir." He turned and walked out of the office, closing the door behind him.

"You already did choose sides, Peter, whether you know it or not," Satori said to the empty room and then began to laugh.

Chapter 19

Peter Smith woke as the morning sun pierced the window of his room and struck him between the eyes. He rolled over to escape its glare and pulled the sheets over his head, desperate for more rest. He had been in this resort on Maui for two days already, and the nights had been blissfully dream free, or at least he had forgotten them like everyone else on Earth. He wondered if his proximity to the Satori and Prospect families had intensified his dreams or whether he was just experiencing a temporary respite. "Just a few more minutes," he said to himself as he tried to clear his mind and fall back to sleep. Several minutes later, he began to hear an argument in the next room. The words were muffled by the wall so he could not understand, although the tenor of the discussion was clearly unpleasant. Then came the sound of running water, but it was too close, as if coming from his own bathroom. He sat up straight and strained to hear any other sounds. Slowly he climbed out of bed and walked silently toward the bathroom door, which was slightly ajar. The shower was running and the curtain closed. His nerves were on edge and he wondered what he should do next. Perhaps it would be better to leave the room and contact security. How could anyone get into his room? He checked the main door and the security lock and chain were still secured as he left them when he went to bed. He inched forward toward the shower although he did not know why he was doing this. Anyone or anything could be inside. He should be running the other way, but his feet moved forward. His left hand rose to grasp the shower curtain and he flung it open.

"Hello Pete," Sheila Farness said. She was standing in the shower nude with the water pouring over her head and down her body. "Why don't you join me?"

He sat up in bed, still trembling in fear. He jumped out of bed and checked his room, finding nothing. He sat on the chair by the desk and gasped for breath with his heart beating rapidly. He glanced out the window and noticed the sun had not yet risen, although the sky was beginning to lighten. The entire episode had been a dream, but thankfully, there was no death or destruction, only the invasion of his shower by a beautiful woman. He opened his laptop and signed on. He had pulled all of his savings together for this escape, but had chosen an expensive hotel. He remembered Satori's promise to give him some money, but to date, nothing had happened. He thought about going back to Iowa and living with his parents, but that would mean acknowledging that his jaunt to New York had been an abject failure. After he connected to the hotel's Wi-Fi, he signed onto his bank account to check his funds. He sat staring at the screen for a minute, his mouth moving up and down while his hands shook. Last night, he had seen his balance of just over three thousand dollars. This morning, the balance was one hundred million dollars higher. He clicked to look at account details and found two inbound wire transfers, one for one million and the other for ninety-nine million dollars. "I must be the luckiest son of a bitch in the world!" he laughed. He logged off and went to take a shower.

Pete was standing in the shower with hot water running over his head and singing when the realization hit him. He had sold out humanity for money. He really was Satori's pawn now. He put his hands on the wall to support himself as his knees began to buckle. He sat on the floor of the shower and began to cry. "What did I do?" he groaned.

§

A large group of soldiers wearing black uniforms stood in formation near the three Scud missile launchers. A Star of David had been painted on each, as well as the words "Death to Israel" in Arabic. The commanding general paced back and forth in front of his men. "This is a great day for all of us! Today we begin the destruction of the terror state of Israel and reclaim the holy city of al-Quds!" The soldiers cheered, raising their rifles over their heads. The general motioned for the troops to be silent and then said, "Soon, we will march across the desert and take back the land that belongs to us. The Jews will flee or be crushed under our feet!" More cheers broke out as the general pointed at the launch control officers who pressed the final contacts to initiate ignition.

The mass of soldiers cheered wildly as the three rockets lifted off and rose into the sky. After several seconds, two of the rockets turned to the west on a direct course for Tel Aviv. The third rocket moved erratically for several more seconds until it turned south and east. The soldiers kept cheering, but the general knew something was wrong and rushed over to the launch control position. "What's wrong with that rocket? It's going the wrong way!"

"I don't know, general," the soldier said. "It is not responding to my commands."

"Initiate self-destruct, Barsat!"

"I have tried that as well, general. The console seems to be dead. I don't know what else to do."

"May God have mercy on our souls if that rocket hits one of our cities," the general sighed. "Do you know where it's headed?"

"No sir. It is already left our range, but it appeared to be heading into Saudi Arabia. Hopefully, it will land in the middle of the desert."

Fifteen minutes later, the Iron Dome deployed missiles to stop the incoming rockets. One was destroyed almost immediately. The second continued on its way, finally crashing into a major hotel in Tel Aviv and exploding. The building collapsed into a smoldering pile of concrete and steel. The IDF immediately went on highest alert while the origin of the Scuds was investigated.

Another fifteen minutes later and the final Scud streaked out of the sky and slammed into the holy city of Mecca, smashing several buildings and starting a massive fire.

§

Pete strolled into the restaurant in the hotel and was led to a small table where a fresh cup of coffee was poured. As he looked through the menu, he still thought about the money, and wondered if Satori would fulfill his part of the bargain. He heard someone speaking and looked up to see the man at the next table holding a tablet in front of him and listening to the news. The speaker said, "We have confirmation of missile attacks this morning on Tel Aviv, Israel, and Mecca, Saudi Arabia. The source of those weapons is unclear at this point, although all governments in the area have denied involvement and condemned the attacks."

"Hi Pete," said a woman's voice, and Pete looked up to see Isabel Garcia standing at his table. "It's good to see you again."

He stood and shook her hand. "Hi, Isabel, this is a pleasant surprise! Would you like to join me, or are you with someone?"

She smiled and replied, "Actually, I'm here with some girlfriends, but I'll be with them all day. I'll join you if that's okay."

"Absolutely," he said as he pulled out a chair for her.

"Thanks, Pete. That stuff in the Middle East is very frightening, don't you think?"

"I know. I just can't believe anyone would strike both countries. It doesn't make any sense at all."

Isabel sighed and continued, "Well, they call it terrorism for a reason. I guess no one is safe anymore. What brings you to the islands?"

"I just had to get away from it all. I was getting squeezed between the Prospects and Bill Satori. Finally, I chose to get out while I still could."

She laughed. "So, you still think both of them are out to get you? Honestly, if you weren't so cute, I'd think you're crazy."

"You think I'm cute?" he asked, but she never replied. His phone buzzed in his pocket. He pulled it out and chuckled when he looked at the screen. It was Emmanuel Prospect calling. He showed the phone to Isabel who looked shocked, then clicked the connect button. "Hello, Granddad. How can I help you?"

"I know you've left us Peter, but let me ask you one question. Did you dream about the missiles?"

"No, sir, I haven't remembered any dreams since I've been here."

"How about the subway attack?"

"What subway attack, Granddad?"

"I've got to go now, son. Take care," Emmanuel said as he closed the connection. Pete set the phone down and stared into space.

"Pete, what's going on? What subway attack? What kind of dreams were you talking about?"

He reached across the table and held her hand softly. "Isabel, it's a bit of a long story. I don't want to take you from your friends, but I'd be happy to tell you everything. It will take a few hours though."

"What subway attack, Pete?"

"I don't know."

§

Five large vans stopped next to five different Metro stations in Paris at the same time. Six heavily armed men rushed out of each van. Five of each group hurried down the steps into the station, while the sixth stood guard at the top of the stairs, his automatic rifle leveled and ready to fire. The five opened fire on the crowds as they reached the station. People pushed back in panic, screaming and dodging bullets. One terrorist remained near the bottom of the steps while the others smashed through the gates and hurried to the subway platforms, firing on anyone in their path. Once on the platforms, they continued to fire on the crowds, which ran in every direction possible to get away. When the next subway car entered the platform, the men fired on the cars and threw hand grenades into the opening doors. The group then retreated back up the steps and into the vans, which raced away. In less than ten minutes, the Metro system had been shut down and hundreds of Parisians lie dead or dying on the concrete floors.

A police car spotted one of the vans and pursued it through the city, its siren blaring and cars and pedestrians rushing to get out of the way. Narga opened the passenger window of the van and tossed a grenade back at the police vehicle. The grenade landed on the hood of the police vehicle and exploded, instantly killing the officers inside. The driverless cruiser veered to the right and slammed into a crowded sidewalk cafe, crushing patrons and smashing tables and chairs until it crashed into a solid wall and stopped.

§

Pete and Isabel were walking down the beach, hand-in-hand. He had told her everything he could remember, even the dream where they were lovers and both had been murdered in some kind of post-apocalyptic war. She smiled and listened intently, although she was not certain whether the man next to her was a prophet or a lunatic. "That's quite some story, Pete," she said at last as she pulled her hand from his. "You think all of this stuff is real, don't you? Pete, I think you need help."

He stopped and stared at her. "You don't believe me, do you?"

"Pete, I want to, but you have to admit it's pretty outrageous."

"Here, let me show you something," he replied as he pulled his phone from his pocket. It began to ring as he fumbled with it. He frowned when he saw the screen and showed it to her. Bill Satori was calling.

She took the phone from him and clicked the connect button, "Peter Smith's phone. Who is calling please?"

"This is William Satori. Who is this?"

"Really, you expect me to believe that one of the richest men in the world is calling Peter. How do you know him?"

"Frankly, young lady, that is none of your damned business. If you want, have him show you his bank account. Now put him on the line, please," Satori growled.

Isabel handed Peter the phone. He sighed deeply and put it to his ear, "Yes, sir."

"Peter, my boy, I wanted to thank you for keeping your side of the bargain. I hope you liked the nest egg I provided," Bill said.

"It was very generous of you, Bill. Thank you."

"You are quite welcome, Peter."

"Mr. Satori, I thought we had an agreement that you would actively try to stop what's happening?"

The man laughed. "You hurt my feelings, Peter. What makes you think I am behind any of these unfortunate occurrences?"

"So, you're saying you were not involved?"

Satori's voice turned into a low growl. "Peter, what I am saying is that you have lots of my money now. You agreed to go away and avoid the Prospects. Since you have done that, I am going to let you live for now, but don't push your luck. If you like, I can send you a lot more money, but if you go back on your side of the agreement, things will go very badly for you."

"What about the end of the world, Bill? You said you would try to stop it."

"I lied. Enjoy Hawaii and tell Isabel she has the most beautiful brown eyes." The line went dead.

"What did he say, Pete?" Isabel asked.

"He said to tell Isabel that she has the most beautiful brown eyes," Pete replied.

"How does he know my name, Peter?" she exclaimed. "And what did you mean about the end of the world? What was that about your bank account?" She felt weak at the knees and sat on the sand, holding her head in her hands.

Pete sat next to her and put his arm around her shoulders. She leaned into him. With his other hand, he opened his banking app and signed in. He went to the detail of the wire transfer and showed it to her. "This deposit hit my account yesterday."

She stared in disbelief. "Are you kidding me? That says ninety-nine million dollars! What did you do for that much money?"

"I think I sold out the human race," he sighed.

She put her arms around his neck and hugged him tightly and then kissed him on the cheek. "What happens now, Pete? How do we stop this?"

He kissed her lips gently. "I wish I knew, Isabel. I wish I knew."

She took his phone and added her number to his contact list. "Pete, I've got to go meet my friends for a bachelorette party now. Call me if anything else happens and I'll call you tonight."

"Okay."

"Pete, please tell me everything will be all right. I'm not ready for the end of the world. No one is." He only shrugged his shoulders and turned to look out at the ocean.

§

Peter sat on a stool at the bar of his hotel, watching the evening news. There was no doubt in his mind that the end was coming. After the missile attacks in the Middle East and the subway attack in Paris, most nations had gone on alert. Video footage of all the scenes was played around the clock. He took a sip of his beer and stared at the screen. "This just in," the newscaster reported. "Fragments of both missiles have been found by the governments involved, further raising tensions in the area. In Tel Aviv, the fragment apparently was marked with the words "Death to Israel" in Arabic. The fragment discovered in Mecca showed a Star of David. All governments in the region have denied any involvement and denounced the attacks."

"What's the world coming to?" the man on the next stool said. "This is freaking crazy!"

"You got that right," Pete replied. "By the way, I'm Peter Smith." He extended his hand.

After shaking his hand, the man said, "I'm Ben Hanson. What brings you to Maui, Pete?"

"Running away, I guess."

Ben laughed. "Well, this is a great place for that, if you can afford it. Cheers!" The two clicked their glasses together.

"Why are you here, Ben?"

"It's kind of a surprise for my fiancée. She's having a bachelorette party tonight, and her best friend thought it would be funny if I show up at the end," Ben said.

"That's a coincidence. I know a woman here for a bachelorette party, but she's not the bride. Her name is Isabel Garcia."

"She's Katie's best friend! It's a small world, Peter," Ben chuckled.

"This is a Fox News Alert," said the newscaster on the television. "Two airliners have collided over New York and crashed into the city. Several Brooklyn neighborhoods are in flames at this time."

"Mother of God," Ben sighed. "I'm from Brooklyn."

The reporter continued, "Apparently, the two planes were on approach to land at JFK and La Guardia when the incident occurred. There are no other details at this time, but we will interrupt regular programming when we have more information. Once again, two airliners have collided over New York and crashed into the city." The bartender turned off the set, sighed and walked away.

The bartender returned with three shots of tequila and set them down. "This one's on the house, guys. Here's to those poor people in New York." All three drank the liquor and stared at one another, unable to find words to describe what they were feeling.

Pete's phone rang and he clicked the connect button, saying, "Hi, Isabel. I guess you heard."

"Oh my God, Pete! What am I going to do? I'm so scared."

"Where are you?"

"My friends and I were going to the bar when we heard. We don't know what to do anymore."

"Isabel, I'm in the bar with Ben Hanson. You should all come here so we can be together," Pete replied.

"Okay, Pete, we'll be right there, but who the heck is Ben Hanson?" she asked.

Pete was stunned. He looked to the man seated next to him, but the seat was empty.

The group of women entered the bar and Isabel rushed over, throwing her arms around him.

Chapter 20

With the events of the day, all the women decided to stay together with Peter in his room. He was trying to sleep in a chair with his feet on the hassock. He kept waking with different aches in his back and legs and readjusted his position over and again. The air was dense with the perfume from ten women squeezed into the room. Three slept on each of the two beds, with one on the couch and the rest on the floor, using blankets for mattresses. Isabel slept on the floor next to him and he could hear her soft breathing and felt comforted by her closeness. He wondered again about the man in the bar. He had been there and claimed to know Isabel. Suddenly he disappeared. What did it all mean? Minutes later, he was asleep.

When he woke, the air was icy cold, forming clouds of fog when he exhaled. He stood up and saw the women still sleeping. He gently touched Isabel on the cheek, but her face was freezing cold and her body was stiff, as if frozen solid. He moved from woman to woman, and each was the same. Pete ran over to the door and tried to pull it open. The knob was brutally cold, causing him to wince in pain and release it. I must be dreaming, he thought. He heard an odd engine sound and hurried over to the window, throwing open the curtains. A small plane was losing power and headed straight for that room. He tried to move, but the airplane crashed through the window, its propeller slicing the women into pieces and spattering their blood everywhere. When it finally stopped, he could see there was no one in the cockpit. The engine burst into flames and he felt the fire burning off his skin and screamed in pain.

He opened his eyes and found he was still sitting on the chair. He heard an odd engine sound very far away. Pete jumped to his feet and started shaking the women. "Get up! We have to get out of here now!" he screamed. He rushed over to the door and threw it open, blocking it with a chair. "Hurry!"

Isabel shouted, "What's wrong?"

"Get out of here for God's sake!" he screamed. He started grabbing the girls and throwing them toward the door. They were shaking and crying, knowing this crazy man would likely kill them all.

Only Isabel remained in the room, glowering at him. "Pete, what the hell is going on?"

He rushed over to her and threw her over his shoulder and ran for the door. "There's no time, Isabel!" Carrying her, he screamed at the others to run down the hall; they complied, in fear for their lives. There was a tremendous explosion, and a fireball shot out the open doorway, knocking Peter to the floor. He lay there panting for breath and groaning in pain. His shirt was on fire, and Isabel pulled off her top to smother the flames. Pete coughed and asked, "Is everyone okay?"

"What happened, Pete?" she asked as she pulled her top back on. "How did you know that was going to happen?"

He groaned as he sat up on the floor. "I had a dream where a plane crashed through the window and killed everyone. Then I woke up and knew we had to get out."

Several hotel security guards rushed onto the floor and headed for the room. Flames shot out of the interior so they backed off. In the distance, sirens wailed. "Is everyone okay?" the lead guard said.

"No," Isabel shouted. "My boyfriend has been burned pretty badly." Pete looked up at her and she just smiled.

§

Peter was lying on his stomach in the emergency room as a nurse cleaned his wounds. He could see a television relaying the local news. The reporter said, "A local elderly couple died today when their small plane crashed into a local hotel. By a happy coincidence, the guest registered in that room survived with only minor burns. Also, none of the adjacent rooms were occupied."

"You're a lucky man, Mr. Smith," the nurse said. "I think you're all set and ready to go."

"Thank you," he replied. "You know, it feels like I didn't get burned at all. That must be some powerful medicine you used." He sat up and noticed her nametag said "Mary." "Thank you, Mary."

"Nothing but the best for you, Mr. Smith. By the way, my name is Mary Prospect. Your friend Mike is my brother."

"It is a small world," he smiled.

"Granddad wanted me to ask if you dreamt about the airplane," she said.

"Yes I did, except in the dream, there was no one flying the plane," he replied.

"That poor couple could never have known they were marked for death," Mary noted. "Ben and Carol Hanson have lived here for many years and I knew them both."

"Did you say Ben Hanson?"

"Yes, why do you ask?"

"Last night I was sitting in the bar and a man calling himself that name sat next to me. He was saddened by the collision over New York and said he was the fiancé of Isabel's friend. Then he just disappeared," he related.

"That is a remarkable gift you have, Pete," she said. "What happened is not your fault, but if we would have known that last night, there is a chance they could have been saved."

"But there really was someone sitting next to me," he argued. "I did not dream him."

"That's interesting. It would seem Satori has a sense of humor, or perhaps is hoping to be stopped."

Pete stood and replied, "I think he was testing me. If I told Granddad, he'd know I broke the agreement and kill me."

"Another possible scenario," she noted. "Peter, you have to know he will get to you one of these days. You came within seconds of a horrible death this morning. Don't be stupid and think he is fair minded and won't try again."

There was a knock at the door and both turned to see Isabel standing in the doorway with a shopping bag. "Are you all set, Pete? I bought you some new clothes."

"Good luck, Mr. Smith," Mary said as she walked out of the room.

Isabel closed the door, dropped the bag, and rushed into Pete's arms. She kissed his lips and smiled at him. "My God, Pete, you saved all of our lives. Is all of this true? Did you really dream about the plane?"

"Yes, Isabel, I did. But this means Satori has decided to kill me whether I help the Prospects or not," he answered.

"What do we do now?"

"I think we need to get back to New York, but it's crazy dangerous right now. How do you feel about a road trip?" he asked.

"I have to get back to work, Pete."

"Isabel, I've got a hundred million sitting in the bank, waiting to be spent. Take a month off and we'll drive across America. I think Bertrand Industries will give you a leave of absence," he said.

"I don't understand, Pete. What if they don't?"

He leaned close to her and whispered in her ear, "Isabel, in one of my dreams, all the major cities of the world were destroyed. I saw New York in ruins. Stay with me and stay alive a little longer."

"Pete, what about my friends? Most of them are flying back today. I have to tell them something," she insisted.

"Call them tomorrow when they're back. Honestly, I don't know what will happen or when, but when I know, you can warn them, hopefully in time. We have to get out of here before Satori acts again."

§

At 1:15 p.m. the Satori Industries jet landed at the Kahului Airport, taxied to a small hangar and parked. The door was opened and Sheila Farness descended the steps and entered a white limousine which then drove toward the exit and out into the city. Sheila opened the small refrigerator and removed a bottle of water and took a sip. Then she pressed a speed-dial button. "Hello Bill, I have arrived."

"Excellent!" he laughed. "What is your plan to eliminate the threat?"

"I called the hotel just before we took off and they confirmed that both Peter and the Garcia woman have not checked out. It is unfortunate that Narga's plane accident failed, but I will not."

"Sheila, let's not get too presumptuous. You know Peter's ability. He may have already sensed your plans and changed his schedule," Satori noted. "Let's just say you'll try your best. If he escapes, we will continue to look for him."

"Yes sir, I understand. But if he is still in Hawaii, I will hunt him down. However, you might consider monitoring the local airports to make certain he does not return to New York," she replied.

Bill chuckled. "I doubt he'll come here right away. He has seen the carnage we have loosed on the world and may have foreseen the destruction of this city. That works to our advantage actually. He will be far from me, but also far from the Prospects. Keep me informed." The line was disconnected.

Sheila slipped the phone back into her purse and withdrew her pistol and examined it. She removed the bullet clip, verified that it was loaded and ready, and then put it back in her purse as well. She lowered the divider between the seats and said, "How much longer before we reach the hotel?"

"About a half hour, ma'am," the driver reported.

"Thanks," she replied and raised the divider again. She slumped down on the seat and closed her eyes.

At 1:40 p.m. the Hawaiian Airlines flight lifted off from Kahului Airport and headed east toward Los Angeles. Pete and Isabel sat in the front row of first class holding hands as the plane rose through the clouds. The flight attendant brought them two glasses of champagne, smiled, and continued her rounds. Isabel leaned over to him and whispered in his ear, "Pete, are you sure the plane is safe?"

"I don't know what is safe anymore, Isabel, but we couldn't stay there any longer. Satori already made one attempt on our lives, and he will keep trying until he succeeds. The sooner we get back on the continent, the more places we'll have to hide," he replied.

"Pete, don't take this wrong, but sometimes I wish I had never met you."

He laughed. "I understand how you feel, but you wouldn't be any safer. If the war comes, we all will be in mortal danger."

"What is our plan after we land, Pete?"

"I don't have a clue," he sighed. "I'm trying to decide whether to contact the Prospects, but since I threw my phone in the ocean, that's going to be difficult."

"I was wondering why you did that."

"I don't want to listen to Satori's crap anymore. For all I know, they were tracking me by that damned thing. When we land, I'll buy a new phone," he replied. She put her head on his shoulder, and soon both were sound asleep, allowing the events of the morning attack to fade into memory.

At 2:00 p.m. the white limousine turned up the circular drive leading to the resort. A bellman opened the door and Sheila climbed out and walked into the lobby. She stopped at the front desk and asked for the manager. Two minutes later, Walt Jeffries came from a door behind the desk and approached her. "Good afternoon, madam, how may I serve you?" he said.

Sheila pulled a badge from her purse and showed it to him, saying, "I'm Special Agent Farness of the FBI. I am here to investigate the plane crash this morning."

"Of course, Agent Farness, we are happy to help in any way we can. Several HPD investigators are already on the scene, and we are expecting a team from the NTSB later in the day. Would you like me to show you the way?"

"Later perhaps. I am primarily interested in interviewing the registered guests who may have been in the area at the time," she replied. "We have been told that a Peter Smith was registered to the same room the plane crashed into."

"Yes, it is amazing that Mr. Smith and his guests survived. Somehow, he heard the plane and rushed everyone from the room just seconds before the impact."

"Frankly, that seems a bit convenient to us, Mr. Jeffries. Where is this Peter Smith now?"

"I'm afraid he checked out a couple hours ago. We obviously comped his visit and offered him lodging at any of our other locations, but I do not know if he will take advantage of that," Walt finished.

She frowned and looked at her watch. "You mentioned his guests. Are any of them still in your hotel?"

"No, they all checked out very early to return to the mainland, except a Ms. Garcia, who checked out at the same time as Mr. Smith. Would you like to go to the scene now, Special Agent?"

"I don't think that will be necessary, as I'm certain the HPD will do a thorough job. We will contact their office later for a report. Thank you, Mr. Jeffries," Sheila said as she spun on her heels and headed for the door.

"Safe travels, Agent Farness," Walt called out after her. She did not acknowledge him and left the hotel. The limousine sped away.

Once inside the car, she pressed a speed dial button on her phone. "Master, I'm afraid Pete has already left the hotel. I can call around and find out if he is at another hotel."

"That won't be necessary, my dear," Satori replied. "I'm afraid Peter has gone underground to avoid us."

"Bill, if you give me some time, I know I can find him."

He laughed. "I admire your spunk, Sheila, my dearest. I think it best that we continue with our other plans. Now that Peter knows he's a marked man, he will obviously start to help the Prospects or, if he's smart, he'll avoid them and us and try to survive a bit longer.

That is why we must accelerate our actions. Pete is just one man with one brain in his head. He would have to sleep around the clock to foresee everything we plan to do. If he stops one in five or one in three, the end will still come. My friends are also watching the Prospects. As soon as he contacts one, we will discover where he is. Then it will be your chance to kill him."

"What can I do to serve you now, Bill?" she asked.

"I need you to go to Asia. You need to coordinate the delivery of the satchel bombs. Call your team together, give them their targets, and let's get this thing moving!"

§

The first tremors hit the Los Angeles basin at 5:45 p.m. at the peak of rush hour traffic. Vehicles slid around on the freeways as the ground shook and the concrete buckled. Overpasses twisted and shook until more than a dozen crashed down on the gridlocked cars and trucks beneath them. Gas lines snapped all over the region, followed by massive explosions and out-of-control fires flowing in waves over the suburbs. Hundreds of buildings collapsed as their supports gave way under the moving earth. Hundreds of thousands of people poured into the streets to escape the shaking and flames. The sky filled with black smoke until the afternoon looked like twilight. After ten minutes of violent shaking, the city fell into an agonizing silence, punctuated only by sirens and the screaming of those trapped under the rubble.

The South Coast Plaza shopping center was obliterated by the earthquake. All the floors pancaked, killing or trapping almost all the shoppers and workers inside. The last tremors of the quake tore the wreckage in half, revealing a massive crack in the earth, which quickly grew to one hundred feet wide and one thousand feet long. Noxious smoke belched from the crack, giving an odd greenish tint to the sky over Orange County. First responders rushed to the scene in full hazmat gear. They frantically tried to push the people away from the opening in fear that poisonous fumes or magma would pour forth. Hundreds of police officers cordoned off the area, wearing full riot gear. They formed a human wall between the hole and the panicked residents looking for their friends and family in the wreckage.

By seven thirty, the crowds had begun to thin as more rescue equipment arrived on the scene. Groups of firefighters began the task of removing the debris and searching for survivors and victims. A command center was in place and the Costa Mesa Chief of Police had taken charge of the incident. Similar command centers were set up around the LA area due to the widespread destruction from the earthquake.

A small group of SWAT officers at the collapsed mall were given orders to do a preliminary investigation of the gaping hole in the earth. Major Brent Prospect led the team of four men, wearing self-contained breathing apparatus and carrying high-powered rifles and pistols. At eight o'clock, the group approached the opening and used their lights to see inside. Brent was astounded to see a flat surface leading down into the ground, almost as though it was constructed for people to walk inside. He shrugged his shoulders and began to enter the cave with his men. The corridor continued for more than a mile without change. His gage showed they were several hundred feet underground. His communication link was fading due to the interference of the rock over their heads. Far ahead, he noticed a reddish light and immediately concluded there was a magma pool down here. He immediately sent one of his men back to the surface to report. He had the other two stay at this position to make any needed reports.

Brent continued alone. He knew who his family was and that there was little risk for him but could not allow the others to see what he really believed he would find at the end of the tunnel. As he continued, the tunnel began to narrow slowly. After another twenty minutes, the tunnel ended at a two-foot diameter opening into a large cavern. He removed his breathing apparatus and set it down. Then he climbed through the narrow ten-foot-long tunnel and climbed out and onto the floor of the cavern.

The room was very large, with the ceiling one hundred feet over his head. The area he stood upon stretched hundreds of feet to his left and right. The solid surface gave way to a sea of lava only twenty feet in front of him. The giant red beast was walking toward him on the molten rock. Then he noticed several hundred flying beasts swooping and turning in the smoky air above the magma sea. He stepped back until his spine was pressed against the rock wall. The beast walked out of the magma and approached until it was only one or two feet in front of him. Then it squatted so it could see his face. "Another damned Prospect, just my luck!"

"Satori, what are you doing? Why did you attack this city?" Brent asked.

"This is only the beginning, my boy. Now it's time for the end of this stupid game. Watch me unleash the true nature of your precious humans!"

"But don't you claim they created you? If you kill them, won't you be killing yourself too?"

Satori laughed until he had to hold his sides. "My brother has always thought people were basically good and well intentioned. He is a fool. Scrape the thin veneer of civilization from them and they are me to the core. They will turn on you long before they run out of evil in their souls."

"You're wrong, Bill," Brent replied. "They know the evil you represent. They will forsake you, as has the Creator and my father."

Satori stood and stretched his sore knees. "You may be right, Brent, and that is precisely why I am doing all of this." He began to pace back and forth. "Rather than playing this ridiculous game of waiting to see who turns good and who turns bad, I figured I would expedite the process. I intend to unleash unholy chaos around this ball of rock until both Manny and I know for certain which of us is right."

"The people don't deserve that, Bill."

"It's too late for that judgment, Brent. It has already begun and nothing will stop it." He patted Brent on the head and continued, "You know, I was going to let you choose between a normal disaster, such as a gushing river of lava, and an unnatural one, namely my friends personally attacking. But it's too late for that. I've decided to do both." Bill grabbed Brent around the waist and threw him into the pool of magma. "Gee, that felt good, although it was a waste of time." He signaled to the flying beasts, and they fell into formation and rushed toward the opening. Bill struck the wall with his hand, causing the rock to crumble until the opening was a hundred feet wide. The flying monsters shot forward up the tunnel and out into the skies of Los Angeles.

Satori heard the magma bubbling and turned around. A point of intense white light shot out of the magma and hovered in the air. "You will regret this decision," said Brent's voice as the light shot past and out of the tunnel. He shrugged his shoulders and then raised both arms. The molten rock began to boil and rise. He motioned toward the opening, and a geyser of magma shot out of the tunnel.

Chapter 21

Isabel woke up two hours later, her hand still in Pete's. She turned to look at him and saw his face contorted in pain. A few tears rolled down his face and she wiped them away. She tried to wake him, but he seemed locked in a trance of some kind. Isabel grabbed him by the shoulders and shook him as hard as she could, not wanting to worry the attendants or other passengers. After twenty seconds, Pete's eyes burst open. He was trembling and gasping for air. "Pete, what's wrong? Are you okay?" she asked.

He put his arms around her and held her tightly. He whispered in her ear, "Los Angeles has been destroyed." He sat back and stared at the bulkhead in front of him.

Isabel's mind was racing, not wanting to believe what she just heard. "Perhaps it was just a dream?"

"I hope so, Isabel, but I don't think it was. There was too much detail," he replied.

"Like what?"

"The epicenter was a place called South Coast Plaza, which is a shopping mall in Costa Mesa. The lead SWAT officer involved is one of the Prospects," he said.

"That doesn't mean anything, Pete. You're overreacting."

Pete took her hands, saying, "Isabel, please listen to me. I've never been to Los Angeles. I've have never heard of the South Coast Plaza and don't even know if there is a city named Costa Mesa. Did I make that up?"

Isabel replied, "Pete, those are real places. I've been to that mall several times. Maybe you read about them in a magazine or something."

"I hope you're right," he sighed.

A tone sounded and a voice spoke over the loudspeaker. "Ladies and gentlemen, we are being diverted to San Diego. There has been a swarm of earthquakes in the Los Angeles area and local airports are closed. We have no other information at this time, but will work with our partners to arrange travel to your ultimate destinations. Sorry for the inconvenience."

"Oh my God, Pete, how did you know that?" she asked.

"I don't know. The visions just came to me. But there is a lot more than earthquakes involved here. I doubt anybody will report what is really happening."

"I don't understand, Pete. What could be worse?"

"The end of the world," he replied as he turned to look out the window.

§

It was shortly after 9:30 p.m. when the Hawaiian Airlines flight landed in San Diego after circling for some time due to the heavier than usual traffic. Being first off the plane, Pete and Isabel walked slowly down the terminal toward the baggage claim. The terminal was packed with people trying to make arrangements to get to their next destination. Those who were headed to LA were lining up for buses, even though many of the freeways were still closed at this hour. Everyone they passed was talking about the troubles north of here, and most seemed unsure as to what to do next. "I think we'll have to get a room at a hotel in town tonight, Isabel. I want to buy a vehicle for us to use since we don't know where we're going or when we'll get there," he said.

"Okay, Pete, but with this crowd, finding a hotel room might be a challenge," Isabel replied.

They stood at the end of a long line to use the escalators down to the baggage claim. When they finally stepped on the device, Pete smiled when he noticed Joshua Prospect standing at the bottom of the escalator with a sign that read "Smith-Garcia." They walked over and Pete extended his hand. "How'd you know we'd be here, Josh?"

"You're kidding, right?" Joshua replied. He shook Isabel's hand and said, "How do you do, Isabel? I'm Joshua Prospect."

"It's nice to meet you, sir," she replied.

"Please just call me Joshua, or Josh if you prefer. If you don't mind, could I talk to Pete for a moment? You can go over to the baggage claim. We'll join you in a moment." Isabel walked away and Joshua led Pete out the doors and into the warm San Diego evening. "What's your plan, Pete? I assume you know everything that happened in Costa Mesa?"

"Is Brent okay?"

Joshua laughed. "Yes, he's fine. I can assume you know it all then. Pete, first you have to know that none of this is your fault. Bill Satori is an evil, twisted monster. He's been looking for an excuse to come out in the open for thousands of years. You only gave him an excuse."

"Mary told me I could have saved the Hansons if I had understood that vision. I'm beginning to think this is about me."

"Pete, horrible things happen on Earth every day! Most of the time, it is nature or people doing bad things to each other. Now, Satori has decided to act on his own. He doesn't want you to help my family because he will cause less damage. But he will not live up to his agreement with you. He's already tried to kill you and will try again."

Pete's head hung down. "What do you want me to do? I'm tired of wondering what to do next. Please just tell me."

Joshua reached into his pocket and extracted a phone, handing it to Pete. "You might want this back."

Pete was shocked to be holding his own cell phone again. "But how did you get this?" He saw Joshua smirking at him. "Sorry, that was a silly question. But I don't want that bastard Satori calling me or tracing me with this damned thing."

"He won't be able to trace you, Pete. We've taken care of that. We would like you to take his calls, however."

"Why should I talk to him? He disgusts me."

Joshua put his hands on Pete's shoulders and stared into his eyes. "Do you remember when you and Shirley were chained to the wall in that long chamber?" Pete nodded. "We think that something happened then that is totally impossible, involving you and Satori."

"What?"

"We can't talk about that now, Pete. It may be nothing or it may be the answer to this entire situation, but we need to let things unfold naturally, okay?" Joshua asked.

"Whatever you say, Josh," Pete sighed. "With all the visions, I'm not getting much rest. I was asleep almost the entire flight over, and I'm still dead tired."

Joshua was about to speak when Isabel exited the terminal, pulling her suitcase behind her. He waved her over. "You guys never showed up, so I came looking for you," she said.

"I apologize for that," Joshua said. "Sometimes when I start talking, I just don't know when to shut up." A loud horn sounded and they turned to see two H1 Hummers pulling up to the curb. "Here's our ride. I'll take the suitcase for you, Isabel. You and Pete should get in the back seat of the first vehicle. I'll be in the second one and we'll be following you."

Pete climbed in the back of the first vehicle and sat down. He immediately noticed that Gabe Prospect was driving. "Hey, Gabe, how are you?"

"I'm okay, Pete. I'm glad you made it here. Hi, Isabel, I'm Gabe. I don't know if you remember me."

"At the car crash in New York, I remember," she said as she shook his hand. The two SUVs pulled away from the curb and drove away from the airport. They turned on Grape Street and took the on-ramp to Interstate 5 South. Pete was already sleeping again when Gabe left the freeway to cross the Coronado Bay Bridge. Ten minutes later, the two vehicles pulled into the gate for the Hotel Del Coronado and approached the entrance. Isabel woke Pete, and they left the vehicle and walked into the hotel lobby, followed closely by

Joshua, Gabe, and Mike Prospect, who had been driving the second vehicle.

Minutes later, the group entered the large suite, where Joshua showed Pete and Isabel their bedroom. Then the entire group sat together in the large living room. Gabe poured drinks for everyone and passed them out. Joshua sat with his two nephews on one couch while Pete and Isabel sat opposite them. "What are we doing here, Joshua?" Pete asked. "Isn't this the first place they'll look for me?"

"That would normally be true, but Satori does not know that you left the islands yet. You will both be long gone before he learns the truth. Also, this room is completely safe, I can assure you of that," Joshua started.

"We also have reason to believe that Satori will not spend much time or effort finding you," Mike said.

"Yes, I agree," Joshua noted. "You had the vision about the LA earthquakes, right?" Pete nodded. "Well, there was also a subway attack in Moscow, a devastating tsunami in the Philippines, and two terrorist bombings in Israel that you did not foresee, or at least couldn't remember. Satori knows that you can only see so much, so if he causes several disasters at a time, you can only tell us about one or two."

"And I'm sure he believes that when you understand you can't stop him, you might choose to run away and hide to save your own skin," Gabe added.

"That's not a bad idea," Isabel agreed.

"Unfortunately, what Satori has in mind could lead to the extermination of human life. Hiding won't save anyone if nuclear winter sets in, or clouds of nerve gas and radiation circle the earth for a thousand years," Joshua noted.

"Could that really happen?" Isabel cried.

"Yes, it could, and it has already started," Pete said. "Joshua, what can we do? I certainly don't want anything to happen to Isabel. She got wrapped up in this by accident."

"Isabel, Pete is right," Joshua began. "If you want, you can leave now, and we will guard you for as long as we can. Bill Satori has no fight with you as long as you're not connected to Pete."

"But if the end of the world is really coming, I'll still be dead, right?" The three Prospect men sat still without comment. Pete held her hand and squeezed it tightly. "Well, if I'm dead anyway, I think I'll stay, if that's okay with you, Pete?" He kissed her gently.

"What do we do now, Joshua?" Pete asked again.

Joshua stood and began to pace back and forth. He cleared his throat and looked nervously at his nephews. Finally, he stopped and sat again. "Okay, this is going to be very difficult to believe, but here goes. I mentioned before the time when you and Shirley Manson were chained to the wall in that long corridor." Pete nodded again. Isabel sat back in disbelief. "That place does not exist on Earth."

"What?" Isabel gasped. Pete sat quietly, holding his head in his hands.

"That place is sacred to us. It is the place of atonement for humanity. Each person must atone for the evil in their lives in that place after they die. My brother Luce and his family, except Gabe here, facilitate it," Joshua said.

"It's true, Pete," Gabe replied.

"What does that mean for me, Josh?" Pete asked.

"Living people can never enter there, and before your visit only one has ever left there alive," Joshua continued. "That was me, but it was long ago."

"But Shirley and I did," Pete argued. "I feel fine. Maybe you are wrong about that."

"Well, we fixed it for Shirley by forcing one of the demons to kill her. Then she was brought back to life without the memory of the brutality of her death," Joshua said. "So the line between her life and death was fixed, if you will. Pete, what happened when you left that place with Satori?"

Pete sat quietly for a moment, clenching his teeth and agonizing with the memory. Isabel put her arm around his shoulders and tears welled in her eyes. Finally, Pete sighed heavily and said, "He took me to a mountain overlooking a vast desert. We walked around the mountain, and he showed me a vast forest full of temples. Then we crawled through a cave where he pushed me into a river. As it flew out of the cave I fell impossibly far down." Pete's head shot up. "That's it. He killed me then!"

"I'm sorry, Pete, but none of those places really exist either. He showed them to me as well, back when I was a man like you," Joshua replied. "What else happened?"

"Before the mountain, he showed me several tombs that could be mine depending on whether I help him or not. What does it all mean, Josh?"

"I honestly don't know, Pete. It's as if the sun rose in the west tomorrow and you asked me why. Things like this can't happen. We're faced with a situation that is totally unimaginable," Joshua said.

"Uncle, I disagree," Mike said. "I think this might be our solution. I don't know how yet, but something had to have allowed Pete to be alive today, and that's far more than what Satori or Granddad can do."

"Okay, that's enough for tonight," Joshua concluded. "Let's get some sleep and see what happens tomorrow. Pete, if you have any visions, just yell out and we'll rush right over."

"What I really need is sleep, Josh. Good night," Pete replied as he stood, took Isabel by the hand and walked into the bedroom, closing the door behind them.

§

Sheila Farness walked alone across the desert. She wore black commando style fatigues. The private jet sat two hundred yards behind her. Ahead, a glimmer of light emerged from a cave on the side of a large hill. As she approached, she could sense the eyes on her, but continued forward. Fifty yards ahead, five men stood aiming automatic rifles at her. She smiled and continued until she was fifteen feet in front of them. "I really don't think you need to point those things at me," she laughed.

"What is the password?" a guard shouted as he continued aiming at her head.

Sheila could see the laser points on her chest and she squinted as one moved across her eyes. "Armageddon!" she shouted back.

The lead guard motioned for the others to lower their weapons. "Do you have the codes, Ms. Farness?"

She pulled a piece of paper from her purse and held it up for them to see. "Here it is. Now show me the bombs."

The guards led her to a makeshift staircase that led up the hillside to the open cave. She followed them up and entered the cave. Twenty men clad in black were sitting on folding chairs facing another man who was speaking to them. "This is your day of glory! Today you will bring the infidels to their knees. Your sacrifice will liberate the world!" The men jumped to their feet and began to shout, "Satori, Satori, Satori!"

Sheila walked over to the speaker and said, "Great job, Barsat. Your father will be proud of you."

"Shut up, Sheila," he growled. "I hope you have the codes." She handed him the piece of paper. He reviewed it carefully and then handed it back. "Very well, I'll let you take it from here." He turned and walked away toward a small portable office deeper in the cave.

"Dear friends," she began, "today you will be in paradise! Each of you will take your satchel and deliver it to the sites of the attack. At precisely 1800 UTC you will enter the detonation codes and press the red button. Five seconds later the device will explode and all the infidels within miles will be instantly incinerated. You will have killed the enemy, and by your sacrifice, you will live forever in paradise and your families will be rich. Do you have any questions?"

One short, thin man stood and asked, "What if the device doesn't detonate?"

She laughed. "I find that highly unlikely, however, if that happens, you must drop the satchel in the nearest river or ocean and contact Master Barsat who will give you new orders. If the device fails, we will rescue you, and your family will still get the money. Any other questions?" No one spoke. "Good. Now I will input the coding into each device and verify the detonation codes. Then you can be on your way. We will have twenty jets landing in the next ten minutes to take each of you to your designated city. Good luck!"

Sheila was kneeling in front of the first satchel bomb, typing codes into the keyboard when Barsat returned and stood over her. "Is all of this really necessary, Sheila? It seems pretty extreme."

In one motion, she stood, removed her pistol and pressed it against his temple. "You've always been a damned coward, Barsat. Are you going to openly defy your own father? What kind of son are you anyway?"

"Shoot if you want, Sheila. We both know it won't accomplish anything, except my guards will blow you to pieces. Then the entire plan will fail and it will have been your fault."

Sheila glanced around the room and saw several soldiers aiming weapons at her. She slipped the pistol back into her purse, then kissed Barsat lightly on the lips. "I'm sorry that I overreacted, dear Barsat."

"I was only interested in your opinion, Sheila. Several of my brothers and cousins feel this escalation is misguided, although none of us would ever openly defy Bill."

She patted him on the cheek and replied, "I think we all wonder the same things, Barsat. But if no one will defy him, then we have no choice but to move forward and hope for the best."

"When all of these devices explode, millions will die, radiation will encircle the globe, and the world will plunge into a darkness that may last thousands of years. I just don't see how that helps us."

"It will be okay, Barsat. The radiation will likely kill me, but you will survive. The quarrel between Bill and Emmanuel has reached the boiling point and now must overflow into the lives of all people. There is no going back, Barsat," she reasoned. She tore the sheet of codes in half and handed one part to him. "Here, please give me a hand. I need to finish and get out of here in ten minutes."

§

"Josh!" Peter screamed.

Isabel rolled over and grabbed him. "What's wrong, Pete? Are you okay?"

"Josh!" he shouted again. The three Prospect men rushed into the room. Joshua sat next to Pete on the bed. "Oh my God, Josh! I just had another vision."

"What's happening?" Gabe asked.

"Everyone be quiet!" Joshua shouted. "Sit still, Peter and let me hold your head." Joshua took Pete's head in his hands and leaned forward to rest his forehead on Peter's. The two men sat quietly for several minutes before Joshua released him and rushed out of the room.

Gabe sat next to Pete and asked, "What was it?"

"Satori has twenty small nukes that he's planning to detonate all over the world," Pete sighed.

"What did you see, Pete?" Mike asked.

"It was Sheila Farness. She was somewhere in a desert and met a group of men inside a cave. She had a list of codes and sites. Then she typed the codes into each of the bombs."

"Peter, this is very important. Did you see the list?" Mike queried. Pete nodded. "Was San Diego on the list?" He nodded again as tears welled in his eyes. "Shit, we have to get you two out of town now!"

"What about the people?" Isabel asked. "You have to warn them to get away!"

"Isabel, we will do what we can to stop any of it from happening, but first of all, you and Pete have to get out of town now," Michael replied. "Gabe and I will leave you two alone so you can shower and get ready. Don't take too much time, okay?" The two men walked out of the room.

She took Pete's face in her hands and turned his head to face her. "Pete, are you sure that's what you saw?"

"Yes, I remember every detail," he sighed.

"Pete, was New York on the list?"

"Twice. I saw Manhattan and Queens."

"We have to do something, Pete. Can I call my friends and family?" she asked.

"Yeah, but try not to panic them. Make up some story about meeting up with us upstate somewhere. Tell them we're getting married there today or something that will make them leave quick, okay?" he asked. "I'll take my shower first while you do that. My only friends in New York are the Prospects and you, Isabel." He kissed her on the cheek and walked into the bathroom.

§

Two brilliant points of light flew through the night sky over a remote desert in Western China. After a moment, they plunged toward a single light source on the side of a hill. The elder Michael and Gabriel Prospect appeared in the cave. The guards opened fire, but the bullets bounced off of them. Michael waved his arm and the guards flew across the room and slammed into a wall. Barsat rushed them with a large blade and swung it at Gabriel's head. Michael reached out and grabbed the blade in his hand. "Barsat, you are a fool. Where are the others?"

"Long gone, you dolts!" Barsat shouted.

Michael surveyed the scene. Twenty guards and ten bombers huddled against a wall. The ten satchel bombs sat in a row on the opposite side of the room. He walked over to the weapons and examined them one by one. "Two megaton yield, I see. You father is a very bad man, Barsat. How can you help him with this? It's an abomination!"

"I can no easier defy my father than you can yours!" Barsat spat. "We'll get more weapons and there is nothing you can do to stop it."

Michael squatted next to one of the bombs and asked, "Is this the course you would have taken, Barsat?"

Gabriel walked over to join his brother. "Yes, Barsat, if you were in charge, would you have done this?"

"Of course, my father is never wrong!"

"Then why did you tell Sheila this action was misguided?" Michael asked.

"She told you that? I knew that bitch was trouble. She's a double agent, isn't she?" Barsat argued.

"No, Sheila is more loyal to your father than you, I think," Gabriel noted. "We have other sources of information."

"Ah, Pete Smith, I should have known," Barsat said. "That man will die very soon at my father's hands. Then this battle will be unleashed and you will have to fight."

"We'll leave that in God's hands," Michael said.

"I suppose you'll be taking my bombs then?" Barsat asked.

"I think not," Michael said. He typed four letters into the keyboard and pressed the red button.

The hillside was vaporized by the detonation, leaving a thirty-foot hole in the earth. Earthquakes shook towns and cities within a hundred miles, and the thick, black mushroom cloud rose quickly into the sky. The concussion blast raced across the desert, smashing and igniting scrub brush and tossing boulders through the air. The other bombs were blown to pieces before any more could detonate. Cities within a hundred miles could see the cloud rising in the sky, foreboding the end of the world.

Chapter 22

Pete and his group were standing next to the two SUVs. Gabe was showing some of the features of the car which Pete and Isabel would be taking out of town. Isabel was nervously looking around as though the nuclear blast could occur any moment. Joshua came out of the hotel and walked over to join them. He took Isabel's hand gently and led her away form the group. "Isabel, you need to calm down. You're making Pete nervous."

"Josh, we could all be blown up any second, and you want me to calm down?" she said. "My whole family could be dead already and I wouldn't know it."

"Your family is just fine now. My father is watching over them personally. He called your parents and said he was officiating at your wedding later today and offered to send limousines to collect them all," Josh said.

"Thank you, Josh."

"Don't thank me yet, Isabel. My brothers were able to destroy ten of the bombs before they started their trip, but we have no way of knowing which was headed where. Things are going to be very bad soon. You and Pete have to find a place to hide far from here, and Pete has to keep us informed of what Satori is doing. That means you'll have to do your share of driving and navigating. Stay out of big cities for now. Once the other ten bombs are out of the way, we'll know better where you can go."

"By out-of-the-way, you mean after they explode, right?"

"Isabel, we are looking for those men in all twenty cities on the list," Joshua said. "Maybe we can stop all of them. That's what we're trying to do."

"What do we do if we run out of gas or have car problems? I don't know if credit cards will mean anything after the bombs go off," she asked.

"First of all, the car cannot break down and doesn't need fuel. We have taken care of that. We have also placed stockpiles of currency and gold in the car just in case. Make sure Peter shows you everything so you can handle things if he has a vision," he replied.

"Josh, do you think this will all work out okay?"

He sighed and looked around the area. "I honestly don't know, Isabel. Satori has chosen a path that only leads to death and destruction. The end of the world may still come, no matter what any of us does."

"I still don't understand why any of this is happening?"

"My uncle honestly believes that people are basically evil, while my family sees the good in them. We've been sitting on the sidelines for ages watching to find out for certain. Good things happen and we think good is winning. Bad things like war and terror happen and Satori is convinced he is right. We are satisfied to let people grow in their own way. Now, I believe Satori sees that he is losing and wants to end the game once and for all by killing everyone," Joshua noted.

"Isabel, we're ready to go!" Pete shouted from the driver's seat of one of the vehicles.

"Joshua, I hope your side wins," she said as she hugged him.

He kissed her on the cheek and replied, "I'm afraid we're all going to lose now. Take care of Pete and yourself. Be well." She walked away and climbed into the passenger seat and buckled her seatbelt. Pete waved at the others and closed his door, pulling away from the curb and heading down the driveway and onto the streets of Coronado.

"Where to, Pete?" Isabel asked.

"Out into the desert, I think," Pete answered.

"Joshua said to avoid big cities for a while," she replied.

"What time is it now?"

"Just about 9:00 a.m."

"That gives us three hours until the remaining nukes go off," he said as he looked at her, far away on the long front bench seat.

"What's your plan?"

"I think we'll take Interstate 15 North toward Las Vegas. Neither Vegas nor LA were on the list, which makes perfect sense because LA is already smashed and Vegas is pretty small on a global scale," Pete said.

"There could be other events we don't know about."

"There isn't anything we can do about that, Isabel. We have to just keep moving and hope for the best."

"I don't feel very hopeful right now, Peter," she noted.

§

Ten miles outside Barstow, Isabel's cell phone rang. She pulled it from her purse and pressed the connect button, saying, "Hello?"

"I'm sorry about the plane crash, but Pete was supposed to be alone in his room," a male voice replied.

"What? Who is calling please?"

"This is Bill Satori, Isabel."

She held the phone against her chest and whispered to Pete, "It's Satori. What should I do?"

"Just find out what he wants to say and then hang up," Pete replied.

She put the phone to her ear and said, "Mr. Satori, how can I help you?"

"I want you to leave Peter Smith. I have no fight with you. If you stay with him, you will die with him, but that will be your decision, not mine," he said. "You have to know this is all about Peter. If he comes to me willingly, no further deaths and destruction need to occur."

"What about the nukes, you monster?" she shouted.

"There is still time to stop them, Isabel. Please listen to me. Peter Smith is an evil demon who will kill you himself soon. Don't trust him!"

"Why should I believe you?"

"All of this started when Peter moved to New York. Now he has drawn you into his web. You will be his next victim. I am willing to destroy the world to eliminate the stain he will make on humanity. It's up to you, Isabel," Satori said.

She closed the connection and turned to Pete. "He said you were the demon and not him. He said he would stop the end of the world if you surrendered yourself to him."

"What do you believe, Isabel?"

"I don't know anymore. It's the end of the world, Peter. None of this makes sense."

Pete slowed the vehicle down and stopped on the shoulder and motioned for Isabel to join him outside. It was brutally hot in the high desert with the sun almost at the zenith. The small city of Barstow, California, lay at the bottom of the slope in front of them. Pete opened the tailgate and opened a metallic box. He pulled out a pistol and checked to make sure it was loaded. Then he walked over to Isabel and handed her the weapon. "Isabel, redial Satori and tell him I have surrendered to you and where we are. Do it quick too, it's almost noon!"

Isabel was trembling and could not press any of the buttons. Pete walked over and pressed the redial for her. Seconds later, Satori's voice said, "It seems we were disconnected, my dear."

"Mr. Satori, Pete has surrendered to me. I have him covered with my gun. Please stop the nuclear attack."

"Of course, I have already stopped it when I saw you calling me. There is nothing to be afraid of, Isabel. Several friends of mine will be arriving at your location within ten minutes to take the monster from you. If he attempts to escape before they arrive, you must kill him, understood?"

"Yes, sir, if he attempts to escape, I'll shoot him," she said with tears streaming down her cheeks. "You swear the attacks have been stopped?"

"On my sacred word of honor, Isabel, the devices have been deactivated. My friends will reward you well. Goodbye," Satori finished as he closed the line.

"Pete, he said he has stopped the bombs and his friends are coming to collect you. Do you think he was telling the truth?" she asked.

"No. He was lying to get rid of me. Nothing else will change and his accomplices will kill us both," he said.

"How can I know for sure, Pete? The world might be destroyed, and I may have just helped the Devil win?"

Pete glanced at his watch, which read 11:58 a.m. "Isabel, it's two minutes to noon. When did he say his friends would get here?"

"Within ten minutes."

"We need to get back in the truck, Isabel. It's armored or something to protect us. You keep the gun on me. I'll get in the back while you get in the driver's seat, okay? Then turn on the radio so we can hear what's happening."

Once they were back inside, Isabel locked the doors and turned the engine on. A local station was playing country and western music. She was trembling violently and almost dropped the weapon several times. Pete sat quietly in the back with his head in his hands. "Pete, what am I supposed to do now?"

"That's up to you to decide, Isabel. If Satori upholds his bargain, then I don't mind if you give me to his thugs. If my life can save millions, it will have been worth it." He sat back and chuckled to himself. "You know, this is funny in a sick way. I was really falling for you, and now we'll be dead, or at least I'll be dead in a couple of minutes."

"I'm sorry, Pete," she replied. "I like you a lot too."

"Isabel, look at the clock. It's 12:02 p.m. If something was going to happen, it just did," he sighed.

A large group of motorcycles came up the freeway from behind them. They slowed and pulled onto the shoulder just in front of their truck. Four black SUVs pulled to a stop behind them. Several dozen men wearing black uniforms surrounded the vehicle. All were carrying machine guns, which were aimed at the windows. One yelled, "Good job, Isabel. We'll take Pete now and then you can go. Open the door!"

"Pete?"

"Just a few minutes more, okay Isabel?" he asked.

"Open the door, Isabel!" the man shouted as he tapped the barrel of his weapon against the glass. "No one needs to be killed here today. You have an agreement with Mr. Satori that you have to honor, Isabel!"

"Not yet, please!" Pete begged.

The group of men began to push on the vehicle until it was rocking violently. Pete and Isabel slid back and forth on the long bench seats. "Honor your agreement, bitch, or we'll kill you too!" one of the bikers shouted.

A loud tone sounded on the radio and an announcer interrupted the music saying, "This just in to our news desk. Nuclear explosions have just occurred in Queens, New York, and Miami, Florida. There are also reports of similar incidents in Sao Paulo, Brazil and Beijing, China. We will provide additional details as they become available. Repeating today's top story, at least four nuclear devices have been detonated around the world."

The men around the truck had stopped the shaking and stood quietly with their weapons pointed at Isabel. "You had your chance, Isabel. We'll see you in hell!" the biker said. All the men opened fire on the vehicle. The bullets ricocheted off the metal and flew back into the group of attackers. Seconds later, most were lying on the ground bleeding and screaming in pain. Compartments in the back bumper opened and rockets shot out and into the SUVs, which exploded in giant fireballs, with wreckage landing all over the road's surface. "Drive, Isabel!" Pete shouted as he climbed over the front seat and buckled himself in. She threw the shifter into gear and smashed the accelerator to the floor. The truck lurched forward, running over several men and smashing a dozen motorcycles until she managed to get it on the freeway and sped away.

Isabel was crying and weaving around on the road while trying to wipe the tears from her face. "I'm sorry, Pete. I don't know why I trusted that bastard. We almost died back there. How could I be so stupid?"

Pete looked out the rear window and could not see any of the attackers in pursuit. "Pull over, Isabel. Let me drive." She pulled over and removed her seatbelt. She was gasping for air and still trembling. Pete pulled her into his arms and hugged her tightly. He kissed her passionately and stroked her hair gently. "It's okay, Isabel. I meant it when I said I'd surrender to Satori if he stopped the attacks. He's fooled me before too. Remember that hundred million dollars that he gave me. At least, now we both know what we're dealing with."

"Thank you, Pete. I'll never mistrust you again," she smiled.

"Don't go too far; I'm no saint," he laughed as they switched seats and buckled in. He pulled back onto the empty freeway and headed north as several squad cars and ambulances flew southward on the opposite side of the freeway.

§

Miraculously, the device in New York City fizzled. While it did detonate, its radius of destruction was only a few hundred feet. No measurable cloud of radiation was detected. The UN ambassadors filled the general assembly to react to the attacks. Members were screaming and blaming one another for the destruction. Several Middle Eastern countries were massing troops near the Israeli border. The Israeli ambassador begged for calm while asserting his country would fight any invaders. Several fistfights broke out as neighboring states blamed each other for the carnage. Missing from the Assembly were the ambassadors from the five permanent member nations of the Security Council, who sat quietly around the table in their own chamber. All of their nations had been attacked, with the USA and China both hit by nuclear attacks. "I just don't know what to say," the US ambassador opened. "Who could be doing this?"

"I certainly hope you're not implying that one of us did this," the Russian ambassador said.

"Please, let us remain calm," urged the French ambassador. "None of our countries stands to gain anything from this destruction. We believe it is a terror network, likely aligned with Al Qaeda."

"Do you have any proof of that?" the US ambassador asked.

"All of this has occurred very recently, so there is no proof of anything at this time. Clearly, we need to focus on securing our own borders. It was only by random luck the device that detonated across the river did not incinerate us all."

"It is interesting to note that only the bomb in New York failed. Perhaps the Americans are behind this, trying to blame their enemies. I did not believe you were capable of such things, Ambassador," the Russian replied, pointing at the American.

"How dare you!" the American screamed. "We have had two nuclear blasts while your country had some hooligans running around in the subways."

"And only China has suffered a major attack in our capital," the Chinese ambassador grunted. "I wouldn't put it past any of you to do such things. Our armies are ready if you decide to attack us!"

"Gentlemen, please!" the American shouted. "The world is in flames and we must remain calm if we are to survive this. The world looks to us to take a reasoned approach and to avoid confrontation."

"The time for talk is through," the Russian said as he stood. "We will protect our motherland. I suggest each of you focus on that as well." He and the Chinese ambassador walked out of the room.

"That didn't go very well," the English ambassador said.

"But I'm afraid the Russian is correct," the French ambassador replied. "As long as our enemy has no face, we have no choice but to institute Martial Law and protect our own. I'm getting out of New York before the next bomb goes off." He shook hands with the other two and left the room.

"Carl, what do you think we should do now?" the American ambassador asked.

"David, I think we should pay a visit to Emmanuel Prospect," the other ambassador replied. Both men walked out of the room.

§

Carl Simpson and David Drake sat at the small table in the steakhouse, nursing their drinks. They looked around the room for any sign of danger. Smaller scale terror attacks were happening everywhere now. No city or village was safe anymore. All armies were put on full alert. Even the New York City Police wore full riot gear and carried automatic rifles as they walked and drove down the streets of the city. David looked at his watch. It was 8:30 p.m. and Emmanuel Prospect was half an hour late, which was totally unlike him. "He's not here yet and I'm worried," he said.

"May I join you?" said a man standing near their table.

"I'm sorry, this is a private dinner," Carl said.

The man sat down anyway. "Gentlemen, I'm Bill Satori."

"We know who you are, Mr. Satori," David replied. "As Carl said, this is a private dinner and we would prefer to be left alone if you don't mind."

Satori frowned at the two men across the table and then his frown melted into a broad smile. "In that case, I shall be brief. Manny is only a couple blocks away, and I'll try to finish before he arrives." The two ambassadors stared back at him blankly. "These are trying times for the governments of the world. I don't know if there have ever been such highly coordinated terror actions on a global basis. I fear nothing will stop it now. The terrorists have attacked several cities with impunity and your police and military seem powerless to stop them."

"It's only been a few hours, Mr. Satori. We will find them and destroy them soon enough," Carl said.

Satori chuckled and continued, "I'm afraid there will soon be too much blood and confusion to waste time looking for culprits. Your governments will be preoccupied with providing safety for the next wave, but they will fail and the cycle will repeat time and again."

"You seem to know a lot about what is going to happen, Bill," David noted.

"I am simply speculating, Mr. Ambassador," Satori smiled.

"As a government could speculate about the involvement of Satori Industries in such activities and freeze its assets?" Carl asked.

"I suppose that is a possibility," Satori affirmed. "But the time for money, business, and civilization is past, wouldn't you agree, Manny?"

The ambassadors had not noticed when Emmanuel Prospect had entered the restaurant and strolled over to their table. He sat on the empty chair between Satori and David. He sighed heavily and said, "No, I would not agree, brother. Your actions are heinous and you and your ilk will be punished."

"I'm shocked that you would accuse me of being responsible for the acts of terror!"

"We both know better, just as we both know your troops failed to kill or capture Peter or Isabel!" Emmanuel shouted.

Carl and David looked around to see if anyone else was hearing the shouted threats from the two men, but the rest of the room seemed separated from them, as though a wall of thin foggy glass had formed around their table. The other patrons were laughing and chatting away as though no one sat at the table.

"Well, I figured it would fail, but I had to try to separate Isabel from Peter."

"You would have killed them both, and you know it!" Emmanuel screamed.

"Gentlemen, perhaps we should tone this down," David begged.

"With all due respect, shut up and be quiet!" Satori barked. He then turned back to his brother and said, "The hour has almost arrived, Manny. The evil inside all men is about to be unleashed. Soon, the mushroom clouds will cover the planet and time will end for these pitiful creatures. The survivors will flood the streets and attack one another in their desperate attempts to obtain food and water. The society of man will revert to its original form, as barbarians out for their own interest and satisfaction. I will have won."

"Emmanuel, is what Satori says true?" Carl squeaked.

"It doesn't have to come to that, Carl. There is still time to defuse the situation and allow calm and sensibility to return. Time is our friend. These setbacks will become memories and mankind will continue," Prospect replied.

"Bah!" Satori shouted. "You might as well listen to my brother. His generous words and kind pats on your shoulders will allow you to sleep tonight. But tomorrow is another day." He stood and walked out of the restaurant and into a white limousine which then rushed away.

"Is that monster really your brother, Emmanuel?" David asked.

"In a way, we are all brothers, David, and I have known him longer than anyone. But he is gone now and we can have some dinner and talk about what we must do tomorrow."

"Things did not go well at the Security Council tonight," Carl said. "I'm afraid that Russia and China will no longer be involved in UN discussions. Their ambassadors have fled the city."

"Did you honestly think they would have stayed after the attack across the river?"

"It's not a matter of what Carl thinks, Emmanuel. We need to work together with them to lower the animosity in that building. They way things are going now, your brother might be correct," David replied.

"We will all do what we can. You need to believe that there is hope. I believe this will turn out for the best."

"Try telling that to the folks in Miami, Sao Paulo, and Beijing," Carl replied.

Chapter 23

Peter drove north on Interstate 15 through Las Vegas and then turned onto US Highway 93. Later he turned onto State Route 318 and headed into the wilderness that is central Nevada. It was getting dark when he pulled off the road and headed out into the unmarked scrub brush and hills. Isabel had calmed down as they were arriving in the outskirts of Vegas and now was sleeping in her seat. Pete found a suitable site halfway up a barren hill and turned the vehicle so it faced the roadway, several miles away. As he opened the door to reconnoiter the area, she woke up and asked him where they were. "Nowhere. That's where we are," he replied. "Joshua thought it would be best to stay away from towns and cities at night. I'm just going to look around."

"You're not leaving me here alone," she said as she opened her door and stepped out into the darkness. Pete walked around to the tailgate and opened it, removing two pairs of night-vision goggles and giving one to her. Then he pulled out a ladder and attached it to the rails on the roof of the vehicle. Both climbed up and sat on the roof and looked around to see if there was any activity on the desolate road.

"Pete, are we going to sleep in the truck?"

"Yes, there's an air mattress and sleeping bags in the back. There's also a port-a-potty when we need one. Tomorrow, we'll continue north until we find a town with a restaurant, although we do have food in the truck," he replied.

Isabel removed the goggles and set them on her lap. She rested her head on Peter's shoulder and put one arm around his back. "This is so surreal. Everything seemed so normal until I ran into you in the bar on Maui."

He laughed. "You're kidding, right? What about the car accident in the city?"

"It was just an accident, Peter, wasn't it?"

"I don't think so, Isabel. I think that was just another attempt on my life by Bill Satori."

"Why does he want to kill you? For your dreams?"

"At first, I think it was that," Pete replied. "Now, I can only see a few things and he is killing people everywhere. I can't really hurt him now. I think he just wants to piss off the Prospects."

"If I hadn't seen what I've seen, I'd say you were crazy, Peter Smith," she said as she kissed him on the cheek.

"We'd better get back inside the truck now!"

"What's wrong, Pete?"

"I have a really bad feeling that something is about to happen," he said as he pushed her toward the ladder. Two minutes later, both were lying down in the back of the secured truck with blankets pulled over their heads. "Are you okay, Isabel?"

"No! I'm scared out of my freaking mind," she replied.

"Maybe it was nothing," he started. "I think my imagination is getting the best of me now."

A massive explosion rocked the truck and filled the sky outside with intensely bright light. When it faded, all the scrub within miles was burning. Isabel was squeezing Pete tight, and both watched the fires all around. She screamed and Pete rolled over to see what she had seen. A ten-foot wooden post was sticking in the ground a few feet away. Joshua Prospect was nailed to the post with large spikes, one in the neck, one in the chest, one in the stomach, and more in each leg. He was gasping for breath and blood poured from his wounds. Pete opened a metal box and removed a machine gun and checked the ammunition supply. He was about to open the door to help his friend when he heard Joshua's voice in his ear. "Pete, do not get out of the truck! You and Isabel are safe there. Don't worry about me!"

Pete and Isabel were both crying as they watched Joshua groaning and twitching from his wounds. Something huge landed on the roof of the truck. The giant red beast jumped to the ground and put its face against the glass. "Come on, Peter, don't you want to save him? If you come out, I will make sure he survives. I swear it." Dozens of winged monsters began to land all around the truck. They pointed their gnarled fingers at the two inside the truck and laughed. "You see, even my children think you are a coward. Be a man, Peter Smith! Come out and fight me!" The winged beasts began to shake the truck back and forth. They pressed their faces against the glass and laughed at the two inside. It continued for a couple of minutes, until Satori shouted, "Enough!"

"This is your fault, Peter!" Satori shouted. He turned and walked over to Joshua who hung limply from the spikes. He ran an index finger down the river of blood on his chest and tasted it. "You had your chance, Peter." He turned and opened his mouth wide. A gusher of fire shot out and struck Joshua and the post. When he stopped, Joshua had been reduced to bones, which collapsed to the ground in a heap. The post continued burning.

The sky filled with white light, startling the beasts. Hundreds of bright points of light shot down from the sky and knocked the monsters from their feet. Now, hundreds of people wearing brilliant white clothes attacked the beasts with long silver swords. Several of the flying monsters were hacked to pieces before the remainder fled. Michael and Gabriel Prospect approached the vehicle, smiling at Peter and Isabel. "Can we come out?" Pete mouthed. The two men nodded.

The air around the vehicle was smoky and smelled of sulfur. Gabriel waved his arms over his head and a gentle rain began to fall. "I'm very glad you stayed in the truck," Michael said.

"But Satori killed Joshua. I should have done something!"

"Peter, everything is not as it would seem," Michael replied. "Neither Joshua nor any of the demons died tonight. That really isn't possible."

"So this is a dream?"

"No, it is not a dream, but it's a bit complicated to explain right now," Gabriel noted. "It's best to worry about more tangible things right now. There is a place north of here in Idaho where you must go now. It is remote and there is an encampment of friends there. You and Isabel can lie low there until things calm down."

"I can't endanger more people," Pete argued. "Look at what happened here! This is my fault. Imagine if this was the middle of a city or your encampment. I can't be responsible for more lives."

"Please, Peter, listen to reason. You have to do this, and you have to keep telling us about Satori's plans. You have already saved millions of lives today!" Michael said.

"I did?"

"Yes you did. There was another bomb that should have destroyed Rome, but we stopped the bomber before he could act," Gabriel replied.

"And the bomb in New York had a limited effect," Michael interjected. "We arrived just as the explosion started. My family was able to contain most of the blast and stop all the radioactivity. Neither of those victories would have occurred without your help. By the way, did you have a vision about this attack tonight?"

"It wasn't a vision actually. Isabel and I were up on the roof, and I had a feeling something terrible was about to occur," he said.

"That's excellent!" Michael replied. "Next time, press and hold the nine key on your phone. That will summon us immediately, okay?"

"I wish I knew what was going on," he said.

"I think you do, Peter. You just don't want to believe it yet," Michael noted. "You two should get some sleep now. I'll leave some men here to make certain you are not disturbed. You've got a big day ahead of you tomorrow."

§

Peter woke as the sun poured through the windows of the truck. Isabel was not there. He looked outside and realized they weren't in the wilderness anymore. The truck was parked in the lot for a small restaurant. He climbed out of the vehicle and walked around to the front of the building. When he looked in the window, he saw Isabel waving to him. She was sitting at a table with a man whose head was turned away from him. He went inside and walked over to the table and froze in shock. Joshua Prospect was sitting with Isabel. "But, Josh, you're dead!" he gasped.

"That's funny, I don't feel dead," Joshua laughed. "Pete, please sit down and have some breakfast."

After sitting, he turned to Isabel and said, "Did you drive us here?" She shook her head. "What's going on?"

"Pete, after what happened last night, we decided to give you both a head start and brought you here to Elko. You're a lot closer to Idaho so you don't have to drive as far," Josh noted. "Things have gone from bad to worse while you were sleeping. Did you have any dreams?"

"Nothing I can remember."

"I suppose that stands to reason. I don't think Satori was directly involved in anything that's happened. I believe your gift is a direct connection to him and not a general vision of occurrences in the world."

"What happened overnight, Josh?" Isabel asked.

The server approached and placed a plate of food and a cup of coffee in front of each. She frowned at Pete and walked away. Pete followed her with his eyes, wondering why she looked at him that way, but decided not to say anything.

"Ignore her, Pete," Joshua said. "Darlene is a bit of a psychic. She probably senses your connection to Satori." He held his hand over Pete's plate for a moment and then removed it. "The food's okay, go ahead and dig in."

"How did . . ." Pete started to say until Joshua flashed a smirk at him.

"Last night the Russians and Chinese decided the attacks were from Muslim fanatics. They are moving large military units to their borders with other central Asian countries. The Middle East is on fire. The Israelis blame Iran for the attack on Tel Aviv while the

Saudis blame Israel for the attack on Mecca. Armies all over the region are building on Israel's borders. Nothing can stop the next Middle Eastern war now," he said.

"This is insane!" Isabel exclaimed.

"It's to be expected, Isabel," Joshua replied. "The first duty of every government is to protect the people. If they think the enemy is over there, they go get them. But there's more. The EU is on the verge of collapse. Each country is closing their borders and buying arms as fast as they can. Even here, the army is now guarding both international borders, and battle fleets patrol both oceans and the Gulf of Mexico."

"So, it's over," Pete sighed. "Satori has won."

"The end of the world," Isabel gasped.

"Please eat your breakfast," Joshua urged them. "I have faith there is another way out. Remember what I told you about the violation of the place of atonement? I think that is why Satori has not stopped coming after Peter. None of us know why, but it was a contradiction of what must occur."

"So it's all about me again," Pete said.

"I'm afraid so, Peter. I just hope we figure out what it means before he gets to you," Joshua said.

Without them noticing, Darlene was approaching the table again and was scowling at Joshua. He looked up at her and smiled. "Yes, Darlene?"

She pointed at Peter and shouted, "How dare you bring the Beast into my restaurant? I can feel the evil pulsing through him and the sinister darkness that surrounds him."

"I'm no beast!" Pete exclaimed.

"Don't speak to me, demon!" she shouted as she pulled the crucifix from her blouse and pointed it at him. "Stay back!"

"Darlene, please let Peter touch your cross," Joshua demanded.

"The Beast wouldn't dare!" she growled. "He would be stricken down instantly and he knows that."

"Peter, touch Darlene's cross," Joshua said.

Pete reached out his hand very slowly. He could see the waitress was trembling in fear even though she maintained her stern expression. When his hand was an inch away, she gasped and held her breath. Pete took the cross in his hand and rubbed it gently. Darlene's scowl melted into a look of abject shock. "But I felt it, I really did," she moaned. "What have I done?"

"It's a beautiful cross, Darlene," Pete said as he released it and put his hand back on the table.

"I don't understand, Joshua. What happened to me?" she asked.

Joshua stood and put his arm around her back. "It's okay, Darlene, we have all felt that same presence within Peter. But it is not him. It's as though the Beast is connected to him in some way."

She looked at Peter with tears in her eyes. "I'm so sorry, sir. I've never been wrong before. I've made a fool of myself."

Pete took her hand for a moment and then released it. "Please don't be upset, Darlene. What you felt is real and I feel it too, all the time." The waitress smiled slightly, turned and walked back into the kitchen.

Isabel took a deep breath and exhaled. "Wow! I half expected Pete to burst into flames or something."

"Me too," Pete laughed.

§

"What is going on?" Sheila shouted.

"Calm down my dear," Satori replied.

"It took me a long time to gain the confidence of those men who died on the side of the highway two days ago! How am I supposed to get more to help if they keep being slaughtered?" she asked.

"I'm sorry, but I had to take a chance on Isabel turning him over to us," he argued. "The timing was just poor and it was my fault. If I would have called her sooner, they both would have been dead before the bombs went off."

She snarled at him and walked over to the bar, filling a glass with whisky, which she then swallowed. "I am so pissed off right now, Bill!"

"My dearest, what is really bothering you?" he asked. "I've never seen you so upset over a bit of blood. You know how the world is and where we are going. You can find as many cold-blooded killers as you could ever need. What is wrong?"

She covered her face with her hands and sobbed. He walked over to her and put his arms around her, holding her tightly. "There, there, Sheila. Please tell me."

"Bill, I'm really scared," she confessed. "You're trying to destroy the world! What happens to me when the air is radioactive? I'll die just like everyone else!"

"You know I won't allow that to happen, darling," Satori replied as he stroked her hair gently and kissed her neck. "If things get that bad, I'll marry you and you will be immortal like me, okay?"

She stopped crying and wiped the tears from her face. "Why not marry me now, Bill? Then I can stop being afraid."

"You can stop being afraid already. You have my word that I'll protect you more than all others, Sheila. But I want to save our wedding for after our great victory! You will prove to my family that you are worthy, and then they will all celebrate our nuptials."

"What can I do to gain their confidence, honey?"

Satori laughed. "You can kill Peter Smith, once and for all. And you might as well add that Garcia woman too. They both make me sick!"

"Tell me where they are and I'll go do it right now!" she exclaimed.

"No, the time is not yet right," he replied. "You know what happened in the desert with my sons? It was a slaughter and Peter still lives. But I can sense a moment of weakness approaching. We will destroy them both and anyone who tries to stop us!"

"Do you know where they are?"

"Yes, they are traveling north through Nevada, and I have a suspicion about their destination. My brother has an affinity with a group of people living lives of seclusion from the things of man. They are well protected by my nephews, but I am planning an all-out assault that will pull most of them away. When Peter is at the most vulnerable point, you will strike!" he shouted.

Sheila kissed him passionately. "It will be my pleasure, Master."

§

The sky over the border between Russia and Azerbaijan was lit with the first glimmers of sunlight when the line of Russian tanks surged across the border, headed south. The defense forces dropped their weapons and ran for the hills. Two thousand miles to the east, an even larger force of the Chinese army poured over the border and into Kashmir. When the invaded countries protested, the only response from the invaders was "we're just passing through." Further to the west, Bulgaria and Greece closed their borders with Turkey, inciting all three countries to move troops to the borders. To the south, a column of Syrian tanks approached the Golan Heights while a force of Egyptian troops and armor massed at the border with Israel. Hundreds of rockets took to the air landing randomly over the Israeli countryside. Two fleets of Russian warships left Odessa. The first blocked Turkish port cities while the second left some ships to secure the Bosporus, while the remainder sailed toward Syria and Egypt. In New York, the Director General of the United Nations begged for calm while insisting that any military actions get Security Council approval. None of the nations involved would reply.

Across the planet, small scale terror attacks raged. Car bombs exploded throughout Europe while groups of armed thugs robbed and killed civilians in North and South America. Poison gas attacks hit most major Asian cities while wildfires closed in on Sydney and Melbourne, Australia.

Barricades were set up throughout Washington, DC, and Army and Marine units patrolled the streets. Public schools were closed in most cities and millions stayed home from work to try to escape what was happening. All churches, mosques, and synagogues were overflowing with the faithful and newfound faithful, praying for an end to the bloodshed.

Pete and Isabel drove north. A few hours after leaving Joshua in Elko, they entered Twin Falls, Idaho. The streets of the small city were empty, as though the entire city had been evacuated. The only cars to be seen were police squad cars that seemed to sit on major street intersections looking for trouble. Soon, they were out of town again. Isabel was trying to find a station on the radio when a newscasters voice said, "Pakistan has filed a complaint at the United Nations for a violation of their territory by the Chinese Army. The President of Iran has issued a stern warning to the Russians and Chinese to stay out of their borders. There are sketchy reports of incursions into Israel by Egyptian and Syrian forces, although those reports have not been confirmed. On the local scene, the Mayor has asked residents of Twin Falls to shelter in place for the next seventy-two hours."

Isabel switched the radio off. "This is really it, Pete! I never dreamed anything like this could happen."

"Unfortunately, I have," he replied while watching the road ahead.

"Go north on Interstate 84 in two miles," the GPS system said.

"Where do you think we're headed, Pete?"

"I have an idea, but I hope I'm wrong," he replied.

"What do you mean?"

"I had a dream some time back where I woke up in a barracks inside a cave. I found you in the cafeteria and joined you. There was an attack and we were both killed," he said.

"I don't think Joshua would send us here to die. He could have let that waitress do it herself!"

Pete laughed and smiled at her. "She looked ready to do the deed, that's for sure." He slowed down and pulled over. "I'm bushed. Could you drive for a while, Isabel?"

"Sure, no problem." They switched seats and buckled in. She pulled out onto the road and Pete put his head against the doorframe and closed his eyes.

Chapter 24

The massive Chinese force easily smashed the Pakistani defenses. Pakistan threatened nuclear retaliation, but knew a nuclear strike from China would kill most of their people. As the Pakistanis fell back, the Chinese surged forward on a direct line for Islamabad. Flights of bombers flew ahead to soften the defenses and demoralize the citizenry. Entire neighborhoods in the capital city were burning, and the highways to the south were clogged with refugees.

The Russian Army fought tough resistance from elements of the Iranian Revolutionary Guards, making scant progress on their race toward Tehran. Several Russian destroyers guarded the fleet as it moved southward along the Caspian Sea. A few ships moved further south to bombard nearby cities and any columns of reinforcements attempting to reach the front lines.

Rockets rained down on Israel from both the Gaza Strip and Lebanon. The Iron Dome stopped about half, but villages were burning and riots broke out across the West Bank. Halfway between Beirut and the Israeli border, a terrorist accidentally detonated the satchel nuke he was carrying. All buildings within a five-mile radius were incinerated or vaporized by the blast. The Lebanese government condemned Israel for the strike. Egyptian tanks rolled across the Israeli border but were quickly pushed back by the superior firepower of the IDF.

Ten infantry divisions led by tank battalions surged across the DMZ into South Korea. Stealth bombers from the USA were launched to soften the attack while the South Koreans tried to stop the enemy from reaching Seoul. The North Korean leader swore he would reunify the peninsula under his leadership or all of Korea would face nuclear destruction.

Peter Smith had slept through it all with no visions. He only woke when Isabel shook his left arm. He opened his eyes and saw four men wearing camouflaged fatigues standing in front of the truck with automatic rifles pointed at them. They had pulled up to a massive fence with razor wire on the top edge. "Where are we, Isabel?" he asked.

"The GPS said we were at our destination, but I don't like the looks of this," she replied.

Pete looked carefully at the four and then his eyes opened wide. "I know two of those guys." He opened the door and climbed out. He walked over to two of the men and shook their hands and then waved to Isabel to join them. She reluctantly opened the door and climbed out. All four men had slung their weapons over their shoulders. "Isabel, this is Sam and Bob. They work for the Prospect Enterprise."

"I'm Isabel Garcia. How do you do?" she said.

"We've been waiting for you two," Bob replied. "Let's get back in your truck and we'll tell you where to stow it." After getting in, Sam drove through the gate and down a gravel road. Looking out the back, Pete could see the other two men closing the gate again and moving out of site of any passersby. "Pete, Gabe wanted me to ask if you've had any other dreams."

"No, not at all. Did something else happen?"

"The planet is coming apart at the seams," Bob said. "There's been more fighting and a few more nuclear blasts over the last several hours."

"I guess that means Satori isn't directly involved. Perhaps we've reached critical mass and nothing will stop it now," Pete replied. The gravel path left the forest and crossed a wide grassy field, which ended at a bridge. The river had dried out, leaving a muddy ravine in its place. Steep mountains rose above them and the truck began to climb up the side of one. "What is this place, Bob?"

"Shangri La!" Sam laughed.

"Granddad thinks this place is just remote enough to survive the end of the world," Bob said. "I hope he's right. The Prospect

Enterprise built this in the 1920s as a retreat from the rat race. Now it's more like an arsenal and hideout." The truck continued up the slope, which was becoming quite steep. "The Prospects are gathering people and equipment to stop or survive the war."

"But won't Satori build his own army and come here to kill us all?" Pete asked. "I had a vision some time back when I was in a giant cave when these soldiers came in and killed everyone, including Isabel and me."

"I hope not," Sam said.

The truck pulled into the opening of the cave. The chamber was very large and several concrete buildings had been constructed to house the residents. "Oh shit! This is the place from my dream," Pete gasped.

"Are you sure, Pete?" Isabel asked.

"It's identical in every detail. That building over there is where I woke up. The one next to it is a cafeteria when I joined you for breakfast," he replied.

"Do you remember anything else?" Bob asked.

"No."

"Well, then it can't be helped," Bob replied with a shrug. "I'll talk to the commander and let her know. Perhaps she can increase the defensive perimeter during the morning hours, or something. Let's get you two unloaded."

Several other troops unloaded the truck which was filled with several dozen rockets, thousands of rounds of ammunition and hundreds of pounds of gold. At Pete's recommendation, the empty truck was used to partially block the entrance to the cave due to its relative indestructibility. While Sam took Isabel to get them assigned to bunks, Bob and Pete walked over to the commander's office, which was far at the back of the cavern for security, to discuss his vision.

§

Satori, Barsat, and Narga were laughing uproariously in Satori's living room. Each had a bottle of whisky in front of him. Sheila Farness scowled at them as she crossed the room and sat next to Bill. "Please let me in on the joke, Bill."

He wiped the tears from his eyes and put his arm around her shoulders. "Don't you see, my darling? We have won!"

"How so?"

"None of us have done anything all day long and the humans are killing and hating each other like never before. We reached the tipping point and now civilization is heading back to the Stone Age where it should have remained," Bill replied. "My brother thought they would discuss their issues, come to a reasoned solution and find peace. What a moron!"

"What about Peter Smith?" she asked.

"I'm glad you brought him up, dear. Narga, tell Sheila about your pal, Peter."

Narga swallowed a gulp of liquor from his bottle and said, "Peter is in Idaho at a place the Prospects think is safe. Soon we will launch an attack there and kill every man, woman, and child."

"And that's where you come in, my dear," Satori interjected. "We believe they have around five thousand people there. I need you to gather a larger force and converge on that site as soon as possible. If Peter survives the initial onslaught, I want you to be the one to kill him."

"How much time do I have, Bill?"

"Two or three days at the most, I think," Bill replied. "While the world is burning today, there is always the chance that Peter will turn the tide with his stupid dreams. If we wait too long, the UN actually might become useful and convince world leaders to stop fighting. We cannot afford for that to happen."

"Wouldn't it be simpler to have your boys here go there and destroy them?" Sheila asked.

"That's what I said!" Barsat shouted.

Satori stood and began to pace back and forth. "No, I don't think that's a good idea. If the humans do all the fighting, we will prove our point and not signal the Prospects to join the battle. If they become involved again, Peter may well survive and all of our plans would be at risk. I want my family to stay on the sidelines for now."

"I think you are taking too much risk if you leave it to the humans completely," she noted. "Perhaps there is another way."

Satori sat back on the couch and put his hand on her knee. "Please go on."

"Humans are basically cowards, Bill." Narga and Barsat nodded their heads in agreement. "Generals don't mind sending soldiers to their deaths, but when their own lives are at stake, they will sue for peace. Perhaps one of your children can join the circle of command in each military now fighting. They wouldn't give any orders, but they could influence and inspire the generals to keep fighting by appealing to their basest instincts."

Narga and Barsat sat slack-jawed. "That's brilliant!" Bill shouted. "They just feed into the mistrust and fear of their enemies and keep stirring the pot. Fantastic job, Sheila. Make it so, boys!" The two demons disappeared in a swirl of black smoke. Bill offered his bottle to Sheila, who took a long drink and passed it back. "Now I have another reason to love you, Sheila. You have just sealed the fate of this planet." He pulled her into his arms and kissed her passionately.

"I will do anything to serve you, Master," she replied.

"In the morning we'll go to Tiffany's to pick a ring, my darling," he said as he lifted her into his arms and carried her out of the room.

§

Peter woke in the middle of the night. Someone was gently shaking him. In the dark, he could see Emmanuel Prospect standing over him. "Peter, please come with me," the old man said as he turned to walk away. Pete looked over at Isabel in the next cot. She was sleeping and snoring very softly. He smiled at her and climbed out of bed, hurrying to catch up to the other man. Granddad walked into the mess hall and grabbed a cup of coffee and then took a seat. Pete got his own coffee and joined him.

"What are you doing here, Granddad?"

"I missed you, Peter," he said. "So much has happened and nothing for the good. Too many people are being slaughtered and blown to bits by bombs. I feel so bad for them."

Pete took a sip of coffee and replied, "Can you stop this craziness, like you stopped the Satori clan in the desert?"

"I'm afraid we do not interfere in people's decisions. If Satori is directly involved, we can act. Other than that, people have to figure these things out for themselves," Emmanuel sighed.

"Even if they destroy the world?"

"Humanity was given hegemony over this planet, Pete. This is the place where you are born, live, make your choices, and ultimately die. My family and Satori's try to influence people to make certain decisions, but only a human can decide."

"The two doors, right?"

"It has always been so, Peter. Unfortunately, many are choosing poorly at the moment. We are working with governments around the world to stop this madness. All of this is just beginning. It could end in a second, or last a thousand years."

"How long do you think it will last, Granddad?"

Emmanuel chuckled and said, "I'd rather know what you think, Peter? You are one of the folks who will be making decisions, after all."

Pete looked into the distance and thought a moment about the state of the world. "I think it will end soon, Granddad. Right now, everyone is very emotional and caught up in the anger of explosions and invasions. Soon, they will realize that war is an abomination and find a way to stop it."

Emmanuel patted Pete's hand. "I hope you're right, Pete. If more people thought like you, it never would have happened."

"Thank you, Granddad," Pete smiled.

Emmanuel's expression became very stern. "Peter, I want you to know that Satori is building an army to come here and attack this place."

"I saw that in my dream."

"I know, and now you have more choices to make. You and Isabel could flee and avoid the battle."

"But he will keep coming until he kills me, won't he?" Pete asked. Emmanuel nodded his head. "Is he sending his army of monsters?"

"No, he won't make that mistake again. He wants my family to stay out of it."

"Then I think I'll stay here," Pete said. "There is no sense going somewhere else to die. These folks are going to be attacked, but it can end here and no one else will have to suffer."

"The world is on fire, my boy."

"I still think that will change soon, Granddad," Pete replied. "Do you know when Satori's army will arrive here?"

"The day after tomorrow, I presume," the old man said. "You don't plan to surrender yourself to them, do you?"

"No, but since there will be no demons among them, I do plan to negotiate to end all of this," Pete replied.

"I have faith in you, Peter Smith," Emmanuel said.

"Granddad, I need to ask you a few questions," Pete began.

Emmanuel held up his hand and stood. "I'm sorry, Peter, but I think I know the questions and cannot answer them now. Perhaps in two days we can chat."

"If I'm still alive."

"Either way." He turned and walked away. Gradually, the old man began to fade away. By the time he reached the door, he had completely disappeared.

Pete sat quietly looking at the door when Isabel pulled it open and walked in. She walked over and sat where Granddad had been sitting. "Pete, I woke up and you were gone."

"I had a visit from Emmanuel Prospect," he replied.

"I didn't know he was here."

"Well, he's gone now and it's kind of a long story," he replied.

She reached out and grabbed his hands and stood up. "Come on, the sun will be up soon and I want to watch it rise with you." They walked out of the mess hall hand in hand and left the cavern and walked until they came to an overlook toward the east and sat down on a large rock.

He put his arm around her shoulders and pulled her close. Isabel nestled her head on his shoulder and sighed. "Pete, this place is so beautiful. How long do you think we'll be here?"

"Another couple days, I guess," he replied.

"Only two more days? Why?"

"Satori is building an army to come and kill us," Pete said.

She stood up and glowered at him. "Two days! Is that all we have?"

"We have to try to reason with the enemy," he said.

"We can reason with those flying monsters?"

"It won't be them. It will just be people like you and me," Pete finished as the first rays of sunlight illuminated the horizon.

§

Peter was standing inside a prefabricated building. The air conditioning was on high and he could feel the goose bumps on his arms. He looked at his body and saw he was still wearing the tee shirt and shorts he had worn to bed. The walls of the room were lined with soldiers looking at computer screens. There was a large table in the center of the room where a group of high-ranking officers were looking at a map. No one seemed to take any notice of him, so Peter figured this must be another dream. He walked over to the table and listened to the conversation. At first, the words seemed foreign, but gradually the sound changed into English inside his head. "General Aleed, we must regroup and ask for reinforcements," a man said.

"What are you blathering about, Ibrahim," Aleed began, "clearly our tanks are no match for the Israelis. Our men were like sitting ducks out there. You want us to send more men to their deaths. This is a battle we cannot win."

"Are you suggesting we retreat?" another general said.

"No, of course not, General Ali," Aleed replied. "But we must realize that if we invade, our forces will just be pushed back again."

"We have to bring overwhelming odds to the fight, General Ali," Ibrahim barked. "They have fewer tanks than we do, and the Syrians have vowed to invade soon to avenge the nuclear attack in Lebanon. That will pull more tanks from our front and we can take them out!"

Aleed laughed. "I can't believe you think the Israelis detonated that device, Ibrahim. It blew up a few villages and burned some trees. That does not seem like one of their surgical strikes to me. If Beirut or Damascus were in flames, perhaps I would believe Israel launched the attack."

"At a minimum, we need to invade Gaza to add their forces to our own," Ibrahim said. "There are many there who would love the chance to invade Israel. We can't just sit here and lick our wounds."

As the soldiers continued to argue, Pete's eyes kept being drawn to Ibrahim. Pete had never known any Egyptians, but there was something very familiar about that man, although he could not be certain.

"Perhaps if the Syrians invade and distract the Israelis, we will have a chance," Ali offered.

"And we could launch some airstrikes to test their defenses," Aleed suggested.

"That's risky," Ali countered. "We know the Americans give Israeli their best weapons and save the second rate goods for us. The Great Satan would never give us an advantage over them."

"I just can't believe my ears," Ibrahim said. "This is the one chance in our lifetimes to reclaim Palestine and you two are whining about the risks."

"You'd better watch your tongue," Aleed scowled. "All of us would love to roll into al-Quds and eliminate the pestilence there, but how many of our brothers must die to pursue that dream?"

Ibrahim walked between the two men and put his hands on their shoulders. Pete could have sworn his eyes flashed red as he said, "Every last one, if that's what it takes."

One of the soldiers monitoring a computer screen turned and said, "Generals, the Syrian Army has crossed the Golan Heights!"

"When will the reinforcements arrive?" Ali asked.

"Within the hour, sir," Ibrahim replied.

"Well, it looks like you might get your wish, Ibrahim. May God have mercy on our souls," Aleed said.

Pete opened his eyes. He had fallen asleep next to the stone he and Isabel had been sitting upon. She was nowhere to be seen. He pulled his phone and pressed and held the nine key. "Hello, Peter, it's Michael. What's up?"

"Michael, I had a vision. I was in a command center for the Egyptian Army near the border with Israel. The generals were deciding what to do next, but there was another soldier there who kept telling them to attack."

"Okay, what do you think that means?" Michael asked.

"Michael, I don't think it was a man. I think it was the demon Narga in disguise. I recognized his face," Peter reported.

"Very well, I understand and will tell my father as soon as we hang up. Take care of yourself, Peter," Michael said as he disconnected.

Peter stood up, stretched and walked back to the cave to find Isabel.

Chapter 25

Twenty-four hours had passed since the North Korean Army invaded South Korea. Seoul had been captured, but the onslaught by the North stopped five miles south of the city. Both sides were fortifying and adding reinforcements to their positions. Then something strange happened. The UN Security Council, in a rare act of unanimity, voted to condemn the actions by the North. Ten thousand Chinese tanks crossed the North Korean border and headed south, followed by one hundred thousand soldiers. A squadron of fifty stealth bombers dropped ordnance on the front lines of the North, forcing them to fall back into the city. A few hours later, Pyongyang fell, and the North Korean President was forced to surrender.

Bill Satori was seething with anger. He stomped around his living room, grabbing pieces of furniture and smashing them against the walls. Barsat cowered in a corner of the room, covering his head with his arms to avoid his father's wrath. Sheila had fled for her life when Bill heard the news from the Korean Peninsula. When most of the furniture was destroyed, Bill panted for air and walked over to the bar, removed a bottle of Jack Daniels, and chugged it down. He looked around at the devastation and saw his son crouched down in the corner. "I'm sorry, Barsat," he began. "Please come over here and get drunk with your old man." He chuckled. The young man walked over, gingerly stepping over piles of wood, upholstery, and shards of glass. Bill removed two more bottles of whisky and handed one to Barsat.

"What do you think happened there, father?" he asked.

"Narga was uncovered," Bill said. "He made the mistake of being videotaped with President Kim. One of the Prospects saw him and proved he was one of us to the President of China and the Security Council. I'm sure they showed the proof to the North

Korean soldiers as well. Once China knew the truth, they convinced Russia to join them, and the rest is what it is."

"Peter Smith told them, didn't he?" Barsat asked.

Satori took a long drink from his bottle and replied, "Who else? I need that bastard dead now!"

"I'll do it, father!"

"No, son, we must find a way to get another human to do it or the damned Prospects will interfere. Is Sheila here?"

Barsat shook his head. "She ran for cover when you blew up."

"I can't say that I blame her," Satori laughed. "Please go find her and ask her to forgive me. Also tell her that I want her army in Idaho tomorrow, not the day after. With Peter confounding our actions, the sooner he's dead the better."

In a puff of smoke, a winged monster appeared in the room. He held his head down and was trembling as he said, "It wasn't my fault, father. I swear it wasn't."

Bill smiled and walked over to the monster with his bottle in his hand, which he offered to it. "Narga, I know you did your best, and I still love you. There was nothing else you could do."

"Thank you father," Narga said, and then took a drink of whisky. "What can I do to help now?"

"Gather your brothers," Satori said. "There is a chance that Sheila and her army will fail. We need an overwhelming force to make sure Peter Smith dies tomorrow. If we face retribution from the Prospects, so be it. Peter must die."

§

General Ali climbed out of his Humvee and walked over to the portable command post and went inside. All the soldiers stood up and saluted. He saluted in return and walked over to the large table. "Aleed, it's good to see you again," he said.

"General, welcome to the front lines," General Aleed replied as he shook the other's hand. "This man is Colonel Ibrahim, my attaché." The two men shook hands. "I'm afraid the news is quite bad, sir. Our tanks did not stand a chance against the Israelis. The Americans have also given them A-10 Warthogs. We had to retreat or be annihilated."

"So, what's your recommendation?" Ali asked.

"I see no choice but to stay on our side of the border now," Aleed sighed.

"General Aleed, we must regroup and ask for reinforcements," Ibrahim interjected.

"What are you blathering about, Ibrahim," Aleed began, "clearly our tanks are no match for the Israelis. Our men were like sitting ducks out there. You want us to send more men to their deaths. This is a battle we cannot win."

"Are you suggesting we retreat?" Ali said.

"No, of course not, General Ali," Aleed replied. "But we must realize that if we invade, our forces will just be pushed back again."

"We have to bring overwhelming odds to the fight, General Ali," Ibrahim barked." They have fewer tanks than we do, and the Syrians have vowed to invade soon to avenge the nuclear attack in Lebanon. That will pull more tanks from our front and we can take them out!"

Aleed laughed. "I can't believe you think the Israelis detonated that device, Ibrahim. It blew up a few villages and burned some trees. That does not seem like one of their surgical strikes to me. If Beirut or Damascus were in flames, perhaps I would believe Israel launched the attack."

The command center was filled with a blinding light. When it faded, the elder Gabriel Prospect was standing in the room. The soldiers pulled their handguns and pointed them at him. Gabriel began to glow from within. He became brighter until he seemed more vision than actual man.

"What is the meaning of this? Who the hell are you?" Ali shouted.

"I am Gabriel and I am here to tell you that you are being used," he replied. He looked around the room until he saw Ibrahim cowering in a corner. He pointed at him and said, "This man is an imposter!"

"What are you talking about?" Aleed asked. "Ibrahim has been with me for years. I know his parents!"

"Get out of here, Prospect!" Ibrahim hissed. "You are nothing here."

Gabriel laughed and walked over to General Aleed and gently touched his forehead. "That man has clouded your mind with lies, Mohamed. Think carefully about how long you have known him."

"I've never seen that man before," Aleed admitted. "Who is he anyway, Gabriel?"

Gabriel walked over to Ibrahim who shouted, "Stay away from me, Devil! Men, shoot him!"

"Belay that order!" General Ali commanded.

As Gabriel approached, Ibrahim's eyes began to glow red. His body twitched and contorted, with his skin reddening and becoming rough and scaly. By the time Gabriel was next to him, Narga had emerged as a giant red monster with bat-like wings. "You will pay for this, Prospect!" Narga shouted. He threw the soldier next to him across the room and smashed through the wall of the command center. Once outside, he stretched his wings and flew away. The soldiers were frozen in surprise as the giant beast flew across the sky.

The light in Gabriel faded and he turned to see the soldiers on their knees before him. "Please stand up," he said. "There is no need for that. I am here to help you." He helped General Ali to his feet.

"Are you an angel from God?" the general asked.

Gabriel smiled and said, "I am your friend. I am here to stop the war. The beast was here to incite you to fight, but he had no desire to see you win or even survive. He only wanted death and destruction to prove humans are not worthy."

"You're not suggesting we surrender to Israel, are you?"

"No. You are all intelligent people, and you must know all the terrible things happening around the world right now. That isn't normal. The beast that was here and his kind are trying to destroy the world. I want you to negotiate for peace with Israel. You know your forces cannot defeat them. By attacking, you are only sacrificing your own loyal soldiers who will die with no hope of success."

"We can never have true peace with Israel, even you know that!" Ali exclaimed.

"Well, let's leave that to time to resolve. I would like to believe all men can live as brothers. At this time, people are being coerced into fighting for an immoral cause. Once things return to normal, then the governments of the world can decide what they will do," Gabriel noted.

"That seems fair," Ali agreed, "but the final decision must come from Cairo."

"Yes, I understand that," Gabriel replied. "My only purpose here was to unmask the beast. Be happy and enjoy your life." He faded away until the soldiers were standing alone in the room.

§

Peter walked back into the cavern and saw Isabel talking on her phone. He walked over and stood in front of her. She smiled and motioned for him to wait. He heard his own phone ring and pulled it from his pocket and pressed the connect button. "Hello Granddad, how are you?"

"I couldn't be better, Peter," Emmanuel said. "I want you to know you have helped us a great deal. Millions more lives have been spared from Satori's wrath."

"That's great, Granddad!" he replied. "What happened? I haven't seen any news here yet today."

"Egypt and Israel have signed a cease-fire. North Korea was defeated by the Chinese. Both China and Russia are withdrawing their forces to their own territory. In every case, one of Satori's children was inciting the fighting."

"I'm glad I could help, Granddad," Pete said, smiling broadly.

"I'd better let you go now. I think Isabel wants to talk to you," Emmanuel said. Pete looked up and saw her standing in front of him. "But one more thing first, Peter. Satori's army will arrive at your location tomorrow. Things have changed since we spoke last. Goodbye." The line was disconnected.

"What's wrong, Pete?" she asked. "You looked like the happiest man in the world until ten seconds ago."

"Satori's army will be here tomorrow, not the day after," he said.

Isabel threw her arms around his neck and held him tight. "I guess there's not much time, Pete, and I have a million things to say to you." She took his hand and led him toward the back of the cavern. She opened a door and led him into a small conference room and closed the door. Isabel kissed him passionately. "So this is it, huh, Peter? I just met you and now we're going to die."

He kissed her face and caressed her hair. "We don't know that, Isabel. We could come out of this just fine. We have to have faith!"

"You're not the only ones with dreams, Pete!" she cried. "When you fell asleep outside, I took a nap too. I saw us in the middle of a muddy ditch. There were dead bodies all around. The air stank of death and sulfur. Then there were those winged monsters surrounding us. We both died in my dream, Peter!"

"Isabel, I had a dream like that some time ago too, but you weren't there. I woke up in the ditch with four bullet holes in my chest. It was unreal, but you were not there," he replied. "Maybe you should get out of here, Isabel. I don't want anything to happen to you."

She sighed heavily and put her head on his shoulder. "I'm not leaving you, Pete. I know the timing stinks, but I'm in love with you." She looked up and tears were streaming down her face. "I'm willing to face death for you."

He kissed her and held her tight. "I love you too, Isabel, but for my sake, please get out of this place. According to Emmanuel Prospect, the situation is improving around the world. This whole mess will be over soon. But Satori won't give up while I'm breathing. You have your whole life ahead of you."

"You really think he'll stop when you die?" she asked. "I think we've had this conversation before, Pete. The universe doesn't revolve around you. Maybe we should both leave this place."

"Please sit down," he said as he pulled out two conference chairs. After they sat, he put his hands on her knees. "I wish it was that simple, Isabel. Do you remember when Michael told us how my trip to the place of atonement should never have happened?" She nodded. "Something happened there, and now Satori and I are linked in some way. Either he or I have to die to break the link. Unfortunately for me, he is immortal."

"I need you, Pete. Please run away with me! I'm begging you!" Isabel cried. "Don't believe everything the Prospects tell you. Maybe they're wrong!"

"Isabel, I love you very much, but this is my fate. I have faith that everything will be okay. If I run away, Satori will kill most of these people. Then he'll find my hiding place and kill everyone there too. Every time I run, I'll be condemning many others. I can't live with that," he said. "Please save yourself."

"What do we do now?"

"First we have to tell the commander about the attack tomorrow. Then, let's get some breakfast. I'm starving."

§

It was just before dawn in the bleak desert landscape and Satori, the giant beast, was pacing back and forth at the edge of a cliff. Sheila was standing ten feet behind him with Narga and Barsat. Fifty feet below, at the base of the cliff, an army of tens of thousands of giant winged monsters stood waiting patiently.

Torches were positioned around the crowd and on top of the cliff, providing an eerie glow. Satori did not acknowledge any of the crowd and seemed lost in his own thoughts. None dared interrupt his concentration and they stood quietly waiting. The first rays of light began to illuminate the horizon and Bill seemed energized by it. He raised his head and waved his arms to welcome his family. The crowd began to whoop and cheer madly. After several minutes of cheering, he raised his arms again to quiet the group down so he could speak. "Good morning, my children," his voice bellowed.

"Good morning, Father," they chanted in unison.

"As we all know, we have been stymied at every step by the Prospects and their prophet, Peter Smith," he said. The crowd booed and hissed and screamed for Peter's death. Satori smiled and motioned for quiet again. "Well, my children, we all feel the same way. I do apologize to those of you where were revealed by the Prospects, but in truth, that was the best thing possible! For too long, the stupid humans have fought each other and made statues to their leaders and adored their celebrities because they thought the universe belonged to them. Now they know differently!"

The crowd cheered and several thousand took wing and flew around the area cajoling their comrades to fight. Bill waved and they quieted again. "Today, we begin in earnest to destroy their fragile civilization. Today, we take the fight to the Prospects. Win or lose, the battle now belongs to the immortals!" Bill watched contentedly while his family cheered and danced in joy. "Some of us have a singular goal today. My fiancée, Sheila Farness, will lead an army to kill Peter Smith. Sheila, please come up here." She walked forward and stood next to him. The audience was dead silent. None of them would trust such an important task to a mere mortal. "I know what you're thinking," Satori sneered. "We all know that the Prospects will not interfere with human conflict, unless we become directly involved. Sheila has executed her responsibilities perfectly. I have little doubt she will succeed." He bent down and kissed her on the head and motioned her to move back. "In the event she fails, a group of you will accompany me to finish the job. No matter what else happens today, none of you can relent until Peter is dead!"

Minutes of wild applause and cheering filled the desert as the sun started to cross the horizon. Satori motioned for quiet. "Your brother, Barsat, will now take Sheila to her army. Then he will join my team. Each of you has been assigned to a target or to a team for a larger target. Your job is to cause as much disruption, death and destruction as you can! You will draw the Prospects away from Idaho. If Sheila's army fails, you will redouble your efforts. When the Prospects are as stretched out as far as possible, I will finish Peter Smith myself! I love you all and wish you the best of luck!"

The group took to the air, howling and shouting and play-fighting among themselves. Barsat took Sheila in his arms and flew north. Narga and Satori flew down the cliff and joined in the revelry.

Chapter 26

Peter woke up in his bunk. He rolled over and noticed Isabel's bunk was empty. In his heart, he prayed she had left. He climbed out of bed and walked out and into the cavern. He crossed quickly to the mess hall where he saw Isabel waving to him. He turned and ran out of the room. He ran up to a fire alarm panel and pulled the lever. Sirens wailed and people rushed out. "This is it!" he shouted. "The attack is coming!"

Two helicopter gunships raced toward the cave opening with their Gatling guns firing. Bullets flew through the air and everyone dived for cover. Pete jumped into the SUV and started the engine. He spun it around so the rear was facing the cave opening. Panels in the back opened and two rockets screamed away. The helicopters turned hard to escape, but both were destroyed by the exploding missiles. In the cave, soldiers donned their Kevlar vests and helmets, grabbing rifles and pistols and headed out of the cave.

Pete was strapping on his Kevlar vest when Isabel ran up and threw her arms around his neck, kissing his face. "Pete, promise me that you won't forget me, no matter what happens!"

"I promise I'll never forget you, Isabel," he replied and then kissed her again.

"You two get to the back of the cave!" Commander Jackson shouted.

"I'm sorry, Cindy, but I can't do that," Pete replied. "We have to contact them and sue for peace."

"They don't look ready to give up yet, Pete. If you're not going to hide, then get out there and start shooting!" she replied.

"I've got another idea," he said as he grabbed Isabel's arm and pulled her toward the SUV. "Get inside!" he shouted.

"What are you doing, Pete?" she asked as she buckled herself in.

"Cindy's right, you know," he replied. "They're never going to surrender if they think they can kill me or win. Let's show them what they're up against." He slammed the truck into drive, spun it around and headed out of the cave.

The soldiers had reached their emplacements and were firing down on the advancing army. From this view, it looked like ten thousand or more were coming with tanks, artillery, and more helicopters. Pete raced down the hill. Small arms fire ricocheted off the metal. The truck dropped into a ditch and came up the other side twenty feet in front of a tank, which fired a high explosive round from point-blank range. The projectile exploded as it struck the windshield. Pete and Isabel froze. The smoke cleared and the SUV smashed into the front of the tank. The truck and windshield were undamaged. The tank tried to back away to fire again. The tank commander manned the machine gun on the turret and fired at the truck. Bullets bounced off and in all directions, killing several soldiers nearby and the commander.

The truck lurched forward and began to pass between two tanks, which turned their main guns to attack. Pete slammed down on the accelerator just as they fired, and the crossfire destroyed the two tanks. Soldiers dived for safety out of the way of the truck.

More tanks turned to join the chase when they started taking incoming rounds from the artillery outside the cave entrance. Two tanks were now in pursuit. Their machine guns were firing nonstop. But their rounds bounced off and struck their own forces, forcing them to cease fire. Pete was approaching the enemy camp and slammed on the brakes to avoid striking a field hospital. The two tanks lined up on either side of the truck. They rushed forward, trying to crush the truck between them. Pete grabbed Isabel and they both dived for the floorboards. The tanks slammed into the truck, but it held. Pete looked up to see both tanks on fire and the crew members scrambling for cover.

The Gatling guns on two more helicopters peppered the ground with bullets, but they ricocheted off the truck. The bumper panels opened again and two rockets were launched. They turned upward and slammed into the helicopters, which exploded in flames. Burning wreckage fell all around them. Pete backed the truck away from the broken tanks and stopped, breathing hard and sweating. Isabel was visibly shaking and groaning. "Are you okay?" he asked.

"Are we dead, Pete?"

"Not yet."

"Then I'm okay," she smiled and squeezed his hand.

Dozens of soldiers surrounded the truck. All were leveling their weapons at the truck. Pete and Isabel could see the looks of loathing and hatred on their faces. "Don't do it!" Pete shouted.

A voice shouted, "Stop! Don't shoot!" Pete saw Sheila Farness rushing toward them, hollering at her soldiers. The soldiers did not care about her opinion and opened fire. The bullets ricocheted off in every direction. Sheila dived for the ground. The gunfire stopped after a couple of seconds, but all of the attackers lay dead or injured. Sheila climbed out of the mud and walked over to the truck. "Hey Pete, it's good to see you again," she said. She turned and walked over to a large winged beast, which took her in his arms and flew away.

§

Three winged monsters landed in front of the United Nations Headquarters. People ran away screaming. The beasts pulled long black swords from their belts and began to hack away at anyone they could reach. One smashed the doors to the UN and the three rushed inside, setting fires and attacking anyone in their way.

Three more landed along the Champs-Elysees in Paris. They tossed cars full of people into the open patios of sidewalk cafes. They swung their blades, chopping terrified Parisians into pieces. One flew into the air and attacked the base of the Eiffel Tower. Police sirens wailed and everyone rushed to escape the carnage.

Ten minutes later, the Eiffel Tower collapsed onto the ground with hundreds of people still on it.

One winged beast flew over Mount Fuji. It dove downward into the center of the dormant volcano and pushed down until it reached the fluid magma. A geyser of molten rock flew up into the sky, along with the beast, which was now glowing red from the heat. It landed on the rails of a high-speed railroad and waited. Three minutes later, a train shot toward it at over two hundred miles an hour. It slammed into the beast, which did not move. The locomotive exploded in a fireball and the cars buckled and flew into the air.

Four beasts flew in the air ten miles from the Chinese coast. They flapped their wings as fast as they could until the sea was frothing and surging. They pushed the water into a hundred-foot wave that surged toward Shanghai. The wall of water smashed into the city, toppling skyscrapers and washing people and cars down the streets and out into Yangtze River.

Five beasts descended on Mumbai. Two went to sea to raise another tidal wave, while the rest dispersed to set fires and slaughter as many people as possible. Another five circled above the Java Sea. They grouped together and dived downward, hitting the ocean with incredible force. A massive tsunami moved away from the epicenter and the entire region shook from the earthquake.

Six beasts flew over Mexico City. Three separated and moved toward the volcanoes surrounding the city. The others dove into the city and began to attack everyone they saw. The three volcanoes shook and rivers of lava poured down the slopes toward the doomed cities below.

Emmanuel Prospect and his board sat around their conference table. There were hundreds of reports of attacks worldwide. Most major cities had been attacked and tens of thousands were dead. The earthquakes and volcanoes were out of control. The only good news was that the attack in Idaho had failed. The attackers surrendered when they realized who they were supporting. The two sides had even agreed to have a large celebration of their victory.

"What do we do, Father?" Gabriel asked. "We can't ignore this escalation."

"Gabriel is right, Father. We must fight the demons now!" Michael exclaimed.

"What about Peter, Father?" Joshua asked. "He is what this is all about, don't you remember?"

"Joshua, we all know you're right, but we cannot ignore what Satori and his demons are doing. We have to stop them now," Emmanuel argued.

"I know that Peter is just one man, but I still think these other attacks are a diversion," Joshua noted.

"Michael and Gabriel, please rally our forces to stop these attacks," Emmanuel said. The others disappeared, leaving Joshua and his father alone. "Joshua, this is a battle without a victor. The Creator would not allow us to ignore global destruction to save a single man's mortal life."

"I understand, Father."

"But I still think a solution will arise," Emmanuel continued. "We have to have faith too."

Joshua smiled and said, "I hope that will be enough, Father."

§

The two armies filled the large grassy field. All the weapons were stowed and a large bonfire burned in the center of the gathering. People from both sides mingled and expressed their happiness that the battle was over. They had all seen the winged beast fly away with Sheila Farness, although most thought it had to be an illusion of some kind. Pete and Isabel were sitting at a table with Cindy Jackson having a drink in the warm late-afternoon air. An older man approached the table and said, "Hello, I'm Sander

Kauffman. I was the commander of this group. That's some truck you have there, Mr. Smith."

Pete stood and shook his hand, saying, "Just call me Pete, Sander. Please sit down."

After sitting and pouring a drink from the bottle, Sander said, "You know, I still can't believe that demon was making us attack. He told us you were the Devil himself! The instant I saw his true form, I knew who the Devil really was."

"I'm just glad more people didn't have to die here," Pete said. "I hear there is craziness going on everywhere today."

"We heard the same thing, Pete. Hopefully it will end soon. What do we do now?"

Pete did not reply. He was staring into space and his hands were shaking.

"Pete, are you okay?" Sander asked.

"Pete, what's wrong?" Isabel said as she took his hand.

"Run for your lives!" Pete shouted as he jumped to his feet. A thousand winged monsters filled the sky and began to dive toward the army. Pete grabbed Isabel's arm and pulled her along. The demons were everywhere, swinging their blades and growling and howling at the terrified people. "We've got to get to the truck!" he shouted. He could see it ahead, just on the other side of a small ditch. The soldiers rushed to their armory, but the beasts beat them to it and began to pepper the crowd with automatic fire. People were screaming in pain and falling all around them. A mortar round exploded twenty feet behind them, knocking them to the ground. The grass was almost gone and the field was a bloody, muddy mess.

"I think I twisted my ankle, Pete," Isabel groaned. He stood and threw her over his shoulder and headed down into the ravine which was more like a mud puddle now. He struggled to pull his feet from the muck and keep moving. Pete realized it had suddenly become very quiet as he started up the ravine. When he reached the top, he saw the giant beast Satori standing between him and the truck. Sheila was standing next to him.

Satori rushed forward and knocked Pete back into the ditch. He was laughing hilariously. "Well, at least you tried, Pete!" he bellowed. Pete looked around. The edge of the ditch was lined with winged beasts that were all laughing and pointing at him. Pete helped Isabel to her feet, but she was limping badly. "You are a persistent son of a bitch, Peter, I'll give you that!"

"To hell with you, you sick bastard!" Pete shouted.

"Hell? I think not. The last time I was there I got into a bit of trouble, but that ends now," Satori said. "Sheila, go earn your paycheck."

She pulled her pistol from its holster and moved toward them. "Pete, this could have been a lot easier, you know," she growled.

"Pete, I love you," Isabel said.

Sheila raised the weapon and fired. The bullet hit Isabel in the forehead and she fell backwards dead. "I'll kill you for that," Pete spat.

Sheila walked up to him and pressed the barrel against his forehead. "Just shut up already, lover boy. You'll be with her soon enough."

"Sweetheart, make this quick, the Prospects are on their way," Satori said.

She turned her head and replied, "It won't be a second, my darling." Seizing the moment, Pete grabbed the gun and began to wrestle with her. "You dumb shit, you can't beat me," she snarled. They struggled back and forth while the winged beasts cheered and hollered.

"It doesn't have to end like this," Pete groaned.

"Yes, it does!" she shouted. The pistol fired twice. Sheila looked at Pete and winced. She released the gun and fell to the ground and died.

Many of the winged demons exchanged smiles, glad to be rid of the mortal woman. Satori was in shock. He wiped tears from his eyes. His expression turned from pain to seething hatred. "You worthless piece of shit!" he shouted. "You've taken the one woman I love and killed her! I am going to pull you apart limb by limb!" He started moving toward him. Pete raised the pistol and pointed it at the beast. "Go ahead and shoot. I'm as powerful as your truck over there!" He walked forward.

Pete fired the pistol four times. Satori stood frozen for an instant. He looked down to see four gaping holes in his chest. Black blood was pouring out. He took half a step forward and fell to the ground dead. The winged demons were frozen in shock. They had just witnessed the impossible, the death of an immortal. Pete felt a sharp pain and looked to see four bullet holes in his chest. Blood had already soaked through his shirt. The demons did not move. He dropped the pistol, stumbled backward and fell into the mud next to Isabel and died. With nothing left to do, one by one the winged monsters flew away, leaving the battlefield to the fallen.

Chapter 27

Pete woke with a start and found himself lying in the muddy ditch. His shirt was soaked with blood. He pulled open his shirt and saw the four holes in his body, but did not feel any pain. The dead beast was just in front of him. He walked over and touched it. It felt more like a marble statue, hard and cold, than a body. He came back and knelt next to Isabel. He could see her, but when he tried to touch her face, it was as if she wasn't there at all, just the illusion of Isabel. The air was thick with smoke and the smell of gunpowder. He climbed up the side of the ditch toward where the SUV had been parked, but it was gone. It was deathly quiet and the sun was just rising to the east. As the first beams of light hit his eyes, he saw thousands of bodies all around him. The soldiers had died horrific deaths. Many were missing limbs or heads. Their bodies were shredded by machine gun fire. There were groups of soldiers who huddled together to avoid the monster attack. Toward the west, a line of destroyed tanks sat burning. He turned and began to walk toward the fires.

Clouds of flies swarmed the area, laying their eggs on the dead bodies. They bit him everywhere, and he swatted them away from his face as he stepped around and over the fallen. After twenty minutes, he passed the burning metal hulks. But the carnage did not end there. Slightly rolling hills continued to the horizon, and the view never changed. Mud and death was everywhere. How could this happen, he wondered. He kept walking. After two hours, the fly swarms seemed to dissipate and he could quicken his pace. Another hour later and he reached a forest and the end of the battlefield.

He could hear birds chirping in the trees and the warmth of the sun gave him new strength. The quiet of the field of battle was gone. Bees buzzed and birds sang. He came along a gentle stream flowing through the forest and stopped. He pulled off his clothes and stepped into the water. It was cold but very refreshing. As the water rose to his chest, he felt an odd tingling and looked down. The water was healing his wounds. Within seconds, he was whole again and wondered how a creek could do such a thing. He climbed out on the opposite bank and noticed a white tunic and leather sandals on the grass. He slipped them on and looked back to where he had come. A fog bank had descended and the other side of the river was obscured. "Thank God for that!" he shouted. He turned back and walked up the bank and back into the forest. He heard a strange and beautiful sound and headed toward it. After ten minutes more, the trees gave way to a grassy glade with a small pond and a marble temple. Five women were standing together and singing a melody he had never heard before. They smiled as he approached. They were glowing white and seemed to have long, brilliantly white wings. When he was a few feet away, he recognized one as Mary Prospect from the hospital in Maui. She patted him on the shoulder and pointed behind him.

Emmanuel Prospect was entering the glade. He smiled when he saw Pete and walked up to him, grabbing and hugging him close. The women formed a tight circle around him with their wings enveloping the group. After a moment, they walked away into the forest, leaving the two men alone. "Granddad, am I dead?" Pete asked. Emmanuel pointed to the temple and motioned for Peter to go there. "Granddad, are you God?" Emmanuel only pointed to the temple again and pushed Peter in that direction. Reluctantly, Peter walked up the steps and into the temple. It was exactly like his dream. He walked to the throne in the middle of the room and sat down. He was overcome by weariness and closed his eyes. Peter remembered his entire life while he slept, but his mind focused on what had happened since Satori had taken him to the place of atonement. "That means something," he thought.

Pete opened his eyes to find himself back in the place of atonement. He was chained to the wall. Satori was chained across from him. The giant beast seemed smaller than he remembered.

Sheila was chained next to the beast. He looked to his left and saw Cindy Jackson chained to the wall. He looked right to find Isabel chained. He strained against his chains to touch her, but she remained just out of reach. Resigned to being here, he looked up and down the corridor, which seemed to stretch to infinity in both directions, and people were chained along both walls to the ends. "So much death," he thought. "That must be why Satori died."

He looked at Isabel. There was a pool of blood beneath her and some still oozed from her head wound. He was filled with loathing for Sheila and raised his head to spit on her. He was shocked to see her gradually fading away. He looked back at Isabel and she was also fading. He strained his joints, but still could not reach far enough to touch her one last time. Within a minute, the hall was empty, except for Pete and Satori. Pete heard footsteps approaching on the stone floor, but the hall seemed empty.

After another few minutes, a figure in a hooded robe approached. He walked up to Satori and shook his head. Then he turned to Peter and removed his hood. It was Luce Prospect. "Hello Pete," he smiled.

"Uncle Luce, I'm so happy to see you!" Pete exclaimed. "Where did Isabel and the others go? Can you bring her back?"

"No, but that's a good thing," Luce replied. He waved his right arm and the chains on Peter dissolved. Luce caught him as he fell from the wall.

"What do you mean? Am I dead? Is Granddad God?" Pete rattled as he regained his footing.

"Peter, frankly, I'm going to be a bit busy with the big guy over there," Luce said, motioning toward Satori. "I brought along someone else to explain everything."

"Hi Pete," Joshua Prospect said.

Pete spun around to see his friend and hugged him. "Oh, Josh, it's great to see you! Where's Isabel?"

Joshua put his arm around Pete's shoulders and led him away. "Let's go, Pete. You don't want to be around Satori now. He has to atone."

"But what about me? I'm dead too, don't I have to atone?"

Luce said, "No, not at this time, Peter, but Joshua will explain it. Now get going!" A wall grew in the corridor, separating them from Luce and Satori. Just as the wall was filling the last gaps, the most terrifying scream, saturated with fear and pain, filled the chamber. It stopped instantly when the wall was complete.

"Poor Satori," Josh sighed

"Poor Satori, are you kidding me? He killed all those people and didn't give a damn for them," Pete argued.

"Have a heart, Peter. I know you don't understand—since birth, life, and death are integral to your existence—but once a man dies, we must show some remorse for his passing."

"I'm sorry, Josh, I suppose you're right, but it just seemed moments ago when Sheila shot Isabel dead," Pete said.

"Isabel isn't dead, Peter, and neither are those others in the chamber with you," Joshua began. "You still remember being here the first time?" Pete nodded. "You came here alive and left alive. That is not possible."

"I've heard this before."

"Pete, when that first impossibility occurred, there was a hole in reality, which could only be plugged by your death."

"Joshua, who shot me? I don't remember anyone shooting at me," Pete asked.

"Pete, when the impossibility occurred, you and Satori were linked together. As part of that link, he lost his immortality. Since you were linked, if either one of you died, the other would die the same way," Joshua said as they kept walking down the corridor, which stretched further than the eye could see.

"So, if Sheila would have shot me, then he would have died too?"

"Yes, Peter. And when you did die, you plugged the hole in reality, and reverting all of existence back to the moment of the first incident."

Pete stopped in his tracks and said, "And that's why Isabel and the others disappeared! None of the attacks ever took place!"

"That is exactly right, Pete," Josh announced.

"But I'm still dead, right?" Pete asked.

"For now, yes," Josh replied. "I intend to take you back though, once you've asked all your questions."

"But no one will remember what happened. I know for most that's a good thing, but I don't want to forget anything. This has been the most amazing experience of my life."

"Everyone will remember, but it will be like a dream. Everyone dreams and usually forgets them, but this dream will stick. It will be up to them to decide what to believe though. My father has allowed you to retain all memories. To you, everything that happened will be with you your entire life," Joshua said.

"Thank him for me, please."

"Do it yourself, Pete. He's coming to Gabe's for dinner when we get back," Joshua laughed. "You didn't think you'd avoid the Prospects, did you?"

"I just thought you all were done with me, Joshua. With Satori dead, I don't know what help I can be."

Josh started walking again. "Don't be silly, Peter. You are my friend for life. And just because Satori is gone, don't think the rest of his family won't be causing trouble. We're hoping your ability will help us for a long time."

"Josh, what about Sheila Farness? Won't she try to kill me again?"

"The rest of Satori's family hates her. They were jealous of her for stealing their father's affection. She is also being allowed to remember all details. We hope she will come to us for help. Maybe even she can be saved," Joshua replied. "Any more questions?"

Peter yawned. "You know, I just woke up and I'm dead tired again. I don't understand it."

"It's normal, Peter. When you can't walk, I'll carry you. When you fall asleep, I'll return you to your bed in Gabe's apartment. Do you want to ask me anything else?"

"Joshua, is Granddad God?"

"I knew this moment was coming. No, Emmanuel Prospect is not God." Pete's head was drooping, so Joshua picked him up in his arms. "When the Creator made the universe and your planet, life flourished according to His design. As life progressed, it became apparent that existence would be difficult, with life consuming life, herbivores eating the plants and carnivores eating the herbivores and each other. It stands to reason that when humans came along, they still had the desire to control their environment and each other, which led to war and crime, and ultimately the existence of Satori and his clan."

"I remember him," Pete yawned and nestled his head on Joshua's shoulder.

"We were given the responsibility to keep him at bay. We allowed people to make their own choices, but tried to keep him from involving himself directly in human lives. It was our job to help humanity improve and evolve. We gave them hope and something greater than themselves to believe in. We created the balance between good and evil."

"Josh, you told me you were born a man," Pete said with his eyes closed.

"Well, I'm an exception. My father allowed me to live as one of his sons and help others, which is all I ever wanted. Anything else, Peter?" But there was no reply. Peter Smith was asleep.

§

A knock at the door woke Peter. He rolled over and said, "Come in."

Gabe Prospect stuck his head in the door and said, "Let's get going, sleepyhead! Granddad will be here in an hour!"

"Okay, thanks Gabe," Pete said as he sat up on the edge of the bed and rubbed his eyes. What an amazing dream, he thought.

The door opened again and Gabe said, "And it was no dream, Pete!"

Then he remembered it all. The memories poured through his mind and he trembled at the memory of each attack and the death of Isabel Garcia. He pulled up his shirt, but there were no marks from the bullets. He stood and looked out the window. It would be sunset soon and was surprised he had been sleeping in the middle of the day. He walked to the bathroom to take a shower.

Half an hour later, he walked into the open room and froze when he saw Gabe and Sheila Farness sitting on a couch. When she saw him, she jumped up and ran over, throwing her arms around his neck and kissing his cheek. "Pete, I'm so sorry! I can't believe any of that happened either. Can you ever forgive me?"

"Sheila, none of it did happen. Let's leave it at that, okay?" he replied.

She released him and walked back to Gabe who was now standing. "I think that's enough for today, Sheila. I don't think my Granddad is ready to see you just yet," Gabe said. She kissed his cheek and walked into the waiting elevator car and the doors closed. "It will be okay, Peter. With Satori dead, she's not under his spell anymore."

"Be careful yourself, Gabe. She was an unholy bitch for a while."

"Don't worry about me, pal. But we have a little surprise for you. Do you like surprises, Pete?"

"That depends," he replied.

The doors to the various rooms opened and two dozen members of the Prospect family came out applauding. The elevator doors opened and Emmanuel, Luce, Gabriel and Michael came out applauding as well. They formed a circle around him and began to cheer. Emmanuel walked over and hugged Pete. Each of the others took their turn to do the same. Pete was blushing from all the attention and affection. After a few minutes, they quieted down and Emmanuel spoke. "Tonight, we are all honored to be with Peter Smith, the man who stopped the end of the world and saved most of mankind." He walked over to him and handed him a box and shook his hand. "Peter, I'm sorry to tell you that most people will not remember what happened, but we will, and Satori's clan will remember as well. Please open the gift, son."

Pete tore off the paper and opened the box. Inside were a set of keys, a bankcard, a ring, and a watch. "Thank you all very much," he replied.

"Peter, let me explain," Emmanuel said. "The keys are for the SUV, which we have parked in the basement. Your quick thinking and the capabilities of the vehicle changed the world! It seems only fitting you should have it. The ring holds the Prospect family crest. It officially makes you a member of our family." Everyone applauded again. "The watch has the same crest. Both the ring and the watch will keep all of us connected to you at all times. You don't even have to call us anymore. Just think of one of us and we will be there, okay?"

"Wow! That's amazing. Thank you."

"And last but not least is the bankcard," Emmanuel said. "I hope you know that the desire for money is the root of all evil, but that being said, a man's got to eat!" Everyone laughed. "Each of us has one of these cards. They give us access to the combined worth of the Prospect Enterprise. Please use it as you will, and trust me, no matter what you buy, it won't affect the funds available."

"Thank you, but I don't think I can accept this. It's too much!" Pete balked.

"Nonsense, my boy," Emmanuel said. "You really don't understand what you did. Peter, you saved the world. Keep the card. If you don't want to spend any money, that's your choice. But if you are ever in need, none of us could live with ourselves if you suffered. Please, keep it for me."

"Okay, but I won't use it unless it's an emergency, I swear," Pete replied. Everyone applauded.

"Let's eat!" Emmanuel said.

Pete sat across from Emmanuel, with Joshua and Gabriel on either side of him. Gabe and Luce sat next to Peter. Maria had outdone herself with this dinner. His steak was as tender as butter and everything was seasoned perfectly. The Prospects were chatting among themselves and telling jokes. Pete was remembering the moment when Sheila shot the love of his life dead. He could still hear her saying she loved him just before dying. He forced back his tears.

"Pete, this is a celebration," Granddad said. "You look sad."

"I'm sorry, Granddad. I just keep remembering how Isabel died."

"She didn't die," Emmanuel said. "You'll see her tomorrow, or did you forget that your job at Bertrand Industries starts at 9:00 a.m. sharp."

"Our entire relationship was part of that dream, and now it's gone."

Luce put his hand on Pete's shoulder and said, "Love is a powerful thing, Peter. If you two are meant to be, she will remember. Even if she does not, she may fall in love with you again."

"I know you're right, but the image was so horrible," Pete said.

"Would you like to forget that image, Peter?" Emmanuel asked. "We can make that happen."

"No. It is part of that reality and I have to live with the whole thing." He turned to Luce and asked, "How did it go with Satori?"

"Thank you for caring, Peter. It was pretty much as I expected but took considerably longer. He has lived for millions of years and had much to atone for, but that is finished. I released his spirit to the Creator and it is up to Him what happens next," Luce replied as he took a bite of his steak.

§

Peter woke as Maria opened the door to announce breakfast would be ready soon. He looked at his new watch, which said it was 7:00 a.m. He rose and went to the bathroom to get prepared for work. After showering and shaving, he put on a business suit and tied the necktie. He put on his watch and ring and slipped the bankcard into his wallet. Then he walked out into the main room and into the kitchen. Maria was putting a plate of *chilaquiles* down as he approached. Gabe and Mike were eating and arguing about the fate of the Euro in a recession-prone market. He sat there quietly, eating his food and trying to come to grips with a world that did not know what had happened. Israel had not been invaded. President Kim was still in charge in North Korea. Los Angeles had not been destroyed by the earthquake and lava flows. It was just another day.

After breakfast, he brushed his teeth again and stood looking at himself in the mirror. The image of his body with the bullet holes in the chest and blood everywhere flooded his mind. He shook his head and splashed water on his face. It was eight-thirty. He wanted to get to work early to make a good impression, so he rushed out of the room and took the elevator to the ground floor. As the doors opened, Bob said, "Do you want the SUV, Pete?"

"No thanks, Bob. I'm just going to work." He waved and walked out onto the sidewalk. The concrete was packed with people headed to work. No one was running to escape an attack on the United Nations or leaving town after the nuclear strike in Queens, or plane crashes in Brooklyn. It was just another day.

He crossed the street and hurried down the sidewalk. Halfway down, he thought he heard someone yelling his name. He turned around to see a woman run out of a cafe and deliver a briefcase to a man ten feet behind him. "You forgot this, Pete."

He replied, "Thanks, honey. I'll see you for dinner."

Two blocks later, he walked into the building where Bertrand Industries was located. He remembered the floor and waited for an elevator and then joined the crowd in the large car. The car stopped several times before reaching the thirtieth floor, where he and a few others exited. He was the only one who headed for the Bertrand Industries glass doors and pulled one open. Before he walked in, he noticed the words "A Prospect Company" had been added. He smiled and stepped inside.

"Good morning, sir, and welcome to Bertrand Industries, how may I help you?" the receptionist said.

"Good morning. I'm Pete Smith and this is my first day working here."

She stood up and offered her hand, which he shook. "Welcome to the team, Pete. I'm Abby. It's good to have you with us. Please take a seat and I'll have someone come for you."

"Thank you, Abby. It's nice to meet you." He sat down and thumbed through a magazine on the table as several of his coworkers-to-be filed in and said hello to Abby. He saw Isabel rush through, but she did not notice him.

Oscar Bertrand walked in and stopped to talk to the receptionist. "Any messages, Abby?"

"No, Oscar, but you have a new employee here," she said pointing to Pete.

He dropped the magazine and stood to shake his boss's hand. "Peter, I've heard many good things from Emmanuel Prospect. I'm very happy you decided to stay here with us."

"It's my pleasure, sir. I'm happy to be here."

"Just call me Oscar, Pete. We're very informal around here. Someone will come get you in a minute, okay?" Pete nodded. "We'll have lunch this week. My assistant will set it up."

"Thank you, Oscar," Pete replied as the man turned and walked away.

A woman walked into the lobby and approached him. "Hi, Pete, I'm Kim and I work with Isabel." They shook hands. "Please follow me." She walked into the large office with him right behind her. "Pete, rather than taking you to Jeff, our controller, our HR Director wanted to speak with you first, if you don't mind."

"That's fine. Whatever you folks need."

She led him to a small conference room and motioned him to enter the room. "Please have a seat. The director will be here soon. There's some water in the refrigerator in the corner if you like." Before he could respond, she slipped away.

He pulled out a bottle of water and sat down. He opened it and took a sip. He felt his phone vibrate and pulled it from his pocket and looked at the screen. There was a text message from Granddad with only the words, "Don't worry." He chuckled and slipped the phone back into his pocket. The door flew open and Isabel Garcia stepped in and closed it behind her. "It's good to see you again, Isabel."

She sat down nervously, wringing her hands. "Mr. Smith, I'm just going to say what's on my mind if that's okay. You'll probably think I'm crazy and walk out, but I don't care!"

"Say what you want to say, Isabel."

She cried, "I'm really sorry. I shouldn't be doing this. You probably think I'm crazy already. I'll leave." She stood and headed for the door.

"Isabel, please don't leave!" Pete begged. She stopped but did not turn around. "You remember everything, don't you?"

She spun around and he could see her tears and the pain on her face. "Do you remember something too?"

"I remember running into you in Hawaii. I remember the plane crashing into my hotel room and how you told the paramedics I was your boyfriend."

She was sobbing and holding her head in her hands. "It was a dream, Pete."

"I remember you in the truck with me when the demons tried to kill us. I remember Joshua nailed to the post. I remember the crazy waitress and how I had to touch her crucifix," Pete continued.

She looked up at him in disbelief, shaking her head slowly from side to side.

"I remember the cave in the mountains and how you told me you were in love with me," he continued.

"And you told me you loved me too."

Pete smiled. "And I do love you, Isabel. But do you know what I remember most?" She looked at him and half-smiled. "I remember you said you loved me just before that bitch shot you dead."

She stood trembling and wiping the tears from her face. "But you said it yourself. I died in that dream. It can't be real. Look at me. I'm here and I'm breathing."

"It wasn't a dream. It really happened and that's why you remember it so well," Pete replied. "I died then too, and my death made it all go away. Now, here we are, both alive and both able to make our own choices." He stood next to her and took her hands. "Isabel, I know this is hard for you. It's hard for me to understand too." He pulled his phone and showed it to her. "Look at this message from Emmanuel Prospect."

"Don't worry," she chuckled. "What's that supposed to mean?"

"We have to have faith, and we have to believe what we both know to be true," he answered. "We have another chance!"

"I'm still confused, Pete. I want to believe it, oh God, I want so bad to believe it . . ."

"Look at my contact list and let me look at yours," he said. A moment later, he said, "You have my number in your list. How about that?"

"You applied for work here, silly," she replied but froze when she saw her number on his. "I put my number there. I remember that distinctly. That means it did happen."

"It also means that we're both still in love, Isabel. I don't ever want to lose you again," he said as he took her in his arms and kissed her lips and face.

"I love you too, Pete."

About the Author

Karl J. Morgan

Karl Morgan has a lifelong fascination with stories in the science fiction and fantasy genres, whether it was the Tom Swift novels by Victor Appleton he read as a young boy, or television like *Lost in Space* and *Star Trek*, and especially films like *Star Wars*, *Harry Potter* and *Lord of the Rings*. All of those tales put the protagonists in terrible situations where the odds are against them and, yet, somehow they prevail. The reader/viewer is always left with a sense that something greater than ourselves is watching over us.

The reliance on Divine Providence, the power of friendship, and the desire to learn and grow are cornerstones of the author's Dave Brewster and *Heartstone* series. That continues in the Modern Prophets series, only the unseen forces are now out in the open.

These are tales of reluctant heroes who have been given powers they do not yet understand, and challenges that would seem overwhelming. Still, the hand of Fate is firmly on their shoulders, and friends arise just when needed most to prevent the most despicable of evils.

Karl lives in the San Diego area with his wife, Aida, and their beloved puppies. Their two grown children have fled the nest and started their own adventures in life.

To read more about Karl and his projects, please visit his website and blog: www.karljmorgan.com
facebook: www.facebook.com/karlmorganauthor
twitter: @karljmorgan.

Other Books By
Karl J. Morgan

The Dave Brewster Series

Showdown Over Neptune
ISBN: 978-0-9860270-0-0
(Book 1)

The Second Predaxian War
ISBN: 978-0-9860270-1-7
(Book 2)

The Hive
ISBN: 978-0-9860270-2-4
(Book 3)

Tears of Gallia
ISBN: 978-0-9860270-4-8
(Book 4)

The Accord
ISBN: 978-0-9860270-6-2
(Book 5)

Heartstone

Heartstone: Sentinels of Far Sun
ISBN: 978-0-9860270-3-1
(Book 1)

Heartstone: The Time Walker
ISBN: 978-0-9860270-5-5
(Book 2)

Modern Prophet Series

The Reluctant Prophet: A Love Story
ISBN: 978-0-9860270-8-6
(Book 2)
Available for sale fall 2014

Hand of God
ISBN: 978-0-9860270-9-3
(Book 3)
Available for sale winter 2014

Individual Book

Remembrances: Choose to Be Happy and Embrace the Possibilities
ISBN: 978-0-9826461-9-9

www.ingramcontent.com/pod-product-compliance
Lightning Source LLC
Chambersburg PA
CBHW070117120726
47909CB00002B/636